HUNTING MEDUSA

ELIZABETH ANDREWS

One murderous mission. One killer case of PMS. Who said "the curse" was a myth?

The Medusa's Daughters Trilogy, Book 1

Ever since the original Medusa ticked off Athena by bragging about her beauty, her cursed daughters have been paying for that mistake. To this day, successive Medusas play cat and mouse with the descendants of Perseus, known as the Harvesters.

When Kallan Tassos tracks down the current Medusa, he expects to find a monster. Instead he finds a wary, beautiful woman, shielded by a complicated web of spells that foils his plans for a quick kill and retrieval of her protective amulet.

Andrea Rosakis expects the handsome Harvester to go for the kill. Instead, his attempt to take the amulet imprinted on her skin without harming her takes her completely by surprise. And ends with the two of them in a magical bind —together.

Though their attraction is combustible, her impending PMS (Pre Magical-Curse Syndrome) puts a real damper on any chance of a relationship. But Kallan isn't the only Harvester tracking Andi, and they must cooperate to stay at least one step ahead of a ruthless killer before they can have any future, together or apart.

Warning: A hunter who's fallen for the woman he's bound to kill, a Medusa who must trust him with her life, and a magical curse only love can break.

Hunting Medusa
Copyright © 2014 by Elizabeth Andrews
Original:ISBN: 978-1-61921-837-6
Second Edition Ebook ISBN: 978-1-7346689-2-6
Second Edition Paperback ISBN: 978-1-7346689-3-3
Edited by Holly Atkinson
Cover by Valerie Tibbs
Series Graphic and additional cover design by Aleisha Knight Evans

First Samhain Publishing, Ltd. Electronic publication: January 2014
First Samhain Publishing, Ltd. Paperback publication: January 2015
Second Edition Electronic and Paperback publication: July 2021

In all the years I've worked toward this goal of becoming a published author, I have had a lot of support along the way. As I sat down to ponder this dedication, I realized much of that encouragement has come from the men in my life. So I have to dedicate this to the men who have been my biggest supporters and real-life heroes:

To my dad, who not only bought me my very first typewriter many years ago, but whose name is on this book;

To my husband, who never, in many years of rejections, ever said, "maybe this isn't meant to be", but offered sympathy and encouragement, and then celebrated with me— first when I found an agent who wanted to take me on, and then when we sold this book;

And to my two sons, who have never—at least in my hearing —complained because dinner was just leftovers, or was going to be late because I got caught up in writing or revising, and who I suspect will become terrific heroes in their own right in a few more years.

Thank you all very much for everything on the way here! I am so happy I get to share this milestone with all of you.

Medusa knew he was coming. She always knew when the next one approached to try to kill her. But she had not been ready to die—until now.

While listening to the soft, sneaky sounds of his footfalls on the rocky path, she studied the golden goblet. It had not rid her of Athena's curse, but it would help her daughters. As long as one of them had it, the amulet would stop them all from suffering constantly as she had all these years, limiting the effects of the curse to only a few days each month for the keeper of the goblet. Until the Goddess forgave Medusa's foolish bragging.

Her killer drew nearer, still attempting to be quiet. Something about his deliberate pace—unhurried, careful—made her grateful she had already finished her protective spell for her children. This one would not have died as easily as the rest.

She looked around, from one statue to another—men of all ages and sizes, various weapons in their hands or tucked into their belts, all wearing the same horrified expression. Her eyes burned. She knew she was a monster. She had known not to brag so about her hair. Athena did not suffer braggarts. She had ruined Medusa's hair, had cursed Medusa to live in exile this way—on this Gods-forsaken island, with no company but her own—as well as all her offspring.

Medusa despised living this way. She was not meant to be alone. She had never enjoyed her own company more than others'. When this hunter came, she would let him kill her.

He did not come into the clearing as the others had, charging forward recklessly. No, he came in with his back to her, watching her reflection in a shield. Clever, this one. She pretended to not have seen him, very aware of each step he took.

Soon. It would be over soon.

And she could not wait for the torment to end.

When he came nearer, she closed her eyes and prayed to Athena for forgiveness.

His blade whistled through the air. Closer, closer…

CHAPTER ONE

I t was one of those days when having the Medusa's fabled power to turn people to stone would really come in handy.

Andrea Rosakis did not, however, have that ability, not this week, anyway. Even though she was the reigning Medusa.

She glared at the man on her back porch, wondering if he could ever understand how lucky he was she wasn't suffering from PMS this week. And why wouldn't he stop talking? Her fingers itched to slam the door.

"…if you just have five minutes, ma'am," he concluded.

She narrowed her gaze on the vacuum beside him. "No, thank you." And how the hell had he found her all the way out here? No one ever bothered to follow her rough, muddy driveway all the way to the top, even if they did ignore the "No Trespassing" signs posted at the foot of it. Not to mention the protective warding she had set at the boundaries of the entire property. Sure, it wasn't the heavy artillery of protection spells, but no one else had ever gotten past it. This man however, had not only ignored the signs and the subtle "go away" protections, but managed the entire bumpy, muddy track into the woods and halfway up the mountain. Just to hear her say, "No."

And he didn't look discouraged. At all.

Andi almost wished she *were* PMSing this week, though it would be a real pain in the ass to have to get rid of a life-sized stone statue of a vacuum salesman.

Or maybe she could keep it. He was very pretty, even if he annoyed her. He was tall and broad, his inky black hair was a tad too long, and his bright green eyes held her attention. At least as stone, he'd be silent and still pretty. She gave herself a mental shake. "I'm sorry, but I don't have time for this—"

"When would be a better time?"

"Never."

He did blink at that, but his smile never disappeared. "I'll have to check my calendar."

She snorted, then clapped her free hand over her mouth. Laughing would not discourage the man. "Look, I'm sure it's a great vacuum, but I don't need it. I don't want to see how it works, and I'd like you to get off my property."

His smile did fade a little bit. "Well, I suppose, if that's what you really want."

She quirked an eyebrow, trying not to smile again. He had the faintest hint of an accent, but she couldn't place it. Not without hearing him talk some more, and she didn't want to encourage that either, or he'd just keep trying to sell her an expensive vacuum she didn't need.

"Maybe I could talk you into meeting me for coffee sometime then," he said.

Her jaw dropped. The cute salesman was hitting on her. For half a second, she indulged the fantasy of a date with the hunk. A real date, maybe ending with a real kiss. Her pulse quickened. Then she remembered one good date led to more, and eventually, it led to guys running away from her, gibbering like idiots when PMS struck. She shut her mouth and ignored the regret burning in her middle. "Sorry, but no."

"You're a hard woman," he said lightly, his bright gaze sliding down to her mouth. "I'll leave my card in case you change your mind. About the coffee, that is." He forced a small card into her hand and picked up his vacuum.

Andi stared after him as he strode off her porch. The bulky vacuum looked like it weighed nothing in his hand, swinging at his side on his way to the shiny, new truck parked behind her car.

When he took one hand from the steering wheel to wave at her, she stopped herself from lifting her hand in response. He turned the truck around and vanished down the drive into the trees. Frowning, she went back inside and shut the door, then locked it and re-armed the alarm. He'd tossed the vacuum into the bed of the truck. A very strong salesman.

Who didn't seem to care the impending rain was going to damage his expensive vacuum.

She turned back to the door and stared out the narrow window beside it, her heart beating faster now with alarm. Maybe he didn't realize. Or maybe he really hadn't come here to sell her a vacuum.

She swallowed hard.

Aunt Celosia had always told the cousins stories of the Harvesters, the men who still hunted for the Medusa. Somehow, Andi had always thought they'd be more frightening. More obvious. Ugly men intent on murder.

If this vacuum salesman was a Harvester, he was sneaky. Of course, if he was a Harvester, he would be sneaky, as Perseus had been when he killed the first Medusa.

She was in a lot of trouble.

She double-checked the alarm, then spun away and grabbed the phone from the wall on her way into the kitchen. She hit an auto-dial number and stared out the window into the woods.

"Hello, Andi."

She took a slow breath. "Hi, Mom."

"What's wrong?" Trust her mother to know something was bothering her. Better late than never, she supposed.

"What do the Harvesters look like?" She realized her fingernails were digging into her palm, as were the corners of the crumpled business card she still held. She uncurled her fingers and studied the crescent-shaped marks in her hand to distract herself from the way her pulse raced with fear. She dropped the card onto the windowsill for later.

Her mother was silent for several heartbeats. "Like men, I suppose. No one has seen one in a very long time, Andi. We've all managed to stay out of their way, because when they come calling, they don't stop to ask questions first."

Andi relaxed, sinking onto the nearest chair and realizing her legs still shook with the rush of adrenaline. Her heart stopped pounding so hard, easing back into a normal rhythm.

"Why?"

"I'm just being silly. Some stupid vacuum salesman actually made it all the way up the driveway." She laughed at herself, though the sound was weak.

Her mother sighed. "Well, if he were a Harvester, you wouldn't be on the phone with me right now."

"I know." She rested her forehead on her free hand.

"Do you want to come to visit for a while? We haven't seen you in almost a year."

She ignored the hopeful tone in her mother's voice. "No, thanks. I'm really fine, and I'm kind of busy with work right now." That wasn't exactly true, as she could do her work anywhere, but she didn't want to go visiting right now. Maybe she should have a gate installed at the bottom of the driveway. It would keep out other salesmen who might be brave enough—or desperate enough—to try the mountain road. And maybe she ought to make her protective wards a bit stronger to keep out hot salesmen who seemed impervious to the existing protective spells.

"Okay." Even that single word was filled with disappointment and residual guilt that Andi pretended not to notice.

"I'll call you in a couple weeks, though. Maybe things will have slowed down by then." She knew after this week she had a lull with her customers, no big orders pending. That didn't mean she'd go visit, however.

"It would be nice. We miss you."

Reverse guilt. Mothers were aces at that. "I miss you, too." She wasn't lying. "Tell Dad I said hello, okay?"

She hung up and rested her forehead on the cool tabletop. It wasn't like her to be scared of little things. She'd been the Medusa for eight years now and scarcely given the legendary Harvesters much thought. It had been generations since a Medusa had been killed by one. That wasn't about to change now. She would be another in a long line of Medusas who died an old woman of natural causes.

Sitting up, she squared her shoulders. Work waited, and then she could take a nice long bubble bath later to relax.

Still, she couldn't quite explain away the tiny niggle of unease in her middle.

Kallan Tassos sat at the foot of the mountain, tapping his fingers on the steering wheel of the rented truck. Getting to the Medusa had been a lot easier than he'd been led to believe. He wondered why.

She was also a lot prettier than he'd imagined.

Sure, he knew the original Medusa had been so beautiful and confident she'd angered a Goddess. But this one wasn't what he'd expected. She had short, dark hair framing very expressive blue eyes. Somehow he'd imagined long, blonde hair for a woman whose hair turned into snakes. And cold eyes like those very reptiles. Maybe not with a mouth that made him wonder how she'd taste.

He frowned, tapping his fingers faster on the wheel. Someone had left out a lot of details in the legends. Or the reality had changed much in the generations since the last Harvester had done his duty in killing the monstrous Medusa.

He shook his head. No, his imagination was simply working overtime. And when he got home to Baltimore—or even when he went to Greece to visit Uncle Ari at the family's ancestral home—he needed to find a willing woman, as it had clearly been too long if he was finding his quarry so attractive.

When his phone rang, he hesitated for a second at the name on the tiny screen. He finally thumbed the button after the third ring. "Stavros."

"I hear you may have a promising lead. It is past time one of us killed this monster." His cousin's everyday accent thickened when he was excited, and judging by the way Greece flavored his words, he believed they were getting close.

"I'm sure one of us will," Kallan said mildly, drumming his fingers on his knee.

"I keep imagining taking her head after all this time. Perhaps before I do, I can make her pay a little for her family's existence."

Kallan frowned. Stavros didn't care who knew about his penchant for cruelty.

"Where are you now?"

Again he hesitated. He rarely lied, and never to his family. "Oklahoma. I've found some information on a young woman closely related to the last Medusa that perfectly fits our profile." He didn't feel bad about the lie, since he knew his cousin would be there within twenty-four hours if he told him where he really was and that he'd found the Medusa.

"Where are you heading?"

"Northeast." He hoped Stavros would be satisfied with the vague answer for now. But he didn't want his cousin breathing down his neck. Stavros had a vicious streak miles wide, had ever since they were children and just beginning to explore and use their individual talents in their hunt for the Medusa. Kallan could undo any lock with just a touch. Stavros could sense and undo any magical spell he found in his path. When they were teenagers, Kallan had seen him use his magical skill to kill innocent animals just because they were nearby. On occasion, he'd used any handy weapon or his bare hands, simply because he could. Kallan knew Stravros's cruelty had intensified in recent years based on things not only Stavros had mentioned, but whispers from his other cousins. While he knew as well as everyone else in his family the sort of monster the Medusa was, he didn't think it necessary to make her suffer the way Stavros would. Especially now that he'd met her.

"Ah. Well, I wish you luck in your hunt, Cousin. Goddess bless our quest."

He repeated the mantra, then thumbed off the phone, thinking. Hopefully his cousin would take the lack of a specific answer to mean Kallan was simply searching and not really onto a solid lead. That would keep Stavros on his own hunt and out of Kallan's way.

He smiled grimly, turning the key in the ignition. Now he

had plans to finalize. Supplies to purchase. He put the truck in gear and steered the vehicle back toward Ellsworth.

Now that he'd found her, the Medusa would die by his hand.

Andi couldn't shake the feeling something was wrong. She'd worked into the night after the vacuum salesman's appearance, until she couldn't see straight to continue with her beading. Then she'd sunk into the bubble bath long enough to be nearly asleep. Today, she'd repeated everything but the bubble bath. Plus she'd driven into town to ship the big order she'd finished early.

Now she sat in the dark beside the front window, watching the forest. Waiting. Trying to convince herself nothing was coming. No one.

When the phone rang, she jumped about two feet in the air, barely keeping in a shriek. She shut her eyes and took a deep breath, forcing herself to laugh weakly as she picked up the receiver. "Hello, Aunt Lydia." She didn't need caller I.D. to know when one of her cousins or aunts was on the phone.

"I didn't mean to startle you, my dear," came the quavering voice. "I just wanted to touch base with you. It's been ages since I've seen you."

Her slightly psychic great-aunt must have spoken to Andi's mother. "I know. I've been busy working." She thought of the small stack of boxed beaded bracelets sitting on her desk upstairs for another customer whose order wasn't even due for a month and a half.

"You're aware you could do that here, too, right?"

Andi smiled in the darkness. "I know. I'm not feeling much like company right now."

"You don't have to visit your parents, you know."

Her laugh escaped before she could stop it. "That isn't very nice of you, Aunt Lydia."

"Maybe I'm getting selfish in my old age." Her great-aunt chuckled. "But I'd like to see you."

"Maybe in a few months."

The older woman sighed. "All right. But I wanted you to know I was thinking of you. I love you."

Andi felt her eyes sting a little. "I love you too."

"Your mother knows she wasn't there for you eight years ago, Andrea. Perhaps it's time to let her be there for you now."

Andi's eyes dried. "I need to go, Aunt Lydia."

"Of course, dear. I hope you'll come soon."

She looked back at the window and murmured, "Maybe. I've got to go, Aunt Lydia."

Something had moved outside.

Something too tall to be one of the does that frequented the clearing each evening, though not tall enough for the bull moose who came occasionally. Just the right size for a sneaky Harvester posing as a vacuum salesman.

She thumbed off the phone and sat up straighter, her other hand coming to rest on the dagger across her knees. For a long moment, she didn't see anything. Then a dark shape slid between the trees, a few yards nearer to the house.

Her heart hammered against her ribs and she curled her fingers around the dagger hilt. That was no animal. At least not of the wild variety. No, this was a two-legged animal, and she had the terrible feeling this one really was a Harvester, no matter what her mother had said yesterday.

Let him try, she thought, setting the phone back on its base. He'd find this Medusa wasn't going down quietly. She only wished she were PMSing so she could take him out without too much effort. Or mess. If only he'd waited just a few more days to make his move…

She stifled a hysterical giggle at that last thought, glad she'd listened to her instincts this evening.

The shape disappeared again in the dark trees, and she held her breath. Then he reappeared for a few seconds, much closer to the house this time. Her pulse pounded in her ears. He was determined. And now out of her line of vision.

A loud, sharp beep indicated her alarm system had shut down, and was accompanied by the sound of every appliance in the house also turning off. He'd killed her power at the junction box outside.

Bastard.

Andi got to her feet, then tried to decide which door he'd come in. She heard the soft sound of a footfall on the back porch. She crossed into the kitchen, not needing to feel her way around the furniture, and positioned herself beside the refrigerator. He wouldn't make it far into the house, and then he was hers.

Kallan wiped his sweaty hand down his jeans, hoping the shriek of the Medusa's alarm shutting off hadn't wakened her. He didn't want her prepared for an attack. He'd prefer to kill her quickly and get the hell out. He could be back in Baltimore by supper tomorrow with the amulet in hand for Uncle Ari to destroy, ending the protective spell for the rest of the Medusa's descendants.

He touched the doorknob, felt the locks disengage beneath his hand, then turned the handle and swung the door wide.

Silence greeted him, and he took that as a good sign. No creaking came from upstairs, as there would be if she'd wakened. Good. Nevertheless, he stepped inside cautiously, listening hard. He took another step after a few heartbeats, trying to remember just where the kitchen table and chairs stood from his limited view the day before.

He made it past the furniture and paused to listen again. Still nothing. He frowned. With the power off, the house was too quiet. Surely the sudden and complete silence would wake her, even if she hadn't heard the brief noise of the alarm shutting down. He slid one foot forward on the smooth wooden floor, and suddenly she was there. Fiery pain shot up his left arm. He grunted, realized she'd stabbed him deeply. He swung his other hand up, managing to hit her on the side of the head.

She cried out but didn't go down, swinging her blade again. He caught her wrist, but she managed to get another slice to his already-injured forearm before he yanked her arm behind her.

Her booted foot connected with his knee—hard—and he bit back a string of curses at the pain, but didn't let her go. Why wasn't she barefoot? If she'd been sleeping, she should be barefoot. His left arm was nearly useless, blood pumping steadily from his wounds, so he crowded her up against the nearest surface. The refrigerator. He shoved hard, hearing her moan when he twisted her arm a little more.

Her blade hit the floor between them. She kicked backward again, and her foot hit his knee from the other side this time.

"Dammit," he muttered, flattening her between his body and the appliance's cool metal surface. His arm burned, warm blood dripping from his fingers.

"Get off me, you murdering bastard," she said, her words slurred slightly from her face being mashed into the refrigerator.

"Well now, that's not very nice. Especially since I've never murdered anyone. Yet," he added darkly, tightening his grip on her wrist. The bones in her arm were fragile and he was fully aware he could crush them, render her arm as useless as she had his. But he didn't. He wasn't Stavros.

"You're not going to start with me, either, Harvester."

Mouthy. He grinned at the back of her head. Even trapped and defenseless as she was now, she didn't stop fighting, even verbally. He had to work to keep from laughing as she continued to threaten him. No one had warned him the Medusa would be talkative. Or soft, he realized when her bottom shifted back into his groin. He concentrated on breathing evenly when his nerve endings all came to life. He'd never imagined he might be aroused by the Medusa.

"Wh-what are you doing?" she asked suddenly.

Kallan realized he wasn't moving—or most of him wasn't. He shut his eyes for a second, clenching his jaw. Her ass now cushioned his throbbing erection.

"Hey!" She shrank closer to the fridge, making a soft sound when the move forced her arm higher behind her.

He shifted, easing her wrist a little lower. This wasn't going at all as he'd imagined it. "Stop moving." He forced himself to unclench his jaw.

"If you think I'm going to make it easy for you to kill me, Harvester, you have another thing coming." She didn't stop wriggling.

Growling, he flattened her completely between his body and the refrigerator again.

She froze, and he could feel her pulse beating crazily in the wrist he still held. Fear? He imagined that was one cause. Anger too, probably.

He doubted she was having the same unexpected reaction to him that he was to her.

Not that it was a bad thing that she wasn't suddenly aroused, too.

He just needed to stop thinking about it.

Concentrate on the task at hand.

Kill the Medusa.

Feel how soft her ass was against him. If he shifted his hips just a little—

No. He growled again, and she shifted, just as he'd imagined so her softness cradled him even more.

"Get off, Harvester," she whispered.

"Stop calling me that." He hated hearing it from her lips for some reason. Yes, it was what his name meant. It was what he was destined to do. But the contempt in her tone… He didn't like it at all.

As though the Medusa had room to be contemptuous of him.

"It's your name." Her voice was stronger now, as if she'd somehow sensed his unexpected inner struggle. "Why shouldn't I use it?"

"You won't be alive long enough to worry about it." He ignored her behind against his groin for the moment and took a slow breath, trying to remember his plan.

Get in, find her, kill her, get the amulet, and get out.

Well, his plan was not going very well at all.

He didn't want to be the first Harvester in so many generations to finally find the Medusa and then fail at his job.

"Really?" She didn't sound as worried as she should. "I'd have thought a big, strong man like you would have already done the job."

So would he.

But something in him resisted destroying her.

"Where is the amulet?"

"The what?"

Kallan frowned in the dark. "Don't play stupid. It's hardly befitting one of your stature."

"I don't know what amulet you're looking for."

She didn't sound as if she was lying. But how would he know? He didn't know her, and ten minutes on her front porch yesterday afternoon hardly qualified him to make such judgments. He hesitated. If he killed her now, he'd have to spend time tearing up her house to find the goblet, and who knew where she could have hidden it? Or if she'd secured it somewhere else?

"Seriously, Harvester." Her tone was even more confident now. "No amulet here."

"You lie. I know the current Medusa always has possession of the amulet." He tightened his grip on her wrist, but didn't wrench it higher.

She sighed. "I'm not lying. I think I'd know if someone had sent me an amulet when Cousin Annis died. Instead all I got was PMS from hell and—" She stopped suddenly.

"And?" His heart beat faster, and he realized blood still pulsed steadily from his wounds.

"And a new tattoo," she whispered.

"A tattoo?" He kept his grip on her wrist. "Where?"

She hesitated.

He pulled her arm upward again and heard her quick gasp.

"My back."

Kallan considered for a moment. Surely the tattoo was just a tattoo—his own tattoo of a scythe was just a tattoo. But if she'd gotten hers when she became the Medusa… He needed to see it. He released her wrist. "Don't move or I'll kill you here." Without stepping away, he fumbled his left hand into one of the loaded pockets on the side of his pants, and found what he needed, surely leaving bloodstains as he did so. He snapped one end of the handcuff onto her wrist, then the other onto his own wrist.

"Hey!"

He shook her a little. "We need the lights back on, and I can't trust you to stay where I put you."

She inhaled shakily, but remained silent as he eased away from her.

He dragged her along with him, back to the door he'd left open. He could see better outside, with the stars and moon shining high above them. In the light from the crescent moon, the Medusa's face was pale but set. Determined. He bit back a smile. She still thought she could get out of this. He admired her spirit, but he had a job to do. His urge to smile vanished.

He strode along to the side of the house where he'd shut off her power at the main box, then reversed the lever to allow electricity to flow into the house again. Even from here, he could hear the hum of appliances restarting inside. And the beeping of her alarm.

"You need to shut that off," he said shortly, grabbing his backpack from where he'd dropped it earlier below the junction box before he dragged her back inside.

She did as he asked, then flipped on the overhead kitchen light, her bright eyes narrowed on his face. "You're making a mess all over my kitchen."

Kallan smiled faintly. "Whose fault is that?" He tilted his head to look at her. "Where is your tattoo?"

"I told you—on my back."

He spun her around and used their cuffed hands to immobilize her against the wall while he yanked her shirt up.

All he could see was the tip of a red flower peeking above the waistband of her jeans.

He shut his eyes for a few seconds, steeling himself. "Unbutton your pants."

"No."

He glared at the back of her head. Then reached between her belly and the wall for the button on her jeans.

She bucked backward, trying to kick him, and he pressed her flat again between himself and the wall. "Get off," she snarled.

He wrestled the button free and fumbled for the zipper as well, then wrenched the denim down.

She growled at him, making him smile as he eased away. His gaze slid down her bare spine, from where their joined hands held her shirt up, down over creamy skin to where her hips flared outward, to the highly stylized tattoo decorating the lower left side of her back. It started even below the elastic edge of her silky white panties, then reached upward, the snake almost hidden in the cluster of detailed flowers. And in the middle of the bouquet, the snake's body coiled around the stem of the gold cup.

The amulet was in her skin.

How in Hades was he supposed to retrieve that?

He exhaled slowly, his gaze riveted to the cup. No one had ever mentioned this. And if she'd gotten this when her cousin had died, then he couldn't take the goblet after killing this one.

But he couldn't take it while she lived.

That was too gruesome to envision. Instead, he focused on her creamy skin, soft against his fingers when he traced the tattoo. Goosebumps rose up beneath his touch.

"Stop it."

He blinked, his gaze lifting from where his finger still burned against her back to her nape. He had no right to touch her this way. He shouldn't even want to. But he did. He let his finger slide over the warm spot again, then frowned, realizing the cup heated further at his touch. He slipped his finger over the flowers at the top edge of the tattoo. Nothing. Her skin was cool. Lower, he grazed the cup again, and her skin flared hot there.

"Ow." She jerked closer to the wall. "What are you doing?"

"Just deciding how I'm going to take the amulet," he murmured, though he frowned. It was an impossible task.

She shuddered, and he heard her swallow.

Kallan resisted the unexpected urge to comfort her. If she'd realized the tattoo was the amulet, then she knew what he had to do to take it.

He sighed. He would have to think about this. Nothing he'd planned for had included carving the amulet from a still-living Medusa. The method shouldn't matter. He knew what she was. He knew what he was. He'd been taught and trained all his life to do this job, as had all of his cousins. But he couldn't quite bring himself to do it. Not right now.

He ignored the little voice in his head that pointed out Stavros wouldn't have the same qualms, that his cousin would enjoy her screams as his blade sliced into her skin. Kallan was not his cousin. He would find another way.

He turned her around and refastened her jeans, ignoring her pale cheeks and the questions in her wide eyes. "Reset the alarm. We need to get some rest."

She hesitated.

"Do it, Medusa. I won't kill you tonight." He heard the resignation in his tone and hoped she did not.

She touched a few keys on the lighted pad, then settled her wide-eyed gaze on him again. "My name is not Medusa," she said after a moment.

"I know what your name is." He knew everything about her. Or he'd thought he had. Obviously, he'd missed a few things in his copious research.

"I don't know yours."

He lifted one brow, studying her ashen cheeks. "I am Kallan Tassos."

Her mouth flattened. "Harvester."

His own lips tightened. For some reason, hearing the translation of his name coming from her mouth bothered him. "As long as we each know who we are." He tugged on their joined wrists. "Come." He towed her along behind him, farther into the house.

Turning on lights as they went, Kallan dragged her up the stairs until they reached the bathroom. He searched for and finally found her First Aid supplies, then started to clean up his arm. The blood flow had slowed, but when he ran his arm under the hot water, rubbing his wounds gently with the soap, he hissed in a quick breath at the sting. "Vicious," he whispered, shooting her a sidelong glance.

She glared at him, trying to keep her cuffed hand out of his way. Out of the water.

Deliberately, he tugged her wrist along with his under the full force of the water so she sputtered a protest. He hid his smile as he bent to clean his wounds. Neither cut was too deep anymore. Not deep enough to require stitches, anyway. His body was nearly the same as normal human males, but he did have a quick healing ability for most non-fatal wounds. He ignored the stinging in his arm as he shut off the faucet and reached for a towel—a move that dragged her arm across his body, forcing her nearer. "Here," he said, putting a handful of bandages in her free hand. "Open these."

Her glare would have turned him to stone another time.

"You made the mess—you can help clean it up." He kept his tone light as he dabbed antiseptic cream onto his arm. Two straight gashes, one only two inches long and nearly as deep, the other about five inches long and shallow. Neat, no ragged edges. The Medusa kept a sharp blade.

Which he needed to retrieve and put out of her reach. He took a bandage and opened it himself, as she still stood there with the handful of unopened packages. "Thank you," he said.

She growled.

Kallan didn't bother to hide his grin this time, applying the covering to his wound, and continuing to open more bandages and stick them onto his arm until both cuts were covered.

Now what?

He'd planned this down to the smallest detail—cutting the power, disengaging the lock, finding and killing her, searching for the amulet, then making his escape before anyone was the wiser. His discovery of the amulet's location, however, put a real wrinkle in his plans. A much bigger problem than the Medusa's defensive attack on him in the kitchen.

He'd been told all his life he was destined to hunt and kill the Medusa. The notion bothered him somewhat. It always had, knowing his family existed to appease the angry Athena by committing murder. Cutting the amulet from Andrea's skin while she lived— well, that bothered him quite a bit more.

He needed to think about this, and he couldn't concentrate with her attached to him.

"Time for bed."

Her jaw dropped. "Excuse me?"

Kallan gave her a bland smile. "Time for bed." He guided her out of the bathroom and steered her into the next doorway, flipping on the light as they went. Her bedroom.

The bed loomed large in the middle of the space,

reminding him uncomfortably of being pressed up against her back in the dark kitchen.

She balked, then stumbled when he gave her arm a gentle yank. "I am not sleeping with you."

"I'm sorry, I don't recall asking you." He pushed her toward the bed.

She tried to dig her feet in, but she didn't get any traction with her boots on the hardwood and skidded into his side.

He nudged her onto the edge of the bed. "Boots."

She stared up at him, appalled, for a long moment. "You are insane."

One of his eyebrows shot up. "Excuse me?"

"I'm not sleeping with you."

"You really don't have a choice, Medusa." He sat down and caught one of her knees, lifting her leg to untie the shoe and push it off.

She struggled against him, making him grunt when she elbowed one of the slash marks on his arm.

He wrestled her other shoe off and then dragged her onto the bed before stretching out beside her.

She sat up, tugging on her arm. She could go nowhere so it was a futile effort.

Kallan smiled at her. "It's been a long night. Lie down."

"I'll kill you."

He laughed. She never stopped. "I think that's my job, my Medusa."

"I'm not your Medusa. I'm not your anything. My name is Andi."

He put his free hand behind his head and studied her for a long moment. "Andrea Rosakis. I know your name."

"How did you find me?"

"I don't think we'll discuss that. But I suppose I should

inquire as to whether there are any weapons in your night-stand I need to worry about tonight."

Her look of disbelief made him sit up. He crawled over her, then straddled her and tried not to think about the position while he used his free hand to pull open the drawer. A flashlight, hefty enough to bash him in the head. He tossed it away so it clattered across the floor and landed near the closet. A tattered book. He flipped it over to look at the cover. A romance novel—the half-naked hero on the cover ravishing the slightly more dressed woman in his arms. The worst she could do with that was give him some paper cuts. Or another painful erection.

Kallan cleared his throat and dropped the book back into the drawer, where there were still some scattered papers, a pen—which he threw in the direction of the flashlight—a black satin sleep mask, and way in the back… He closed his fingers around something more substantial than the pen.

A vibrator, he discovered when he pulled it out of the drawer.

He shot her a quizzical glance and found her face averted, but not enough that he couldn't see the hot color staining her cheeks. He glanced back at the toy, imagining her using it despite his best intentions. He could understand a woman like the Medusa having the same needs as other women. But why wouldn't she indulge them with a flesh and blood man? She only suffered the effects of the curse for a few days each month. He flipped the tiny switch on the bottom of the vibra-tor, and the thing hummed to life.

Under him, she stiffened, turning her face further away.

He shut it off and dropped it back into the drawer. "Well, I don't think I'd consider that a weapon," he said lightly. He was suddenly aware of how close she was again, her breasts a scant inch from his belly, her thighs pressed tight between his knees. Her scent teased his nose—something with wild-flowers and herbs. He sniffed. Basil, maybe. And sandalwood. Something else. He resisted the urge to lean nearer to find out what and climbed off her, ignoring his body's protest. It had definitely been too long since he'd indulged his own needs if he couldn't control these urges around the Medusa for even an hour.

"Lie down."

When she didn't immediately obey him, he gave her a gentle push until her head hit the pillow. She glared up at him, her cheeks still bright pink.

"You're going to need your rest. We have work to do tomorrow," he said.

She averted her gaze.

He had to find out if any of the lore talked about the amulet being embedded in the Medusa's skin. And if so, why hadn't he seen it before now? Why had no one mentioned it?

He stretched out beside her once more. "I hope you have something in the refrigerator for breakfast." He hadn't planned on spending the night, after all.

"You don't really think I'm feeding you, do you?" Horror and anger mingled in her tone.

He didn't look at her, though he really wanted to see her expression. "I have two good hands. I can feed myself. I'm just hoping you have breakfast food here for me to do that with."

"Unbelievable."

He grinned, restraining the laugh that tried to work up from his chest. His Medusa was a lot of fun. A lot more fun than anyone he'd encountered in a long, long time.

She huffed and shifted. "Unbelievable," she repeated, under her breath this time. She inched away from him on the mattress—cautiously, slowly—then lay still for a long moment.

Andi tugged uselessly at her wrist, but his arm didn't move from his side. "Hey, Harvester."

The obnoxious grin slid off his face. "Stop calling me that."

"It's your name."

He glared at her, then folded his arms over his chest, dragging hers along and forcing her to half roll toward him again.

She yanked away but he put his other hand over her wrist. "Go to sleep."

She shot him a disbelieving glance. "I'm sorry. I'm not used to sleeping in handcuffs. Or with all the lights on. And I'm not tired." That last sounded rather childish, she admitted to herself, but the man had nerve.

He observed her for a long moment, until she wanted to squirm under his scrutiny. Then another slow grin started at one corner of his mouth, gradually curving his full lower lip all the way to the opposite corner. "I bet I can fix that."

"I don't think so." She leaned as far away as her trapped arm allowed.

He moved fast, flipping her on top of him before she realized his intent.

Andi blinked, then felt her heart pound faster. The Harvester had muscles on his muscles.

Not the best time to be noticing that, perhaps.

She watched him warily as he shifted under her, settled her close, then stretched their cuffed wrists away from their sides. She put her free hand on his shoulder and pushed herself up a little. "What are you doing?"

"Getting you tired." His other hand slid up her spine to

the nape of her neck, where his fingers started massaging the tight muscles.

"Stop it." She shifted her head to one side, then the other, but his strong fingers continued exactly what they'd been doing. She frowned down at him.

He smiled innocently.

"That doesn't work for me." It did feel good, though. Not that she'd tell him.

Kallan's bright gaze slid down from her eyes to her mouth, almost like an actual touch on her lips.

She swallowed. "Don't even think about it."

"Too late," he murmured, using his grip at her nape to bring her closer.

Andi sucked in a startled breath when he brushed his mouth along hers. "You're sick."

It was his turn to blink. "What?"

"You're here to kill me, right?"

His brows dipped into a frown.

"You're not supposed to be...screwing me too." She blushed.

His frown disappeared. "I'm not trying to screw you. Just kiss you, Andrea."

Her mouth dropped open in shock.

"Well, that makes it much easier," he said softly, lifting his head to catch her lips.

His kiss wasn't what she'd expected. Not that she'd been imagining it. Not really. His lips were warm and soft on hers, not demanding or ruthless—although she was certain he possessed both qualities, and probably far worse, knowing his gene pool. His kiss was more an exploration. A gentle caress.

And for a moment, she decided, she could enjoy it. It had been a very long time since a man had kissed her.

She shivered when he nipped at her lower lip, then heard

a soft sound escape her throat when his warm tongue soothed the bitten spot. At her nape, his fingers still moved gently, and the friction sent unexpected heat rushing down her spine and into her belly.

Gods, it had been so long. She leaned into his caress, just a little.

And his kiss shifted into something a lot more demanding.

Hot desire exploded in her middle, reaching out to all her extremities—to her face, tightening her nipples and making her press them into his chest. The hand she'd had propped on his shoulder slid up to his hair.

She knew this was a really bad idea. The man was an assassin. Her assassin.

But his kiss… It was a kiss unlike any other she'd experienced. Ever. And apparently, her impending PMS had already set her hormones in motion. She wouldn't be able to use the vibrator with him here, but this was so much better…

Dark heat expanded inside her, making her forget the danger he posed. Making her wish she could indulge this unexpected attraction. Just for a little while.

Beneath her, his body hardened—even more than it had earlier in her kitchen—and the hardest part pressed just, oh Gods, at the right spot for her to shift her hips against his, hearing a soft moan. She knew it came from her and she didn't care.

His hair was like silk along her fingertips, and his mouth feasted at hers, fueling her own desire.

When they had to part to breathe she could barely force her eyes open, and when she did, she found his dark with need. And wide with shock.

She gulped in some air that failed to cool her desire. It didn't even really sate her body's need for oxygen, but it was the best she could do when her brain wouldn't function properly.

"Tired yet?" he rasped, his thumb sliding along the side of her neck.

An unexpected laugh bubbled from her throat.

He smiled faintly.

Andi swallowed hard. "Have you forgotten who you are? Who I am?" She really needed to remember both of those things. If she could only make her brain work again.

His smile disappeared, and something like regret surfaced in his eyes before he shook his head. "Unfortunately, I have not." He pressed his thumb harder against her neck, and her world went black.

CHAPTER TWO

Kallan shifted as Andrea pitched forward, and ignored the mingled desire and regret burning in his middle. He eased her to his side, wincing when his cargo pants dug into his erection. He deserved far worse for trying to distract her in that manner. Of course, the distraction had been successful.

It had also worked on him, which was not a good thing. He couldn't afford to be sidetracked this way, and certainly not with Andrea. It wouldn't do at all.

He set his hand over the cuff on his wrist and felt the lock give. He eased her arm higher and attached the free cuff to her iron headboard. It wouldn't make her any happier with him or the situation, but he needed to think, and he couldn't do it when he was so close to her. He sat up and swung his legs over the side of the bed, his back to the unconscious Andrea.

The feel of her body against his would be forever imprinted on his brain, he feared. The softness, the quiet sounds she made while the pleasure swamped her.

Growling, he shoved to his feet and pushed his hair out of

his eyes. Reliving it wouldn't make his body stop throbbing painfully.

He forced his mind instead to his impossible task.

Goddess, how was he supposed to take the amulet? He simply couldn't cut it out of her skin while she lived. No matter what sort of monster she might be, no one deserved that.

Kallan paced to the window, his pulse still too quick. He pressed his forehead to the cool glass, his gaze landing on a small group of deer gathered in the dark, just barely out of the trees and into the yard. The animals were watchful, as if aware there was a dangerous predator in their territory. He shut his eyes tight.

He needed his laptop and notes. He had to see what he'd missed in all his research. Surely there was another way.

Ari might know if there was.

But he hesitated to call his great-uncle. The question would require explanation, and Kallan would have to admit he'd found her. Ari would send out reinforcements, including Stavros, and Kallan did not want his cousin near the Medusa. He had done all the work to find her. He couldn't give her over to Stavros now. He'd simply have to find another way to take the goblet. His cousin would look at Kallan's mercy as weakness. Ari would feel the same way.

No, this glory would be his, once he found a way to get the amulet. This was his destiny, not his cousin's.

Inhaling slowly and deeply, he straightened and shot a glance at the bed. Andrea would likely sleep for hours, and even when she woke, she could go nowhere until he freed her. As far as he knew, the Medusas didn't have his ability to undo locks with just a touch, only to do protective spells for their homes. And clearly hers needed to be refreshed. Too late now.

Her dark hair framed her pale face on the pillow. Just a few minutes ago, her cheeks had been flushed with pleasure. Now they were nearly as pale as the wall behind the bed.

He strode back to her, frowning, and touched the pulse in the hollow of her throat. Strong and steady. Relief rushed along his veins. He pushed a short curl away from her temple, then realized what he was doing and pulled back his hand, curling his fingers into a fist.

He couldn't have her. Shouldn't want her.

His only job here was to take the amulet and kill her.

He clenched his jaw and turned from the bed again. He would kill her. He had to. But not until he figured out a way to get the amulet.

He left the room and went downstairs where he'd left his things in the kitchen, turning off lights as he went. He cleaned up the bloody mess from their earlier struggle—and changed into clean clothes so he could wash the blood out of the ones he'd been wearing. At the wooden table, he booted up his computer, trying hard not to think about the very tempting woman he'd left upstairs in her bed.

His enemy.

When Andrea woke in the morning, it was because she'd tried to roll onto her right side and found she couldn't. She opened her eyes to see her left wrist handcuffed to the headboard. And everything that had happened last night came back to her in a rush.

"Bastard," she muttered, scooting toward the headboard and pushing herself awkwardly upright. "Hey, Harvester!" she shouted.

After a second, she heard a thump from the kitchen then slow footsteps to the stairwell.

She glared at the doorway, impatience bubbling. She tried to tamp it down. She needed a plan. Especially now that she *knew* the tattoo was the legendary amulet protecting her family.

She needed her dagger back.

After an interminable pause, his footsteps started up the stairs.

Andi held her breath until he came to a stop in the doorway, his green eyes wary. And bleary. He'd been sleeping. *Good.* "I need to go to the bathroom," she said. If he was still only half-awake, maybe she could surprise him. Something.

He sighed, then came into the room, looking more aware as he fished the handcuff keys from a pocket of his khaki cargo pants.

She watched him carefully, looking for an opening of some sort.

She didn't get one. Instead he climbed onto the bed and straddled her thighs before fitting the key into the cuff on the headboard. Then he captured her cuffed wrist and held it tight, his gaze hard on her face.

"I've made certain you can't lock yourself in the bathroom anymore," he said evenly. "Your dagger is out of reach, and I've put away anything else you could potentially use as a weapon. If you don't come out of the bathroom in three minutes, I'm coming in after you. Do I make myself clear?"

"I can't shower in three minutes," she sputtered.

"You didn't mention showering." His gaze narrowed on hers for a moment, something dangerous flashing in his eyes. "Showering will have to wait. Three minutes."

She swallowed back the frustrated growl working up her throat. "Fine."

Kallan climbed off her, though he kept her wrist in his

grip to steer her out of the bedroom and into the bathroom. "I'll be waiting right here." He released her and pulled the door shut between them.

Andi glared at the wood panel.

"Two minutes, fifty-five seconds," he said from the other side.

She did growl this time, whirling away from the door. While she brushed her teeth, she examined the handcuffs, wondering if she had anything in the house that would pick the lock. Or if he'd left her anything to use.

"Fifty-two seconds." Though his tone was even, she heard the warning underneath it.

She spat in the sink and rinsed her toothbrush under the stream of water. "I'm coming," she muttered, shutting off the water and wiping her mouth on a towel, hating the metallic jingle of the cuffs as she moved.

He stood waiting when she yanked the door open, his arms crossed over the clean white T-shirt stretched across his chest. "Do I need to cuff you to me again?"

"Absolutely not." She folded her own arms, wishing she'd had time to change her clothes too. The ones she'd slept in still had blood smears from when she'd stabbed him last night. Her gaze strayed to his arm, narrowing when she realized there were no bandages left, nor any marks from her dagger. She looked up, irritated by the hint of a smug smile crinkling the corners of his eyes. "What?"

"I'm a fast healer." He caught her wrist. "Let's go. Are you hungry?"

She opened her mouth to say no, then stopped. She had knives in the kitchen. Hell, a fork would work as a weapon. "Yes, starving," she said instead.

He shot her a quick glance as they went down the stairs, but didn't say anything.

Andi worked to keep a smile from her lips until she got into the kitchen and saw her wooden knife block was nowhere in sight. Okay, no cooking knives. He had warned her he'd put away any potential weapons. She inhaled slowly. That was okay. A paring knife could also be used to do physical damage. If she had to, she could gouge his eye out with a spoon.

She tried not to think about that one too much. Instead, she turned to the refrigerator and tugged the door open. Scrambled eggs would require at least a fork.

Except she didn't have any eggs in the house.

Dammit.

Toast. Toast needed butter, and butter required a knife.

She pulled the cinnamon raisin bread off the second shelf, grabbed the tub of butter, and shut the door.

Kallan stood watching her, still looking faintly amused.

Well, they'd see who was smiling in a few minutes.

She started the toaster and leaned against the counter, her irritation growing as he simply stood there, watching her in silence. As if he knew something she didn't. And she had the terrible feeling he might.

When her toast popped up, she pulled open the drawer that held her silverware. But the usual rattle of flatware was much quieter than usual. Not even a spoon lay in the tray, the sections for the knives and forks empty too.

She shot him a glare. "How am I going to butter my toast?"

"I could do it for you, but then you'd know where the silverware is. I guess you're having dry toast this morning." His smile widened.

She punched at him before she realized she meant to, but he caught her fist in his. The swinging handcuff crashed into his wrist, though, making him wince faintly.

"That wasn't very nice," he said, using his free hand to reattach the dangling cuff to his own wrist. "I guess you want to be my sidekick again."

"Bastard." She slapped her free hand at him and found herself pressed close to him, both her arms behind her.

"Andrea, we have to work together for a little while, and that will prove difficult if you insist on assaulting me."

She forced a short laugh, trying to ignore the way he felt against her, as if last night were repeating. "Right. Because you killing me isn't going to put a damper on our relationship at all, right?"

His eyes darkened with anger. "Maybe I need to find a gag too." His fingers bit into her wrist.

Andi felt a tendril of fear slither down her spine.

He released her suddenly, and she would have lost her balance if she hadn't been cuffed to him. "Eat your toast, Andrea. We have work to do."

She rubbed her free wrist for a moment before taking her bread out of the toaster. She'd have a bruise on her arm. *Better bruised,* she mused, *than dead.* "Screw you."

"Tried that, didn't you?"

She sucked in a sharp breath, going still as unexpected pain lanced at her middle. "I think it was the other way around, wasn't it?" she asked after a moment, looking up in time to see his mouth tighten fractionally. "Don't think I'll forget it either, Harvester."

He didn't answer, his gaze sliding away from hers for a second.

Andi took a bite of her toast, but it might as well have been a piece of the kitchen table. She needed to find a way out and fast.

She remained silent when he guided her to the kitchen table and gave her a gentle nudge into a chair, then seated himself beside her. If she could knock him unconscious, she could get the key out of his pocket and be gone before he came to.

As a plan, it sucked.

As her only plan, it would have to do unless she came up with something else.

Forty minutes later, Kallan exhaled sharply, then shut the laptop down and pushed away from the table. Andrea still sat, her face turned toward the window, and he knew she was plotting. He would have been too, in her position. He wondered if she'd come up with a workable solution yet.

Nothing in his research of the notes from the previous generations of Harvesters ever mentioned the amulet being embedded into the Medusa's skin. He'd checked and double-checked. It would explain why his ancestors had failed to secure the cup in millennia. He wondered if anyone else had ever realized its location. Surely his predecessors would have mentioned it if they'd discovered the problem. They would have wanted to make the task easier for those who followed.

"Are you ready for your shower, Andrea?"

Her head swiveled around, her big blue eyes wary.

He waited.

She watched him for a long moment, then nodded slowly.

"Come." He tugged her up and steered her out of the room. He didn't want to think about what was coming. He couldn't afford to. It was too big a distraction.

Upstairs, he waited while she gathered clean clothing from her dresser, pretending not to notice when she stuffed a lacy pair of underwear and matching bra into the middle of the stack of her shirt and jeans. The wariness never left her face, though.

He sighed inwardly and guided her into the bathroom. "I'm going to uncuff you so you can shower, but I'm going to wait right here for you."

Her wide eyes narrowed. "You can't."

"You want to stay handcuffed to me? That will make showering very interesting." Much too interesting.

She swallowed. Apparently, she got the same visual, though, as color bloomed in her cheeks.

He pulled the key from his pocket and unlocked her cuff.

She stepped away from him, rubbing her wrist. He looked closely but there was no mark, so he imagined she was just happy to be free.

"How long before the curse kicks in again?"

She jerked but didn't look up.

"Andrea." He needed to know. If he didn't have any warning, it would be easy enough for her to kill him. Judging by her reaction, it wasn't long. "Today? Tomorrow? Should I just kill you now and start my search all over? I've already compiled a nice list of your cousins to start my fresh search." She didn't need to know he had no intention of doing that, but if it kept her honest…

"A couple days maybe." She slid one hand over the top of her head, her cheeks paling.

Kallan frowned. That didn't give him much time to figure out how to retrieve the cup. Even if he could bring himself to cut it out of her skin…

"Can you at least turn around?" she asked after a moment.

He dragged his occupied mind back to the present, to where Andrea stood several feet away, her expression guarded. "No." He could withstand the temptation for a few minutes.

Her mouth flattened and her jaw set. And she jerked at the

button on her jeans, pulled the zipper down and shoved the denim off her hips.

He stared. He couldn't help it. Her legs were long and strong. He imagined she spent a fair amount of time walking on her mountain.

Then she jerked her shirt over her head, and his mind went blank for a moment.

He'd been very good last night, not touching her in places he'd desperately wanted to touch. Like the creamy breasts over-spilling the white bra she currently wore.

He gulped in some air, working hard to keep his expression impassive.

She glared at him as she reached behind herself to unhook the bra, silently daring him to open his mouth.

He wanted to open his mouth right over those beautiful dark nipples. He could very nearly imagine her taste, was so busy imagining it he almost missed her sliding the white panties down. Until she kicked them toward him.

Sweet Goddess, she was beautiful.

He sucked in a harsh breath as she climbed into the shower and slid the door shut before she turned the water on.

"Do I have a time limit here too?" she called over the spray of the water.

It took Kallan a moment to answer her, blinking to clear the image of her naked ass from his brain, and failing. "I'll let you know when you're pushing your luck," he finally said, hearing how gruff his tone was. He cleared his throat. This was no good. Why had he thought he could manage this? No wonder the Medusas had survived this long. They were not only gorgeous, but smart. Cunning, exactly what Medusa meant.

Against his will, his gaze slid back to the shower door,

through which he could see her pour something onto her hands, then slick them over her body.

This was torture, pure and simple. He was out of his mind to stay and watch.

But he couldn't walk away now. Not when her hands stroked up her arms to her shoulders, then down over her chest, lingering there.

Andi knew he was watching. Even without looking through the frosted door, she could feel his stare. She could tease him.

Thinking of him watching her made her nipples tighten as they had last night when he kissed her. Made the rest of her heat up in ways that had nothing to do with the warm water. Then there was the whole hormonal issue of needing some release anyway, with her period only days away. She decided to indulge herself. Touching herself would torture him at the same time. The only problem was she hadn't grabbed her vibrator on the way into the bathroom. She'd have to do without.

She lingered over her breasts, feeling them swell—aching—but she teased herself with light strokes, fleeting caresses. Until she couldn't stand it any longer and pinched her nipples, tight. The slight pain sent a bolt of heat straight into her belly, making her wet. Wetter. She imagined his mouth on her nipples instead of her own fingers, and a soft moan tried to escape her. She swallowed it back, sliding one hand down over her belly, lower, until she could feel just how slick she was.

She tried to picture his fingers between her thighs. They were strong fingers, hard. She matched her strokes to her fantasy, and soon she had to lean against the cool tile wall to keep her balance.

His fingers would tease her, first with light strokes to her clit, then deeper, harder strokes into her body—not nearly filling her, making her want more.

The climax rushed through her before she realized it was so close, and she gasped for breath, her eyes shut tight, his image still firmly in her head.

Andi gradually caught her breath, pushing off the wall. Outside the shower, Kallan still stood, silent, but the tension in the small room had ratcheted up about a thousand percent. She swallowed hard.

What the hell had she been thinking? She stepped fully under the spray of water to rinse the rest of the shower gel from her body. She washed her hair quickly, trying hard not to think of what she'd just done. Heat rose in her cheeks that had nothing to do with the desire she'd just quenched.

She delayed in the shower as long as she dared, but he never said a word to urge her to finish, so she finally shut the water off and eased the door open only far enough to grab a towel. She dried herself quickly while still standing in the shower stall, resisting the need to peek around the glass to see his face. She'd bet his expression was something far more dangerous than the one he'd worn as she was stepping into the shower.

She took a deep breath. Well, she'd wanted to tease him. Now she'd have to face him.

She shoved the door open and met his gaze, which was shuttered. She blinked. There was no way he hadn't realized... No, not possible. Then she looked closer. His cheekbones wore a dark flush, and his lovely mouth was tight, as was his jaw. She let her gaze slide lower, and she couldn't help the widening of her eyes.

Holy Gods.

She jerked her gaze back to his face, then away, reaching

blindly for her underwear. She stepped into them, then had to take them back off, as she'd put them on backward.

All the while, he didn't speak.

She heard a faint tearing sound and realized she'd yanked the lace so hard, she'd ripped it somewhere, but at least she had the underwear on. She fumbled with the matching bra for a few seconds, finally managing to get that on as well. Why had she grabbed lace? He could see right through it.

She yanked her shirt on over her head, and then yelped in surprise when she emerged from the garment and Kallan was standing within arm's length.

His green eyes were dark, his expression dangerous.

This is what happens when you tease the man.

She froze.

He touched her jaw lightly, his fingers shaking. "You have some interesting shower habits, Andrea."

She exhaled roughly. "It's the onset of PMS," she whispered. That was only partly true.

"Really?" His fingers slid down the side of her throat to her exposed collarbone.

She felt her nipples tighten again. "Yep. Every month, a couple days before the rest of it starts." She gulped in some air when his fingers slid over her shirt, toward one of her nipples. "That's what the vibrator is for." Gods, she should stop talking. She knew she should.

He tweaked the tip of her breast, and her legs went weak. "It would be a shame if you couldn't make use of a flesh-and-blood man while you have the opportunity," he murmured.

Her gaze dropped to the erection still pressing against his pants before she could stop it. Gods, that would be lovely. She curled her fingers into her palms to keep from reaching out.

Then his other fingers slid over the lace between her

thighs, at the same time he pinched her nipple, harder than she had during her shower. A soft sound escaped her before she could stop it. The lace between her thighs was instantly wet.

"Can I help you with that?" His fingers pushed deeper between her thighs, rasping over her clit.

Andi panted, her stance widening of its own volition.

Kallan palmed her sex, and she moaned, trying hard not to rock her hips into the caress.

He tugged the lace aside and plunged one finger right into her core, and she couldn't help but lift her hips into the thrust.

"Andrea?"

She realized she'd closed her eyes and forced them open, finding him even closer now, his heat reaching out to envelop her, almost like an actual embrace.

"Touch me."

The command was impossible to resist. She uncurled her fingers and moved her hand across the scant inches between them to wrap them around the solid length of him. He grunted, his eyes sliding shut for a second, then he met her gaze again and slid a second finger deep inside her.

Andi whimpered, her grip tightening on him.

"Yes?" he breathed, bending nearer.

Her body arched into his next caress without her permission. And the next. The pleasure and tension coiled tight in her belly, shocking her with the intensity and speed.

He kissed her lightly, his hard fingers finding all the right spots to make her desire rush right up to the edge of the precipice, and then he kept her there.

She tried shifting her hips, but his fingers shifted too. She stroked him harder, feeling his hips jerk into her touch, then fumbled with his cargo pants to release his flesh into her hand.

He made a low rumbling sound when her fingers wrapped around his erection, then shifted so her back was to the wall, tugging her shirt up so he could get his hand inside her bra to her bare breast.

She moaned, her body taut with need.

He teased her, sliding his fingers deep, then lightly caressing her clit, his hips rocking into her strokes too. He knew this wasn't a good idea. He'd been certain he could resist it. Resist her. Resist himself. But there was no resisting this.

"Bed," he whispered against her mouth. "We should be in a bed." He rubbed his thumb over her clit, making her whimper into his kiss.

When he thrust his fingers hard into her, she flew apart.

He lifted his head to watch this time, the flush rising from the top of her shirt to the roots of her hair, the deep rose color of the nipple he'd freed from her bra, and the slick evidence of her desire on his fingers with each thrust and retreat. He nipped at her lower lip, then sucked it into his mouth to soothe the sting.

Her fingers on his own flesh were hot, nearly as hot as his erection felt. His hips rocked into each stroke of her fingers, and he knew his own release was only moments away.

Andrea's eyes opened slowly. "Come inside me," she whispered. "Please."

He released her breast to shove his pants down far enough, then tore her panties, dropped the ripped lace somewhere behind him, and lifted her up. She wrapped her legs around his waist and he slid easily into her body, deep, deeper. Around him, her flesh still spasmed. *So good.*

He groaned, dropping his head back for a moment to try

to gather some strength. "Andrea." He met her gaze. "Hard or slow?"

More color washed up her cheeks, but she didn't look away. "Hard."

His body tightened. "As you wish." He slid one hand beneath the soft curve of her bottom, lifting her nearer, and wedged the other between their bodies so he could slide his thumb over her clit.

Her breath caught in her throat, but she still watched him, her eyes bright with desire.

He eased his hips backward—slowly, slowly, till only the tip of his cock was still inside her scalding heat. Then thrust hard, deep.

She cried out.

He repeated the movements, over and over, feeling her body arching into his strokes, her sheath tightening on him, pulsing, burning him until he could no longer resist his own need. When his release thundered through him, he felt her orgasm bloom as well, heard her faint scream. Felt his heart pounding hard against her breast. Her nails biting into his shoulders. Her mouth sliding over his jaw.

He shut his eyes and gathered her close, hoping his legs would continue to hold them up.

When Andrea's mouth touched the corner of his, he turned his head far enough to capture her lips, feeling a last surge of heat rush through him when their tongues met, stroked.

It took a long time for his lungs to slow their wicked pace, for his heart to ease back into a normal rhythm. Equally as long for hers to do the same. He smiled against her mouth. It had been a long time since he'd been so desperate for a woman.

His smile faded. And a very bad time for his libido to kick in, with his quarry as the target of his desire.

As if she'd finally realized their positions, Andrea stiffened in his arms.

Reluctantly, he eased his hips backward—gritting his teeth against the need to stay inside her warmth—then set her on her feet. "Are you all right?"

"I think we're both sick," she muttered, sliding away from him along the wall.

Kallan tugged his pants back up, wincing, and kept an eye on her.

But she just grabbed her own jeans, then stood at the sink, holding them in front of her and looking at her torn panties two feet away.

He felt a surge of satisfaction as he recalled the need that had been coursing through them both when he'd ripped her panties off.

And a twinge of guilt at giving in to the desire with his enemy.

"I'll grab you another pair of underwear," he murmured, noting the faint flash of relief crossing her face. Something ached in his chest.

When he left the room, he heard the sink come on, and imagined her washing. His body jerked as if in preparation, but he tamped down the idea of more. Once was bad enough. At least he knew the Medusas couldn't get pregnant, and—if she had really been without a man all this time—it didn't matter that he had no condoms. He tugged open two dresser drawers before finding her underwear, and blindly grabbed something that turned out to be a shocking pink thong. It didn't matter. He made it back into the bathroom in time to see her drying her inner thighs.

Hot color washed up her throat to her face, and she avoided his eyes as she took the panties.

He knew he should look away, but he couldn't help himself, watching her pull the thong up and on, then the jeans she yanked up, hiding those beautiful legs. And more intimate places.

She sat on the toilet lid, head bowed, and he washed himself while keeping an eye on her. She may attempt an escape, after all.

But she sat quietly until he finished. When he turned to her, he debated pulling the handcuffs from his pocket.

"We can't do that again," she said at last, lifting her head.

He raised one eyebrow. "Really?"

"I accused you last night of being sick, but maybe we both are." She looked away for a second. "I have a perfectly good vibrator for this, and sleeping with the man who's come to kill me is all kinds of stupid."

He pondered her words for a moment. "I don't think you're stupid, Andrea."

A humorless laugh passed her lips. "Right. It doesn't matter. Either you'll kill me before my PMS starts, or I'll kill you when it does. But anything like this between us is foolish." She rubbed one palm on her knee. "At least you know what to expect."

He frowned at that odd statement but let it go. "I think you know I can't kill you before I get the amulet, Andrea."

Her cheeks went chalk-white, and she averted her eyes.

"And I can't take it in the way you're imagining." He sighed. "I need to think about this a little longer. Dig a bit more into the myths."

"You won't find anything about the cup there. Not about how to take it." Her tone was more confident now, and her blue gaze met his again. "If I'm not mistaken, I'm the first of the Medusas unlucky enough to have survived her first encounter with a Harvester, long enough for the Harvester to discover the secret of the fabled Medusa's Goblet." She held his gaze for a moment. "And if you don't kill me without trying to take the cup, you will die when my PMS hits."

"Well, that will be bad for me, won't it?" he said lightly. "Come, let's go downstairs. I need to do some reading." He offered his hand to her, holding his breath all the while.

She eyed his fingers for a long time before she finally put her hand in his and let him pull her to her feet.

He curled his fingers around hers and towed her along the hall to the stairs. It was a dilemma, to be sure. *Goddess, help me*, he thought.

He dug through the same archives he'd dug through during the night, hoping his tired brain had missed something. Anything.

It hadn't.

While he skimmed obscure texts and more modern lore, Andrea sat at the table, an open book in front of her. Kallan knew she wasn't reading though. She hadn't turned a page in more than half an hour, instead staring down at the book blankly.

He debated emailing one of his cousins about the problem, but he didn't want anyone to know he had found the Medusa. Or worse, that he hadn't yet killed her.

Goddess, he'd never find the solution this way.

"Let's go for a walk."

Her head shot up, blue eyes wide. "You think you can keep up with me?" she asked after a second.

He smiled. "I didn't say you'd be walking freely."

Her mouth flattened when he pulled the handcuffs out of his pocket.

To his surprise, she didn't say anything when he bound them together again, just averted her face.

He led the way out of the house, pausing on the front porch to survey the surrounding area. "This way." He strode toward the pathway just visible to the rear of her car. Into the forest.

Andrea kept up with him easily as he climbed over fallen trees and rocks in their way. It would have been simpler, perhaps, if he hadn't handcuffed her to himself, but in addition to keeping her with him, this way she was occasionally forced to accept his assistance, which he enjoyed.

Perhaps he *was* a sick bastard, he mused, slowing his pace as they went deeper into the woods and the trail narrowed. Realizing the woman he wanted most was his enemy had just turned his world upside-down. His family's enemy, a monster created by the Goddess.

He frowned up at the dark canopy of leaves above them. He wondered if any other Harvester had ever been tempted by his quarry. Or had surrendered to the temptation. If so, he was certain he'd never find *that* in the lore.

"Wait."

He stopped walking at her quiet command, his gaze shifting in the same direction she looked. A doe and her fawn looked poised for flight several yards away, the mother watching them closely. Kallan held his breath as the fawn bent back to the small patch of grass. From the corner of his eye, he saw Andrea's smile. He caught her hand in his without thinking about it first.

Her fingers were stiff in his for a long moment, then relaxed a little.

He turned to look down at her, studying her. The top of her head reached his chin, her dark hair curling in the slight humidity. Her bright gaze stayed fixed on the deer, but he knew she was aware of him by the way her pulse skittered in the hollow of her throat.

"Did I hurt you?" He kept his tone low, trying not to frighten the nearby animals.

She didn't move anything but her eyes, shifting her questioning gaze up to his face.

"Earlier. Was I too rough?"

Color washed up her cheeks, and she swallowed, turning her attention back to the doe and her fawn. "No." It was barely a whisper, her reply.

His heart pounded a little harder as he thought about taking her here, right here in her forest. It was foolish. He couldn't. She would never agree to it anyway.

But he couldn't stop the images behind his eyes, not now that he knew what she looked like, what she felt like around him, the way she sounded.

When she turned to look up at him again, he realized he'd tightened his grip on her fingers. Her expression was quizzical, then awareness surfaced, turning her eyes darker, like midnight velvet.

Kallan lifted their joined hands slowly, giving her time to stop him. When she didn't, he dragged his open mouth along her knuckles.

Her lips parted slightly.

He bit one of her knuckles lightly and felt her shiver. "Maybe I am sick," he breathed. "But I still want you."

She shut her eyes, her throat working as she swallowed. "Bad idea, Harvester."

His jaw tightened. For some reason, hearing her use the name his family had claimed many generations ago made him angry. He wanted to hear her use his name instead. Preferably while they were naked in her bed, bodies joined intimately as they had been earlier.

Instead of protesting, though, he nibbled his way down her finger until he could capture the tip in his teeth, then sucked it into his mouth.

Her breath came faster.

Kallan slid his tongue along the side of her finger, feeling her shudder. "Are you wet yet?"

A squeak passed her lips.

He smiled around her flesh and sucked. Her nipples pressed tight against her shirt, and his mouth watered.

The doe had apparently had enough of their intrusion and took flight, leaping into the trees with her fawn on her heels. The sudden movement startled them both, and Andrea tugged her hand free of his lips, blushing.

"Have you had enough walking yet?"

He sighed. "No. I thought maybe being in the fresh air would help clear my head. Help me find a solution." He moved to stand in front of her. "Instead, I find myself ready to take you here against a tree."

She bit her lower lip and looked away.

"Andrea." He wished she would discourage him, as apparently he no longer had a will of his own. That said nothing good about him, he realized. He curled his free hand into a fist at his side instead of lifting it to cup her breast as he wanted.

She met his gaze, her own troubled. "I don't suppose you'd just leave. Let me alone."

Something in his chest tightened, and he shook his head. "I'm afraid not. Besides, I've already found you. That means others can find you as well." Somehow, he hadn't thought of that before, and it unsettled him. Any of his dozens of cousins could be on their way to Andrea's mountain now, following the same vague clues he had, intent on killing her. And none of them knew they couldn't take the amulet after they did.

Somehow, that bothered him less than the idea of one of them killing her.

"You have to figure something out soon then. You only have a day or so."

Then her curse would kick in, and she could kill him instead of the other way around. And with far less difficulty.

Kallan sighed, tipping his head back to look up at the dark green canopy for a moment. "I'll figure something out," he said at last. "Let's walk some more."

She looked away, her mouth turned down, as they began to walk.

He linked their fingers again, ignoring her slight start at the touch, and led her deeper into the forest.

Though they walked for nearly two hours, he couldn't quite find his way around the only solution to present itself thus far: he could take the amulet and then kill her, or kill her without retrieving the amulet. Neither option was palatable, yet it was his duty as a Tassos. The Harvesters of the Medusas, since the first Medusa. To destroy the amulet would break the protection on her family, exposing all of them as monsters his family would eliminate. Somehow he'd never realized exactly what it would mean to kill someone. Anyone.

CHAPTER THREE

Andrea rested her head on her folded arms on the kitchen table, only half listening to Kallan typing on his keyboard. She didn't want to die just yet. She knew for sure she didn't want to be mutilated before she died.

But she didn't look forward to killing the Harvester either.

She never should have had sex with him. She knew it. She'd known it beforehand.

And she should definitely *not* still want him.

When the phone rang, it was a relief. For a few seconds. Until she realized it was Thalia. "My cousin." She didn't think she needed to explain her mental caller I.D. to him.

Kallan held her gaze for a long moment. "Don't try to let her know what's going on," he said at last. "I know where a lot of your cousins are located, and I'm not the only one."

Her heart pounded harder at the implication, but she got to her feet and picked up the receiver. "Hello, Thalia. How are you?"

"I'm fine, Andi, but I think you need to get away for a while."

She frowned, feeling Kallan's presence behind her. Close behind her. Close enough to hear her conversation. "What do you mean?" His body heat teased her.

"The Harvesters are out and about. I'm afraid for you."

Andi shut her eyes for a second, then opened them again when he put his hands on her shoulders. She shot him a glare and moved away, back toward the table. "I'm fine."

"Please don't ignore this, Andi. You know I'm hardly ever wrong."

That was true. But she wondered if her cousin realized she was very often late with her flashes of intuition. Far too late in this case. "Okay. I'll give it some thought, all right? Mom said something the other day about visiting." Gods, had it only been two days ago? "And Aunt Lydia just called yesterday too. I could go to see either of them if anything seems odd."

His hands settled on her shoulders again, massaging the tense muscles there.

She didn't bother to shrug him off this time. He was persistent. "I could even come visit with you," she teased, forcing a lightness into her tone.

Her cousin cleared her throat. "I actually have company right now," she said after a moment, and Andi could almost see her blushing. "You remember I met someone in Athens last summer? Well, he's come again to stay for a while." Even over the phone, the emotion in Thalia's voice was obvious.

One more cousin safe—none of the cousins who'd fallen in love ever had the curse land on their heads. A tiny bit of relief made her relax further under Kallan's touch. "That's terrific, Thalia. When do the rest of us get to meet him?"

"We're talking dates," the other woman said, a hint of a smile in her tone now. "I'll be sure to let you know."

"Good. And thanks for the warning. I miss you."

"I miss you, too. I've got to go, Andi. Talk to you soon. But promise you'll be careful. Danger is coming from more than one direction."

She pushed the off button on the phone and shut her eyes, ignoring the slight sting in them. She was *not* envious of Thalia's good fortune. She was just in an impossible situation here.

His warm breath brushed the top of her head a second before his lips. "That was good."

She wanted to tell him to go screw himself. She wanted a weapon to swing at him. She wanted him to wrap his arms around her and carry her down onto the nearest flat surface.

Her eyes popped open. *Damned hormones.*

His hands slid down her sides and wrapped around her, settling her back against his chest as if he'd read her mind. She hoped he didn't have *that* ability.

"What have you found?" she asked instead, keeping herself upright instead of relaxing further.

"Not a cursed thing."

She blinked. She hadn't really expected he'd tell her, but the resignation in his tone told her his reply was the truth. She inhaled unsteadily. "I guess you have to make up your mind then. You or me."

"There has to be something else." He sounded frustrated now, as if he were gritting his teeth, and his grip on her tightened marginally.

Andi shut her eyes. No matter how torn he seemed to be about his destined tasks, she had no doubt he'd do them eventually. And if not, she'd do what the Medusas had been doing for millennia and eliminate the threat to her. That was *her* destiny.

"We need some supper," he murmured, sliding his face

along the top of her head. "If I let you have a paring knife, will you promise not to try to stab me with it?"

She smiled in spite of herself. "I don't need a knife to kill you, you know."

"We'll cross that bridge when we get there." He squeezed her tight against him for a heartbeat, and she felt her pulse quicken.

Stupid. She moved away. "I'm not sure what's in the house," she said, clearing her throat to get rid of the rasp in her voice.

"You have plenty of food here." He walked with her to the refrigerator and tugged open the top freezer door. "What are you in the mood for?"

She snapped her mouth shut when the first thought that popped into her head was, "sex". Obviously, her hormones were still kicking after the taste she'd had of him that morning. "Fish. Veggies." No, wait—not just from the taste of him earlier, but the regular boost of her hormones before full-on PMS kicked in.

He stepped aside and let her take two packages out of the freezer, then he shut the door while she moved to the island with them. She put the fish into the microwave to defrost. He watched as she found a pan and poured some oil into it, then added the vegetables and fish once it was snapping over the heated burner.

When his phone rang, he took it from his pocket absently and thumbed the on button without looking at the screen. "Yes?"

"Kallan."

His burgeoning smile vanished. "Stavros."

"Have you found her yet?"

"No." He glanced at her when her quizzical gaze lifted from the stove to meet his.

"I'm getting closer. My information is looking good. I've found an excellent prospect, dropped out of college right after the last Medusa died and has never married."

His heart stopped beating. He couldn't tell his cousin the problem facing them. He didn't want any of his cousins coming here. Especially not this cousin. And not just because he didn't want him to know Kallan had found her and not killed her.

"Everything I've found points to one of several women in Maine."

Kallan shut his eyes. Stavros had found the same clues he had followed. *Dammit.* "Ah. My leads are suggesting Ohio, actually. The young woman I was tracking in Oklahoma moved here six months ago and changed her name. Single, reclusive for the last eight years or so, according to everyone I've spoken to so far." He opened his eyes in time to see Andrea's jaw drop. He winked at her.

"Hm. Well, you should follow your own information while I will follow up on mine. One of us will find her this time, take her head."

He clenched his jaw for a second. "Where are you now? Maybe we can pool resources. Compare notes."

"I'm in New York, but I'm heading out tomorrow to drive to Maine. I should be able to narrow down these threads to one location in the next day or two."

Just in time for her PMS to really kick in.

Kallan smiled grimly. If his cousin walked into that, it would be bad. For Stavros. "Oh, what a shame. Maybe next time."

"Sure. After this one is found and eliminated. I've got to

go. I'm meeting someone who may have better information for me."

He shut his phone off and stuffed it back in his pocket. "Bad news, Medusa."

"You tried to send him to Ohio?" She still stared at him, confusion in her blue eyes. "Don't you think reinforcements would be a good thing for you?"

He shrugged. "Stavros has never been one to wait until he has all the information he needs for a job, and I'd prefer he went somewhere else right now. Unfortunately, he's heading this way."

Her cheeks paled, and she dropped her gaze to the frying pan before she stirred the food there.

"He'll be here just in time for you to turn him to stone, if he's being honest about his timing."

"If?" She looked up, fear shadowing her bright eyes.

He rubbed at the back of his neck, hoping to dissipate some of the tension gathering there. "He isn't always." And that was far from the worst thing about his character.

"So now I have two killers after me." She swallowed. "Fantastic."

Kallan glared at her, even though he knew she had a point —he *had* come here to kill her. "Thanks."

"I'm being honest, even if your cousin isn't." She lifted one shoulder in a shrug and set down the spatula.

The scent of their meal filled the space between them, but he ignored it for now. "How about some honesty from me? I'm known for not lying, which is why he'll believe I'm in Ohio. I am not going to let him kill you."

She snorted. "Until you get the amulet."

He clenched his jaw harder and wondered how much more it would take to crack a tooth. He couldn't even protest, as that was his ultimate goal—to collect the amulet that protected the Medusa's offspring so the world could know them for the monsters they were. To make it easier for his cousins to find and eliminate them all.

Except Andrea wasn't a monster.

And he wasn't at all sure now that he could kill her. He never should have given in to the attraction between them.

He watched her pace the small area between the island and the sink. "I had an idea earlier," he said after a few minutes.

She didn't stop walking, only paused to stir their supper. "About what?"

"About you not turning me to stone." He was fairly certain she wasn't going to like it, but he had to bring it up.

She arched one eyebrow at him, silent for a moment. "Let's hear it."

"You have that sleep mask upstairs," he started.

She shook her head before he'd even finished speaking. "No."

"It would involve a little trust on your part," he continued a little louder. "That I wouldn't do anything to you while you were defenseless."

Andrea kept shaking her head. "No."

"What can I do to persuade you?"

She stopped walking and faced the sink, her head hanging as she braced herself on the edge of the counter.

He waited.

"There's nothing."

His heart sank a little. To protect her from his vicious cousin, he would agree to nearly anything. He tried not to think beyond that though, to the reason—whether it was because he still thought he should fulfill his destiny, or because he'd had sex with her. He just didn't want Stavros to get his hands on her. That was enough for now. "There has to be something."

She sighed, still staring into the sink. She unclenched her fingers from the edge of the counter, then traced a pattern on the surface.

"Andrea." His tone was almost a singsong, with that faintest of accents. And it was nearer this time than the last time he'd spoken.

Andi ground her teeth together, counting to ten. It was stupid. She knew it was the start of PMS. She knew she was overreacting. Knowing didn't make it better. She glared at the counter instead of Kallan. And counted ten more.

A small ding appeared in the granite. She shut her eyes. "I think you should go."

He snorted, and it took every ounce of her willpower not to look up at him.

"Andrea." His tone was low now, patient.

"Harvester." Her own was not. Patient, that is. She almost felt like she could spit nails she was so angry. He was asking her to trust him when his sole intention in tracking her here was to kill her. And now he wanted her trust. She stared at the new divot in the granite.

His finger touched the ding. "Stress speeds up the process, I see," he said mildly.

She nodded.

"What can I do to earn just that little bit of trust?" He slid his fingertip closer to her hand on the counter.

"I need a pair of scissors." She didn't know what had made her say it, but she did need them. Very badly. She knew she couldn't trust him, and nothing he could do would change that. But she could pretend for the sake of getting the scissors.

He considered for a moment, his fingertip grazing the side of her hand. "Do you mind if I ask why?"

"I need a haircut." Also true.

He bent nearer, his expression disbelieving. "A haircut?"

She nodded, trying to avoid his eyes.

His gaze slid to her hair, and she knew when he realized her reasoning. Awareness deepened the green of his eyes. "All right."

She gripped the edge of the counter again, surprise coursing through her. "Really?"

He nodded. "And you'll wear the sleep mask."

Andi only hesitated a second before she nodded. It was a small price to pay to prevent the other thing. If he killed her while she couldn't see him—well, that would be her own fault.

Kallan kissed her cheek lightly, surprising her once more. "Scissors tonight, sleep mask tomorrow?"

She nodded dumbly, watching him move away to stir their dinner. Somehow, she hadn't expected him to agree so easily. Or that he would understand.

And somehow, she didn't feel good about either one.

Kallan watched as she pushed her food around on her plate. He plowed through his meal, starved after their trek through the woods. He still hadn't figured out what to do about the amulet, but right now it didn't matter. He needed to get her out of here before Stavros came calling.

Or he needed to delay his cousin.

He paused, fork halfway to his mouth. If Stavros was in New York, there was only one person anywhere who could slow him down. Kallan would have to lie to get it accomplished—a much bigger lie than his fib about his location—

but right now, he was okay with that. He stuffed his last bite of fish into his mouth and shoved his plate aside before he grabbed the laptop to connect to the family's website.

Andrea played with her food for another moment, then rose to dump her plate.

The log-in screen granted him access, and he swiftly typed in his message, leaving tantalizing hints of what he believed he'd found so far, a little brag at the end. He didn't address his post to anyone in particular, but knew his great-uncle would see it and stop Stavros from traveling to Maine, sending him instead to Ohio, on a wild goose chase. Kallan just hoped it would be a long enough delay for him to get Andrea away—he'd need three or four days.

He hadn't realized she'd come back for his plate until she brushed his arm, and he quickly closed the laptop, smiling up at her. Her eyes were wary, though, as she moved away. He watched her, noting the stiff set of her shoulders and jaw. And hoped she hadn't read his message.

Andi eyed the small pair of scissors in her hand. They'd do the job, but she wondered—stifling a giggle—if the Harvester could have found a smaller pair. They looked like the embroidery scissors Aunt Celosia kept in the tiny sewing box that had forever sat beside her wing chair.

As long as they were sharp enough to cut her hair. Her urge to smile vanished, and she inhaled deeply. She made the first cut and ignored the dark curls that fell onto the towel she'd laid across the sink.

Half an hour later, her hair was an inch and a half shorter, framing her face even more closely than any other time of the month. And small tufts of dark brown hair covered the towel.

Andi dumped the towel's contents into the trash, then

dropped the towel into the hamper. Her fingers trembled slightly now that the dreaded task was finished for another month.

Or maybe for the last time.

She frowned at the voice in her head. No, not for the last time. She would still be alive next month. She had to be.

Kallan stuck his head around the doorframe, his expression somber. "Finished?"

She didn't reply, as the question didn't need an answer. Just held out the tiny scissors to him, handles first. And tried not to think of the handcuffs he'd already hung on her headboard to contain her again tonight.

He took the scissors, one eyebrow slightly lifted. "Are you all right?"

"Doesn't matter," she muttered, moving past him.

He caught her arm. "Are you all right?" he repeated, his green gaze capturing hers.

She looked away, aware of the strength of the emotions coursing through her. "Fine. I'm fine." This was also the same man who'd told someone earlier that he believed he'd found the Medusa and hoped to have completed his task in the next thirty-six to seventy-two hours. That didn't help soothe her. She tugged at her arm, but he held on tight enough to keep her in place, but not tight enough to hurt her. She frowned harder—at his fingers though, not at him directly. It wouldn't work yet anyway. In another day, however…

"What's wrong?"

"I just need a little while." Her jaw ached from grinding her teeth together. "Let go." Why was he being so solicitous now?

He didn't release her, but steered her into the bedroom instead.

Andi sighed. "Alone, if you don't mind."

"I don't think so." He sat on the foot of her bed and pulled her down beside him, then slid his hand down to circle her wrist instead of her bicep. "You do this every month?"

She gave up trying to free her arm and stared at the floor. Just beyond the rag rug, a divot appeared in the golden wood. And another when she shifted her gaze. His question didn't really require an answer.

"Does it work?"

Of course he knew why she cut her hair so short. She hadn't had to spell it out for him earlier. "Yes." Somehow, his knowing and understanding without her having to explain that when her hair was this short, it couldn't turn into snakes didn't make her feel better.

"When did you figure that out as an option?" His tone was conversational, as if they were instead sitting on her front porch, talking about the weather, rather than five feet from where he'd be handcuffing her to the bed for the night, and not for anything really fun.

She debated her response and finally decided it didn't matter if he knew more about her now. This man wouldn't be scared off, after all. He only intended to stick around long enough to find a way to steal the amulet and kill her, not long enough to develop a deeper relationship. "When the second man flipped out and ran away." Which was when she'd stopped dating seriously.

He was silent for a long time, and she thought perhaps he'd given up on the conversation. "Most human men might be a little unnerved by it," he said finally.

A short laugh escaped her. "Unnerved? No, this was total mental meltdown. Run away screaming like a girl, never come back meltdown." Which the Harvester wasn't doing. Instead, he was being nice. It was almost enough to make her want to cry. Almost. She hadn't lost complete control to her cursed hormones yet.

Kallan's fingers squeezed her wrist gently. "Had you talked about any of this to him before then?"

"Yes, and I'm sure he thought I was crazy. Not crazy enough to stop dating completely, but a little touched. The snakes, though…" She swallowed. "The snakes convinced him I wasn't lying. Or maybe he just thought he'd had a hallucination. I never got the chance to ask, really." The old pain reared its head when she remembered the way Austin had vanished from her house and her life, almost as fresh as eight years ago.

Warm fingers slid further between her own so his palm touched hers. "He was the second, huh?" He squeezed again, just lightly, sending heat up her arm. "I guess that put a real damper on dating." His thumb stroked over the back of her hand and up the side of her index finger. "And explains the vibrator."

She shut her eyes, smiling reluctantly, despite the pain.

"And the romance novel."

She frowned up at him. "Those are good reads, I'll have you know."

"With sex in them."

She sighed. "I guess I have to give you that one. Still good stories."

"You know there are drawings and sculptures of the original Medusa, with the snakes and her still very beautiful face."

"I'm aware." Her jaw clenched, and she glared at the floor. "Not too many men are in the market for a woman so dangerous, however. Not to mention going out in public like that would be like sending out a worldwide bulletin to your family: 'here I am, come kill me'."

He nudged her shoulder with his own. "I'm attempting to cheer you up, Andrea."

"It's not working, but thanks." A larger divot had appeared in the floor, and she slid her shoe forward to touch the mark with the toe.

Kallan released her hand and put his arm around her shoulders. "Should I distract you in a different way?"

"I thought we agreed that wasn't happening." She didn't move away, though she knew she needed to. Before her hormones really kicked in. She rubbed the bigger dip in the wood floor with her toe again.

"Stop glaring holes into the floor," he murmured, nuzzling the top of her ear.

"Better the floor than you, wouldn't you say?" She tilted her head away from him, but he just bent to the side of her neck.

"You smell good." He licked her skin, sending a shock through her. "Taste good."

Andi jumped when his other hand settled on her thigh. "Harvester."

"That isn't going to work," he whispered, nipping her throat.

"Neither is this." She resisted the need to whimper when his teeth grazed her neck in advance of a slow, open-mouthed kiss over the same spot.

He squeezed her thigh lightly, and heat shot into her middle.

Well, okay, maybe it was working. A little.

When he tilted her back, she let him catch her mouth. Just for a minute. She wouldn't admit it to him, but this really was a pretty good distraction.

His kiss was even better now than that morning. Much

better than last night. It turned her brain to mush and made her pulse quicken. Made her ache.

When his tongue slid along her lower lip, she met it with her own, coaxing him into her mouth, and then the mush of her brain disintegrated into ash. Poof—nothing left.

When the mattress hit her back, she barely noticed, sliding her hands up to twine in his hair and keeping his delicious mouth close. He didn't seem to need persuading, shifting over her so his chest pressed into her suddenly aching breasts, sliding over her tight nipples and sending a rush of need into her middle. Lower.

He murmured something against her mouth, but she didn't know what—didn't really care. The hand he'd had on her thigh slid higher, pushing her legs apart to stroke her through her jeans, which felt damp and in the way. She let him shift her, lifting into his caresses, gratified to hear his groan.

When Kallan moved his own thigh between hers, nudging it against her core, she caught her breath at the explosion of desire. Holy Gods, he knew just where and how to touch her. She whimpered this time in spite of herself when he rubbed over her clit. If she let him, he'd have her naked and under him in no time flat. Bad idea. But that didn't mean she was ready to stop yet. She pushed at his shoulders and rolled him underneath her this time.

He laughed against her mouth, sliding his hand up under the back of her shirt.

She smiled too, just because, pressing her hips down over his. Gods, he felt good.

She didn't want to think about who they were, or why he was here, or if this might be her last few days alive. She wanted this, man and woman, heat and need. Just for a little while. Let her cursed hormones have their way one last time.

When his other hand slid under the front of her shirt to capture her breast, she arched into the caress, lifting her mouth to try to get a bit of oxygen to her deprived brain.

"I want you, Andrea," he rasped, tugging her bra down so he could pinch her nipple tight.

She gasped. "Oh Gods."

"Yes, hard and fast, and slow and easy." He rolled the taut peak between his finger and thumb, then pinched it again so she arched into his touch.

And slammed her hips hard into his erection.

He groaned. "Andrea." He tugged her shirt up and off, then tossed her bra aside too.

She wanted to touch skin. She fumbled with his T-shirt, shoving it up far enough so she could drag her fingers over the hard muscles of his abdomen, higher to the solid muscles of his chest, to the dark little nipples hidden in whorls of crisp black hair. And she bent to one, licking it and enjoying his shocked gasp. She scraped her teeth over the sensitive little bit of flesh, then he tumbled her to her back, dipping to catch her nipple between his teeth and lashing it with his tongue until she begged for more.

He tore at the button on her jeans, and she heard an ominous sound when he ripped the zipper down and shoved the denim away, but she didn't care, because his wonderful fingers found their way inside her panties—*oh Gods* —inside her.

Hard and thick, but still not enough.

Andi forced her eyes open in time to see his midnight black hair sliding over her breast as he kissed his way to her other nipple. She arched into his hot mouth and caught a glimpse of something shiny above her.

The handcuffs.

She shut her eyes for a second at the reminder of her true

situation, feeling her hips jerk up to meet his demanding fingers, her body wet and open to him despite the situation.

And a terrible idea occurred to her.

She swallowed hard, then caught her breath when he pinched her clit as he'd done to her nipples, and fiery shards of pleasure exploded in her belly.

She rolled again and he let her, his fingers teasing her now, his purely masculine smile filled with danger and desire. She shut her eyes when he urged her lower so he could capture her breast, his rough tongue sending goosebumps along her skin when it danced over her aching nipple.

She caught his free hand and stretched his arm out, offering her body into his mouth and wildly hoping it was distraction enough.

"Touch me," he commanded, his breath scalding against her nipple. His fingers slid deep, then withdrew to stroke her wet folds.

Andi reared up, reluctant to release him, but she undid the button on the front of his pants, the zipper. Found him bare and hard. Her fingers lingered over his flesh, tightening around the steely shaft before sliding up to the silky tip, already damp with his desire. She dared a peek and found his eyes shut. And his wrist was within reach of the open cuff attached to the bedstead.

It suddenly occurred to her that he had the keys.

She winced when her next move dislodged his fingers from her aching sheath, but his pants had to go. She pushed them down his long legs and paused to admire the strong muscles of his thighs, then stroked along hair-spattered calves. The boots delayed her a little, but he waited, his green eyes open now and dark with promise.

The man was gorgeous. She pressed a kiss on his knee as she dropped his pants to the floor behind her. He was very nearly a god. She inhaled shakily while she stroked her hands up his thighs and captured his erection between them. His hips jerked up, and she kissed the smooth head, tasting salt and man.

"I want to kiss you again, Andrea. I can't get enough of your mouth," he whispered, holding out one hand to her.

She hesitated, knowing she'd reached the point of no return. She let him take her hand and straddled him, his heavy cock sliding easily along her wet folds. Gods, she wanted him.

But if she could get away…

She bent to catch his mouth with hers, then slid her tongue into his mouth. She moaned when he suckled it, hard. As if it was one of her nipples. "Let me touch you," she breathed against his mouth, stretching his arms over his head —both of them this time. She kissed him while she dragged her hands down from his wrists past the dark scythe tattooed on the inside of his left bicep, to his chest. Still very aware of the erection so close to where she really needed it. She scratched her nails lightly over his nipples, and a rough, startled sound escaped him. She repeated the motion, and this time, his hips lifted, lodging the head of his cock just inside her.

Andi gasped, then shifted up, off, quickly, and snapped his wrist into the cuff before she stumbled off the bed.

She'd done it.

Horrified, she dragged her gaze from the metal cuff around his wrist to his narrowed eyes, one hand clapped over her mouth.

"I didn't know you were into kinky," he said slowly.

Heat rushed to her face, and she shook her head, taking a step away.

"You want my other hand, too? Then you can really have

your way with me." He held out his other arm, a dangerous smile tugging at the corner of his mouth.

"No," she whispered, backing another step away. Still, her brain obliged her by bringing up that image behind her eyes. Her heartbeat stuttered.

"Stop, Andrea."

She froze.

"Come back here and kiss me."

Andi blinked. "I don't have the key on me," she said after a second. *Duh.* Of course she didn't, since she was as naked as he was.

"I'm not asking for the key, but for a kiss."

She knew he wanted the key. But his eyes were still dark with desire. She couldn't stop her gaze from dropping lower. More heat burned her cheeks. *Wow.*

"Andrea." The tiny hint of accent in his voice made her shiver. "Just a kiss. For now." He even stretched his free hand up to grip another bar on the headboard.

She found herself taking a step toward him.

"Come kiss me again, *meli*," he said, his voice even huskier.

She swallowed hard, then moved nearer still.

His hungry gaze made her mouth tingle.

Cautiously, she perched on the edge of the bed at his side.

"I promise I won't touch." His gaze never left her lips.

Andi bent toward him, hearing his breathing quicken. Under hers, his lips parted easily, and his tongue slid along her lower lip before dipping into her mouth, nudging her own.

Another blast of heat exploded in her belly.

"Touch me again," he whispered, nipping at her lower lip. "I want your hands on me, Andrea. I want to be inside you."

Common sense tried to rear its head. He was contained.

He couldn't free himself—at least, not without some effort, and she could be long gone by then.

But her body still ached. Surely she had a little time… She lifted one hand to stroke down the center of his chest, following the thin line of dark hair on his abdomen to the erection that still stood tall, beckoning her.

"Or your mouth."

Her mouth watered at the thought, and she unconsciously licked her lower lip.

"Please."

It was the pleading. That was all. She bent to kiss his chest again, her mouth following the path her hand had just taken, slowly working her way to his groin. His musky scent called to her, enhancing her need—increasing it. When she finally opened her mouth over the tip of his cock, her inner thighs were wet with her desire. She ignored that for now, concentrating on the taste of him.

He was delicious, salty and musky, and all male. She took him deep, then retreated to lick her way around the thick shaft, hearing his groans and the soft words of encouragement he offered.

And when his body tightened, she felt a rush of excitement. His pleasure was entirely in her hands. Or mouth.

"Andrea."

She glanced up at him, sucking lightly on his cock.

"Goddess," he ground out. "I want to be inside you. Please let me come inside you."

A dark flush rode his cheeks, his chest rose and fell rapidly, and his eyes were a deep dark green, full of desire.

She released his erection reluctantly—allowing herself one last lick over the head, which made him jerk toward her —and straddled him once more, this time with his cock standing up in front of her.

She met his gaze, and her heart beat faster yet at the things she saw there. The desire. The promise of incredible pleasure.

"Take me in."

She couldn't resist. She lifted her hips and caught her breath at the first touch of his cock in her wet folds.

"So hot and wet," he murmured. "For me." His accent deepened, his whisper guttural and rough. "Slide down, Andrea."

She hesitated, torn between wanting to impale herself on him and wanting to draw the moment out just a little longer.

His hips lifted, wedging him a tiny bit deeper.

"Oh." She shut her eyes and braced her hands low on his ribs.

"Take it."

She started to ease down, feeling him stretch her sheath with every increment of every inch, her body clenching around him already. "Oh Gods," she moaned.

He jerked his hips upward again, forcing his way in—to the root—and she cried out in pleasure and surprise. "Don't move," he ordered.

Andi wanted to move. Very badly. Her thighs quivered with the need to move. Her release was so close. Oh Gods, so close.

"Touch yourself."

Her gaze flew upward to meet his.

"Like you did in the shower this morning."

Heat burned her cheeks, both desire and embarrassment.

"Show me."

She gulped in some air and lifted her hands to her breasts, cupping and stroking them lightly.

"Are you imagining my hands?"

She nodded.

"Did you imagine me this morning?"

"Yes." She stroked harder, pinching and twisting her nipples. Her sheath tightened on his erection, and she wanted to move. More than she wanted her next breath.

But she resisted.

She stroked and caressed her swollen breasts under his dangerous gaze, until she had to drop one hand to her clit. The hard little bundle of nerves throbbed, and when she brushed a fingertip over it, her hips shifted.

"Not yet."

She bit her lip, tugging at one nipple and her clit simultaneously.

"How much can you take?"

"How much can you?" she countered. Within her body, his cock flexed and throbbed, as if burrowing deeper.

A faint smile curved his mouth. "Not much."

Her fingertip at her clit brushed the base of his cock. "Oh, you feel good," she breathed.

"Lift up."

She shimmied her hips slowly upward, whimpering at the loss of that beautiful erection inside her. She glanced down to see his skin glistening with her wetness.

"Down again. Slowly."

Panting now, she followed his instructions, each torturous movement driving her closer to the brink. Soft, breathy cries escaped her and his chest worked like a bellows, his thighs tight beneath her.

"Please." She didn't care that she was the one begging now—she just wanted him to let her fly.

"Give me your mouth, Andrea."

She bent back to him blindly, sliding one hand into his hair to catch him, and the kiss this time was savage, all heat and reckless passion. When their hips shifted together now, the motion was instinctual, primitive, wild and fast. There was no Medusa, no Harvester. Simply man and woman. Mated. Fated.

And the pleasure was ten times more powerful than what she'd felt that morning. The explosion sent her into the abyss, tumbling freely, breathless.

Andi couldn't stop shaking. Even minutes later, the trembling in her limbs wouldn't stop. Aftershocks made her body tighten on his and his hips shifted against hers. He murmured into her hair, and she heard his wild heartbeat beneath her ear.

She wanted to stay right where she was.

It was the stupidest thing she'd ever wanted. Especially since freedom was not too far away. Just as far as her dresser, clean clothes, the door downstairs.

"Easy." His lips grazed her forehead this time.

Her eyes burned, and she cursed her stupid hormones. She blinked hard and steeled herself. Lifted her hips away from his. Her breath hissed in as he groaned a protest. She felt cold suddenly.

Ignoring that, she clambered off the bed, searching for some piece of clothing to put on. She'd never felt so naked.

"Andrea."

She ignored him too, moving to her dresser and taking out some clean clothes. She didn't even notice what. With her stinging eyes, she couldn't quite see the things she'd grabbed.

"Andrea." His tone this time was harder, more insistent.

She glanced toward the bed.

"Don't do this."

"I have to."

"It's not safe."

She forced a laugh. "Yeah, you're so concerned for my safety. Does it really matter which one of you kills me? As long as it gets done?" She jerked on panties, then jeans before wrestling with a bra.

Kallan sat up, gripping the headboard with his cuffed hand. "Stavros won't be as concerned with how he kills you, or how he gets the amulet."

Andi swallowed as she yanked on her shirt, then froze when he put his free hand over the cuff on his wrist. She heard the unmistakable sound of it releasing before it jangled to the pillow.

Impossible.

He got to his feet, his green eyes dangerous now.

She dashed toward the door. She only made it halfway before he caught her, ripping one of the belt loops on her jeans in the process. She fought, striking whatever she could reach and wishing she'd at least gotten shoes on so she could do some real damage since he was still naked.

But the Harvester was stronger than she was, and he simply held on until she wore herself out.

Andi finally stopped struggling, her head drooping, breath coming hard again, but with far less satisfaction this time.

He carried her back to the bed and snapped her wrist into the handcuff, his mouth set in a hard line. "I have another set, if I need both of your hands out of commission," he ground out.

She didn't bother to answer, struggling still to catch her breath. And against more of the unexpected tears. *Damned hormones.*

He sat down beside her, hands braced on his hair-spattered knees. "I thought we were going to each do a little trusting," he said finally.

She looked at the wall to her left, rather than at him. "I saw the handcuffs and I had to try."

"Was it worth it?"

A scalding tear rushed down her cheek, making her glad she'd turned her face away.

"I know you weren't faking," he whispered, leaning nearer. "You can't fake that."

She bit her lip, swallowing around the giant lump in her throat.

"And neither was I."

She barely kept herself from turning to look at him, but the shock still made her body jerk.

He rose and drifted a kiss on the top of her head. "Try to get some sleep."

Behind her, she heard him gathering his clothing before he padded into the bathroom next door. The water ran briefly, and a few minutes later, she heard him slowly go downstairs.

She lifted her free hand at last to swipe at the tears on her face, closing her eyes.

She should have known this would turn out badly. Who knew the Harvester could undo locks without keys?

Her eyes flew open. What other abilities did he have that she didn't know about yet?

Gods help her.

CHAPTER FOUR

K allan sank onto the hard chair at the table and buried his face in his hands. Tonight wasn't working out at all as he'd imagined it might. Andrea had warned him that morning she wouldn't forget what he'd done last night. A mirthless laugh rumbled up his chest. He should have realized Andrea wouldn't completely surrender. She was a fighter, his Medusa.

He frowned. She wasn't *his* Medusa. She wasn't his anything. Perhaps a temporary lover. And ultimately, his target. His family's enemy.

That didn't mean he'd allow his cousin get to her, however.

With that thought in mind, he booted up the laptop, fingers tapping over the keyboard. Sure enough, Great-Uncle Ari had responded to Kallan's earlier posting, with a command to Stavros to head in the same direction rather than to follow his own lead. None of the cousins ever disobeyed Aristotle Tassos, even now when they were adults and hunting on their own—not even Stavros, arrogant and brutal as he was.

Breathing a small sigh of relief, Kallan idly pulled up his favorite page of the mythologies, one with plenty of photos of ancient artifacts to go along with the stories. Artifacts which had never been seen publicly, items that had instead passed down through generations of Harvesters. Currently, Cousin Demitrios was the keeper of the private collection, though word among the cousins was he wanted to get back in on the hunt and turn the curatorship over to his brother Vasily. That was up to Great-Uncle Ari, and the old bastard never rushed a decision.

He scrolled through several pages until he got to the photo he was searching for. A large urn decorated in great detail, including a scene depicting the very beautiful Medusa about to be slain by Perseus. The first Medusa was gorgeous, with wide eyes and a generous figure. The spitting, hissing snakes atop her head didn't detract at all from her beauty.

He looked up at the ceiling. There was only silence from Andrea's bedroom. He wasn't sure if that was good or bad.

He glanced again at the urn. Perhaps she should see it.

To what purpose, though? The voice in his head sounded very like Ari.

He frowned and picked up the computer, then headed for the steps and ignored the imaginary voice.

The light was still on in the bedroom, and Andrea sat just where he'd left her, her shoulders slumped.

Something in his chest tightened. He reminded himself she'd set this in motion, but he still felt a pang of guilt.

He cleared his throat. "I have something you should see."

She didn't move, didn't jump, didn't give any indication she'd heard him.

Kallan's frown deepened as he crossed the room to her.

She was sleeping. Sitting there exactly where he'd left her, with tear stains on her cheeks.

Goddess, he felt even worse. He put the laptop on her dresser and turned back to the bed so he could ease her down into a more comfortable position. Certainly more comfortable than sleeping sitting up. She didn't wake, just burrowed into the pillow, making an indistinct sound of protest.

For a moment, he watched her, trying to figure out why his chest ached and failing. He gave himself a shake and returned to the computer, then shut it down before he kicked off his shoes and stretched out behind her on the bed, careful not to disturb her. She'd had a rough enough day.

He smiled to himself at that and shut his eyes. They both needed some sleep to deal with what was coming.

Andi realized before she opened her eyes that the Harvester was sleeping with his arm around her. It was why she was so warm.

She frowned and peered through her eyelashes. Early light shone in the window on the other side of the room. The last thing she remembered was racking her brain trying to figure out if the Harvester had any other special talents he hadn't told her about besides the lock thing. Now she was beneath the sheet and blanket, and his body heat warmed the back of her even more.

She shifted slightly, and knew when he came fully awake.

"Good morning, Andrea."

She didn't answer, setting her jaw.

His fingers slid slowly over her belly as he withdrew his arm, and she ground her teeth against the surge of PMS-fueled desire, certain the caress was a deliberate tease. Not that she'd give in to her hormones again. Not with *him*.

"We have work to do today."

She shut her eyes.

"I have something for you."

Something soft brushed her cheek, and she realized it was the sleep mask. She jerked her head away.

"You did agree." His tone was patient.

She glared at the dresser and watched a big gouge mark appear on the side.

"Ah, yes, definitely time for this." He chuckled and slipped it over her head.

Andi kept her mouth shut, hoping she didn't grind her molars to dust.

"Do you want to hear our plans for the day?"

She curled her fingers into a fist beneath the blankets, trying to tell herself it was best if she didn't hit him again today. Not three days in a row.

"No? You're not at all curious?" He adjusted the mask, then touched the short hair at her nape. "I have something I want you to see, but it will have to wait for a day or two now. Today, we're going to figure out a place to go to avoid my cousin when he gets back from Ohio."

She jerked her head in his direction before she could stop herself.

"Mm. Yes, it seems Cousin Stavros got orders from our great-uncle to follow my hot lead there instead of heading here to follow up on his own leads. That gives us a few days to decide what to do."

She turned her head away again on the pillow, considering. She hadn't actually seen the entire message he'd posted, just the part about being on her trail and that he would complete his assignment in the next few days. She hadn't seen where he told them he was.

He patted her hip. "Come on. Time to get up."

She sat up reluctantly, her mind awhirl. It was possible he had actually lied to his cousin. But why? Because he wanted the glory for himself? Because he wanted the amulet even more desperately? She couldn't begin to guess at his reasoning.

His strong hands settled at her waist to lift her to her feet.

She stumbled, off-balance from her imposed blindness, and he steadied her against him.

She took a step back, bumping into the bed, and he chuckled.

"I don't think you'll make it down the stairs this way."

"I'm fine," she said stiffly, reaching out to push him away.

He flattened her hand on his chest so she could feel his strong heartbeat. "I meant with the handcuff."

She clenched her jaw.

He undid the cuff, and she wondered idly if he'd used the key or his handy talent. Then he caught her wrist in his free hand and turned her.

She concentrated on getting out of the room without crashing into anything. Or into him. She made it down the stairs without incident, then sat when he gave her a gentle nudge into a chair at the kitchen table.

"What would you like for breakfast?"

"Your obituary."

He was silent for a few seconds, and she smiled, childishly pleased with herself.

"For a woman who's just missed out on what was bound to be a very unpleasant encounter with Stavros, you don't sound very grateful," he said at last.

"One Harvester or another." She shrugged.

His silence this time was more protracted, and tension filled the room.

She realized he may not just be thinking of his task, but of what had occurred between them already. She felt heat in her cheeks, suddenly grateful he was behind her.

Eventually, she heard him moving on the other side of the island, and she relaxed a little. Her belly twinged, and she stifled a sigh. Right on time. She stood up.

"Where are you going?"

"Bathroom." She felt her way to the end of the table, mentally reviewing the space ahead of her. About fifteen steps to the half bath between the kitchen and living room, and no furniture in her path.

He didn't argue, but his footsteps came nearer, and then his fingers caught her wrist.

"I can get there on my own."

"I'm sure you can." Nonetheless he guided her along the short hallway. "I'd hate for you to bump into anything and bruise yourself." He released her at the doorway.

Andi didn't flip him off as her first instinct suggested, but instead went into the smaller room and closed the door firmly —she hoped right in his face. She flipped the sleep mask up and glanced at her reflection in the mirror over the sink. Her spiky hair would have to wait. Right on cue, another cramp made her flatten one hand low on her belly.

A few minutes later—some aspirin washed down with a little water and her hair finger-combed—she hesitated for a few seconds, then tugged the sleep mask back down and fumbled for the doorknob. He might not still be standing outside the door, so if she walked back to the kitchen without the mask, he'd have time to turn away before she could do any damage to him. And he *had* held up his part of their bargain last night by producing the scissors she wanted.

Kallan met her at the door and guided her back to the table. "Do you need anything else?"

"The couch and a heating pad in about half an hour." She

sat. If he intended to wait on her, then he could really wait on her.

One of his hands brushed over the top of her head as he moved away. "I'll see what I can do about that."

She frowned. "And stop touching me."

He muttered something she couldn't quite hear, then banged a pan onto the stovetop.

She wondered what he'd said. And tried to figure out what he was making for breakfast. She really needed to go for groceries.

Sizzling began a moment later, and then the aroma of fried potatoes teased her nose.

Her stomach rumbled. She was starved. And no wonder, since she'd hardly eaten any of her supper last night.

Then something else scented the air. Bacon.

She frowned. Maybe there'd been some in the freezer? She didn't care where he'd found the food though. It smelled delicious.

She rubbed one finger along the side of the table, feeling a small nick there. She'd have to sand it out once he was gone.

Assuming she was still alive.

Frowning, she gave her head a slight shake. She *would* be alive. Then she could even out the new gouges in the floor and on her dresser too.

A plate hit the table in front of her, and the amazing aromas assaulted her full-on. Her mouth watered.

"How do you think you're going to eat?" he asked evenly.

She felt around for the fork she'd heard him put down.

Nothing.

Annoyance tightened her mouth. "If you go back to the other side of the island, I can eat without the mask on."

"I'm intending to eat my own breakfast."

She squeezed her eyes shut inside the sleep mask. Of course he was.

She heard movement nearby, then the scraping of another chair before he sat down, close enough she could feel his heat. Her pulse quickened.

"Open."

For a long moment, she resisted. But she was hungry, and the potatoes smelled divine. Finally, she opened her mouth, and he scooped some of the food in.

Yum. But she didn't say it aloud. Instead, she took the crisp slice of bacon he put in her hand and ate, silent.

By the time she'd eaten her fill, she was all too aware of the intimacy of him feeding her. Her stupid hormones had her wanting to strip off her clothes and climb into his lap. Except for those damned cramps.

She finished the orange juice he'd given her and pushed her chair away from the table. "Thank you." It was grudging, but she felt a little better after eating.

"Where's your heating pad?"

"Under the sink in the small bathroom."

He caught her hand and led her into the living room to settle her on the couch. "I'll be right back."

Andi shut her eyes behind the mask. It had been years since anyone had taken care of her this way. She wasn't actually sure she could recall when, or who it had been. Maybe when she'd still been a child and her mother was still parentally inclined.

"How hot?"

"All the way."

He handed her the heating pad, then—after she shuddered —covered her with the quilt she kept draped across the back of the sofa. "Do you need anything else?"

She shook her head, rather than give him another smart-ass answer. Her eyes stung, and she was grateful suddenly for the mask that hid her tears.

The Harvester was being far nicer than he needed to be. Far nicer than she would have been if he'd tricked her the way she had him last night.

She inhaled unsteadily and shifted the heating pad closer to the spot where her cramps hurt the worst. Rather than thinking about Kallan Tassos, she put her mind to work to will away the cramping. Not that it had ever worked before. She didn't expect it to work now. But it gave her something else to occupy her mind.

A few hours later, Kallan watched her sleep on the sofa. Her face was pale and strained, and occasionally a breathy moan of pain passed her lips.

He clenched the mug he held. It shouldn't matter if she was suffering. That wasn't his concern. He should be thinking about how to get the amulet. He had to figure it out, dammit.

But his gaze kept straying from his laptop screen to the sleeping woman on the couch. His mind wouldn't stay focused on his search of the internet, instead flashing bits of their heated encounter last night.

She may have intended to distract him with sex, but he knew she'd distracted herself too.

And then he'd revealed his ability to undo locks. That was not the smartest thing he'd ever done.

Then again, sleeping with the Medusa probably didn't rank on the list either. Sleeping with her more than once clearly revealed him to be a complete idiot. His father would be shocked and disappointed if he were still alive. Great-Uncle Ari would be furious.

Right now, he didn't care. He needed her alive in order to

get the amulet. If she died, the search would have to begin anew for the next Medusa.

If she died. If he *killed her* was far more accurate.

He punched a button on the keyboard to clear the screen, then rose to pace. Big windows revealed the bright green clearing in front of the house, then the darker green of the trees around the yard, deepening to black farther inside the forest. A rabbit hopped across the yard, in no particular hurry. When Kallan moved to the smaller window at the side of the room, he could see the driveway winding away into the trees. His truck now sat behind her car, retrieved that first night after he'd knocked her unconscious.

If someone else killed her, he would have to tell his family about the amulet. Which would be difficult to explain.

He frowned. If Stavros really was following the same clues he had, Kallan had to be out of here with Andrea before his cousin realized the Ohio lead was no good.

That meant the truck had to be gone. He pulled out his phone and dialed the rental company. He moved into the kitchen so his conversation wouldn't wake her, and arranged for the truck to be picked up that afternoon.

One problem solved. Posting another mention or two of his trip in northwestern Ohio would hopefully slow his cousin down a little more. Part of another problem solved. Temporarily.

The next step was where to go with her while he came up with a plan to retrieve the amulet.

She shifted on the sofa, making a small sound.

He knelt beside her, touching her forehead, which was clammy. "Are you all right?"

"Need to get up for a minute," she mumbled, pushing the blanket and heating pad away.

He shut off the pad and helped her to her feet before guiding her to the bathroom.

Though she didn't complain, he could see she was suffering. He wondered just how bad the pain was. From inside the smaller room, he heard the rattle of a medicine bottle, then water running.

He moved away from the door a few steps to give her a little privacy. Wondered what else would help relieve her cramps.

Came up blank.

When she opened the door a few minutes later, he took her outstretched hand. "What else can I do?"

She shook her head. "I'll get a shower in a little while, run it as hot as I can. That'll help a little." She bit her lip, flushing.

"What else?"

"You left my vibrator in the nightstand, right?"

His pulse quickened and blood rushed to his groin. "Yes," he croaked.

"That and the shower will help. I want to lie down for a little while first."

He walked her back to the couch, spreading the blanket over her, and all the while, his mind kept conjuring up images of Andrea in the shower. Bringing herself to orgasm.

Sweet Goddess. Sweat broke out on his forehead. He adjusted his pants before he sank into his chair, but there was no comfortable position for the erection that had sprung to life at her words.

He could offer to— *No.* She didn't want him to—

He shouldn't either.

But his body had other ideas.

He dropped his head against the back of the chair and shut

his eyes for a second. It didn't matter how foolish the idea was, he still wanted her.

She moved, rolling onto her back and drawing her knees up a little.

He turned his head to look more fully at her.

Her mouth was pinched, and her cheeks pale, the little color that had tinted them a few minutes ago long gone. Atop the blanket, her fingers rubbed at her belly, as if she could ease the cramping muscles deep inside that way.

His brain gave in then. There was really no help for it. He pushed to his feet. "Come, Andrea. Let me help you." He dropped to one knee beside her and scooped her into his arms.

It was a testament to how miserable she must be that she didn't protest.

He carried her up the stairs and stepped into the bathroom to set her on the closed toilet. "I'll be right back."

Not that he thought she was going anywhere.

He strode into the bedroom and yanked the nightstand drawer open. The vibrator rolled forward, and he took a shaky breath, eyeing it for a moment before he picked it up and shut the drawer.

His next stop was her dresser, where he dug through drawers until he found a pair of black sweat pants and a loose t-shirt, another pair of underwear, and then returned to the bathroom.

Andrea was right where he'd left her, though she had curled forward, her head nearly touching her knees, and a soft moan escaped her.

"Come on, *meli*," he whispered, dropping the clean clothing on top of her hamper before he eased her to her feet. He helped her out of her shirt, ignored all the creamy skin he exposed when he unhooked her bra and dropped it to the floor, then unfastened her jeans. "Okay?"

She nodded. "Turn around for a minute."

He did as she asked, though he now faced the mirror and could easily see her slow, careful movements, something she was clearly in too much pain to realize. He wanted to help her, but he waited until she held out her hand. Then he guided her to the shower, where he turned on the water and tested its heat with his fingertips. It was hotter than he'd like for his own shower.

"Hotter."

He winced when he turned the knob further, but she sighed in relief when she stepped under the scalding spray and braced herself with one hand on the wall.

Steam rose around her.

Kallan reminded himself he was just doing this to ease her pain, not to ease his own growing need.

Still, he tugged his shirt off so it wouldn't get wet. He also retrieved the vibrator from the counter beside the sink. "Let me know when, Andrea." He waited, feeling tension pull the muscles in his shoulders tighter. Painfully.

She only nodded, tipping her head back and shifting so the hot water hit her belly full-on. The water's heat made her skin pink. After a few minutes, the strain around her mouth eased a little. "Better."

His own tension grew, his body hardening still more at the vision in front of him. He *was* a sick bastard, he thought, just as she'd suggested yesterday. And the night before. Goddess, he needed to get a firm grip on his libido.

She sighed, a long, drawn-out exhalation, her posture relaxing a bit more. Then she held out her hand.

"Let me." He knew he shouldn't. But he wanted to.

She dropped her hand to her side, remaining silent.

He took her silence as acquiescence and braced himself on the open shower door before flipping the switch on the vibrator. The toy's low hum made his heart rate quicken still more, and he slid it first across her breasts, surprising her.

"Oh." Her knuckles whitened on the tile wall for a moment.

He teased her until her nipples tightened, darkened. Goddess, he wanted to taste them again. He restrained himself, however, easing the vibrator down over her belly, rubbing the tip in the same area she'd tried to massage by herself earlier. Her breathing hitched.

Smiling grimly, he nudged her thigh with the toy. "Open for me, *meli*."

She widened her stance slowly, and he stroked her inner thighs with the vibe until her hips rocked toward it. Then he slid it up, up to where his body desperately wanted to be. Easing just the tip of it inside her. Flipping the switch to the next level.

"Oh Gods," she whispered.

His jaw tightened. And he eased the toy higher, deeper.

Her hips jolted toward his hand, and the vibrator slid to the hilt.

He groaned at the same time she cried out.

Her free hand settled over his, guiding his thrusts. He let her, watching her face and wishing he could see her eyes as well. Her hips met each drive, rocking faster as her fingers tightened over his, forcing the toy harder into her sheath.

Kallan watched the flush bloom low on her breasts, spread up to her throat, her cheeks, and when she wailed with her release, he felt sweat roll down the back of his neck. And his erection strain behind his zipper.

Andrea sagged against the tile wall, dropping her hand

from his, and he eased the vibrator from her body, shutting it off.

His chest rose and fell as fast as hers, and the sound of their breathing echoed around the room, over the sound of the running water.

"Wow," she managed a few minutes later.

He rasped a laugh, and shut his eyes for a heartbeat. "Better?"

"I think I might be able to rest a little now."

He blindly set the toy on the sink and grabbed a towel from the wall, then shut the water off and wrapped her in the towel.

He was a little surprised she let him tend to her, but he dried her thoroughly and dressed her in the clean things. She remained quiet, her head bowed a little until he'd finished. "Come on. Into bed," he murmured.

She put one hand on his bare chest, where his heart hammered hard against his ribs. "What about you?"

"I'm fine." That was an even bigger lie than the one he'd told his family last night. His cock throbbed painfully inside his pants, desperate for release.

Her hand slid down, discovering his lie. "Let me."

He shook his head even though she couldn't see it. "I can take care of it. Let's get you into bed." He pulled her hand from his groin and herded her out of the small room, then into her bedroom.

She didn't protest, just let him pull the covers back and tuck her in.

He turned away. The bathroom wasn't far enough away to deal with this.

"Wait."

He shut his eyes. "What else do you need, *meli*?"

"If you won't let me, will you stay here to…relieve yourself?"

He whipped around. She lay where he'd put her, a hint of color still in her cheeks, her lower lip now caught in her teeth. "Not a good idea."

"Please."

He felt heat on his own cheeks, imagining the scenario. "Andrea…"

"Come here." She patted the bed beside her.

As if she'd put a spell on him, he obeyed her order, and he sat down beside her. "I shouldn't." But Goddess, he wanted to. "You should rest. I'd only disturb you."

"Get undressed." The quiet command in her voice made his pulse throb faster. There simply wasn't enough fight in him to resist her or his own need.

He fumbled with the button on his cargo pants, then shoved them down, his erection springing up toward his belly. Already, the head was slick. This wouldn't take long. He toed off his boots and kicked off the pants, then slowly stretched out beside her on top of the blankets.

Her warm fingers slid along his thigh, making the muscles there tighten even more. "Wrap your fingers around it."

Unable to resist, he obeyed , groaning aloud. Tighter. He stroked up to the head, then back down, hard.

His breath snagged in his chest.

"Does it feel good?"

"Yes." He repeated the stroke, then again.

"Would it feel better with my hand?"

He didn't reply, his brain already filled with the image.

When her warm fingers settled over his, his hips jerked into the next stroke.

"Goddess," he ground out.

Andrea let him guide the strokes, and he set a punishing pace, hard and fast, occasionally twisting on the up-stroke. His balls tightened, drew higher.

"Oh," she whispered, her grip growing firmer when he squeezed harder. "Let go."

"Say my name," he demanded, tugging their joined hands back down to the base of his cock.

"Let go, Kallan."

At her words, he squeezed firmly on one last up-stroke, and his orgasm rushed through him. He couldn't stop the groan that erupted from his middle.

She didn't let go of him, her thumb sliding over his fingers, then higher, to his super-sensitive head, now drenched with his release, the pad of her thumb slowly dragging over his skin.

His hips jerked one last time before he released his cock. He captured her fingers and lifted them to drag his mouth along her soft skin, before letting their joined hands drop onto his chest.

"Wow," she breathed again, turning her face into his shoulder. "Thank you."

He huffed a laugh, still trying to catch his breath. *She* was thanking *him*. He should be kissing her feet.

When he finally felt like he could speak without sounding as if he'd run three miles nonstop, he heard her soft, even breathing.

She was asleep.

He grinned at the ceiling. Nothing was going as he'd planned.

But he didn't think he was very sorry right now about the changes to his plans.

Andi stretched, wincing at the slight cramping low in her belly, then went still. The Harvester was beside her—sleeping, from the sound of his breathing.

He'd taken very good care of her.

She felt the blush climb her cheeks. And then she'd helped him take care of himself.

The experience had been very erotic, as—with her sight gone—her other senses had been heightened. The feel of his silky skin over his straining erection. The tension in his fingers under hers. The enticing scent of him—spicy, salty, all male.

She swallowed. He was still her would-be murderer. She was just as sick as she'd accused him of being.

"How are you feeling?" His voice was rusty with sleep, and his fingers on her arm were warm.

She wondered suddenly if he was still naked atop the blankets. Heat began to bubble in her belly, competing with the cramps. "I'm okay. Need to make a pit stop and get a drink. And I'm hungry."

He sat up and his fingers disappeared from her arm before they grazed her cheek. "Let's take care of that."

"Why?" She needed to know. She also needed to remind herself of just why he was here.

He didn't answer right away, and she heard the rustling of his cargo pants, then the quiet zip. "I don't know." His tone was tight, frustrated.

Andi was pretty sure he was telling her the truth. "Okay," she whispered, sitting up and throwing back the blankets.

He was waiting when her feet hit the floor to guide her into the next room, where he left her alone.

When she flipped up the sleep mask, she realized her vibrator was still on the sink, though it was clean. After she'd fallen asleep, he'd come back into the bathroom to clean her vibe. Tears stung her eyes, and she turned away from the mirror. By the time she was ready to leave, she thought she'd steeled herself against any more unexpected kindnesses.

Downstairs, she curled into a corner of the sofa with the heating pad. Behind her, in the kitchen, Kallan rooted through the fridge for something for them to eat. She tried to only concentrate on breathing through the wrenching cramps low in her belly.

"How do you feel about soup?" He was no longer in the kitchen, but directly behind her.

She sucked in a quick breath. "Soup is fine."

If she concentrated on listening, she could just hear his bare feet on the wood floor as he went back into the other room. The man was too quiet. Sneaky.

Yeah, sneaky.

She needed to focus on that, instead of him doing nice things for her.

The microwave controls beeped several times, then the ventilation fan started running.

Feeding her. Probably just so she didn't starve to death while he figured out a way to take the amulet.

She ignored the small voice in the back of her head scolding her for that uncharitable thought.

The bell dinged on the microwave, and then a few seconds later, his weight depressed the cushion beside her. "It's hot," he said softly. "Open."

Instead of arguing, she obeyed him, letting him spoon the hot liquid into her mouth. She tried to think of something else, anything else aside from this very intimate act.

Like how much work it was going to be to break and then dispose of the stone statue he would become if she decided to take off the sleeping mask right now. The Harvester was a big guy. It would take quite a lot of effort to break that much stone into manageable pieces to get rid of.

Might be easier to kill him another way.

If she were really a murderer, she would have made sure to stab him fatally the first night. Evidently, she didn't have it in her, at least not where this man was concerned. And she couldn't kill him while he was taking care of her.

His fingers brushed the corner of her mouth.

She shivered.

Where was she? Oh, yes, another way to kill the Harvester. Her mind was blank.

"One more." His warm breath slid over her cheek.

Andi sighed silently with relief when he took the spoon away, then she heard him go back into the kitchen.

"How are you feeling now?" he called.

"Okay." She adjusted the heating pad a little, realizing her cramps were ebbing a bit. She smiled. Thank the Gods.

"Do you feel up to a little walk?"

"How little?" Her smile disappeared.

"From the bottom of your drive back to the house?"

That was quite a walk. And how were they going to get *to* the bottom of the driveway?

"The rental company is coming to pick up the truck." He was nearer again. "I told them I'd leave it at the bottom of the driveway for them. And you might like the fresh air."

Okay, so not really something for her enjoyment. That helped her to feel a little less kindly toward him. "I suppose I can make it."

"Good. I didn't want to handcuff you to the bed."

Definitely less kindly toward him. Her mouth pinched.

He sat down beside her, and she realized he was putting his boots on. And she was barefoot. "I got your sneakers."

Perhaps he did have a little bit of mind-reading ability as well.

She didn't thank him, just let him put them on her, her mind spinning. Outside. She was going outside, unhandcuffed. She knew these woods. She could find a spot, several spots, to hide from him until she could get safely away.

His fingers circled her wrist to pull her up from the sofa.

Her belly cramped again, making her lean forward a little. *Gods, not now.*

He wrapped one arm around her. "Andrea?"

She inhaled slowly but it didn't help. The knotting in her gut only tightened. Athena was a bitch. Still.

Kallan eased her back onto the sofa. "You don't look so good, meli," he murmured, sliding one hand along her cheek and jaw.

She bent forward until her head touched her knees. "Bitch," she whispered. Hot pain lanced her belly.

"What?"

She shook her head, swallowing back a moan of pain at the ferocity of the renewed cramps. "What does that mean? *'Meli'?*" she asked after a second. "You keep saying that." She didn't want this now. *Not now.*

He picked her up, carefully, and strode up the stairs with her. "It means 'honey'."

Her escape was getting further away, and there was nothing she could do about it. Not right now. But it was better to think about that than the casual endearment he'd been using.

Breathing shallowly, she let him settle her back into the bed, then took the aspirin he gave her along with the hot water bottle he must have unearthed while she was taking the medicine.

"I'm sorry, *meli*," he whispered, kissing her temple and stroking her head lightly.

"Not your fault." She gritted her teeth against the next wave of cramping and curled into a tight ball.

He clambered over her, then began to massage her lower back.

She startled at his first touch.

"Easy."

Andi shut her eyes tight and tried to breathe evenly.

His strong fingers were gentle as he rubbed her taut muscles, moving in slow, wide circles that eventually did relax her a little bit.

Rather than dwell on that, however, she thought of the heat from the rubber hot water bottle seeping into her skin. On breathing out the pain.

If she were honest with herself, she thought drowsily, it was mostly the massage that finally let her fall asleep.

Bastard. He shouldn't be so nice to her.

Kallan paced the living room when he got back into the house. Trekking up the driveway had taken the better part of half an hour, and that was with him rushing the entire way.

And she'd been deeply asleep when he raced into her room, just as he'd left her.

He didn't like this.

He hadn't really thought she'd be gone when he got back. She was clearly not feeling well enough to run off if she couldn't even stand up straight.

The part he didn't like was how much he was worried for her.

He stopped walking and stood in the center of the room, breathing roughly.

Sweet Goddess, he was falling for the Medusa.

His heart thudded against his ribs, still too fast from his jog up the mountain, faster still with the shock of his realization. He couldn't fall in love with the woman he'd set out to kill. Still *had* to kill.

He swallowed, his mouth dry, then went to the kitchen for a glass of water. It didn't slow his racing pulse, or his whirl of jumbled thoughts.

He set the glass on the counter and went back upstairs, his pace measured. Slow. Careful. The way he usually did things.

He stood in her doorway. She still lay curled into a ball beneath the blankets, though some of the pallor had left her cheeks. He wondered if the hot water bottle had lost its heat yet. Frowned. He shouldn't care.

His gaze slid over her face again, over features half-hidden behind the sleep mask. Then to her chopped, spiky dark hair. She'd cut her hair to keep it from turning to snakes. Did it every month. What did something like that cost her? And how did she manage this every month when she was on her own? The disabling cramps that had her moaning softly in her sleep.

He had a sudden idea that her whispered curse earlier hadn't been for him, but for the cause of her current distress. *Athena*. And he wondered if he could disagree, seeing her this way.

Andrea stirred a little, rolling to her other side and dislodging the blankets so her back was uncovered.

He went to her, pulling the covers back in place as he also pulled out the now-cool water bottle. After she was bundled back into her cocoon, he stood there, staring down at her.

He was definitely falling in love with the Medusa. With *Andrea*.

What would that cost *him*?

CHAPTER FIVE

Aristotle Tassos waited while the phone rang in his ear, tapping the fingers of his free hand on his desk as he stared out of his office window at the darkness. Sun had set many hours ago, but he was still wide awake. A curse of old age. And of his own busy brain.

"Hello?"

"Stavros."

"Uncle." His nephew's tone held the proper amount of respect. It didn't always.

"How is your hunt going?"

Stavros growled. "I haven't been able to catch up to Kallan for two days. And the things I'm finding don't indicate to me that either of us will locate her here."

Exactly what Aristotle had thought after Kallan's last several messages. Kallan didn't want help from his cousin. Or was it competition, perhaps? "I think it best you return to your own hunt tomorrow if you cannot find a solid lead there."

His nephew was silent a few seconds. "May I ask why you've changed your mind?"

Aristotle tapped his fingers on the desk again. "No. It should be enough that I want you to follow your own leads. The more leads we follow, the better our chances at finding this Medusa."

Stavros sighed. "I'll be happy to return to my own hunt, Uncle Ari. Thank you."

Aristotle hung up his phone and sat back in his chair, turning his gaze back to the family's website. Kallan's messages the past few days had been far more forthcoming than was normal. He rarely shared information about his hunt like this. Something was going on, and Aristotle wanted to know what. He picked up his telephone and dialed another number.

While he waited for an answer, he hoped Kallan hadn't already found the Medusa. Aristotle couldn't be sure Kallan would actually carry out his duty to kill her—not after all the questions he'd asked as a boy and a teenager. All the "why" questions.

He had to be certain someone else found her and finally eliminated the monster. And he needed to know what Kallan was really up to.

On the third morning, Andi felt more like herself. She woke with her face resting on the Harvester's chest, his steady heartbeat beneath her ear, his even breathing riffling through her hair. She rolled onto her back, and carefully stretched out. Only a faint twinge, then nothing.

"Thank the Gods," she breathed, relaxing.

"Better?"

She swallowed. "Yes."

"I was worried."

She didn't reply. She couldn't argue with his claim, as

she'd benefitted from his very solicitous care for the past forty-eight hours.

"I think I have a plan."

Her heart thudded harder. "A plan?" For the amulet, or her?

"Yes. My cousin will only be delayed a day or so at most before he comes back."

Her lungs worked a little faster.

"How well do you know your mountain?"

"Like the back of my hand." Which was why she would have been able to hide from him two days ago without any problem, had her body cooperated.

"Is there somewhere we can go he won't be able to track us?"

"We?"

"You're going nowhere without me, Andrea."

That was a problem. "There are a few places." Including her cave behind the waterfall. But she didn't think taking the Harvester there was really in her best interest.

"Somewhere protected?"

"Yes." The cave definitely qualified.

He sat up, braced himself on one hand beside her shoulder. "How long will it take to get there from here?"

"Hiking?" She considered for a moment. If she took him the roundabout way, she could wear him out and lose him. Maybe. "A day."

He inhaled deeply, and she imagined him pondering the idea. When he exhaled, he touched her temple, just brushing the edge of the sleep mask. "Are you safe now?"

She nodded, wishing just for a second that it wasn't true.

His strong fingers eased the mask up and off, and she rubbed her eyes, blinking against the bright morning light. He helped her to an upright position. "We need supplies if this location will take us a day to hike to."

Andi gave him a long stare, panic making her pulse race. What if she couldn't lose him in the woods? "I have some things in the basement," she said at last. "Water and food." Also true.

He nodded, gaze fixed on hers, and she realized she must be a mess. Self-consciously, she lifted one hand to smooth down her hair. A hint of a smile touched one corner of his mouth, making her blush. "Why don't you shower, and I'll start a list. We should head out tomorrow at first light."

Andi looked away and eased out of bed. She gathered clean clothes from her dresser and headed for the bathroom. Behind her, the Harvester still sat in bed, his bare chest visible over blankets that had fallen to his waist. She wondered if he was naked under her covers.

She shouldn't care.

The bathroom had been straightened up again, she realized as she stripped off her sweats. Her vibrator was nowhere in sight, clean towels hung on the bar, and her hot water bottle lay empty on the sink.

How very thoughtful.

Her mouth twisted and she climbed into the shower, then slid the door shut harder than she needed to. When the water came on, she made it hotter than it needed to be too, to distract herself from how nice he was being. "Come into my parlor, said the spider to the fly," she muttered, soaping up her hands before sliding them along her arms, her torso.

The Harvester could be as nice as he wanted, as sexy as he wanted. But she wouldn't forget why he was here.

She lifted her face into the spray, then turned so her head was soaked next.

Either she would escape him in her woods, or die trying.

Not much as far as plans went, but it was all she had at the moment.

After her shower, she didn't protest the cuff he put on her to keep her in the bedroom while he got his own shower, which was considerably quicker than hers had been. And he'd left her his list to look at while she waited.

Water. Check.

Food. Check.

Camping supplies. She chewed on her lower lip for a few seconds. In the cave she had more than enough, but she didn't really intend for him to get there with her. Perhaps he had some of his own in the backpack downstairs. But the pack wasn't that big. No, he didn't have those supplies.

"What are you thinking?" He stepped into the room, his inky hair gleaming blue-black and wet as he dragged his fingers through it.

She forced her gaze away from his hair and back to the pad on her knees. "I'm thinking it's going to be a long trek."

"You're up to it, right?" Concern darkened his green eyes.

"I'll be fine." She'd get to her cave if she had to crawl there.

He touched the handcuff and it fell away from her wrist. "You're going to need groceries soon."

As if he thought she'd be around for much longer. Or, more likely, she told herself, as if he were trying to lull her into believing it—he still had to figure out a way to get the amulet, which meant he needed her alive. She shrugged. "There's food in the freezer." Which he wouldn't be eating much more of.

She wouldn't be able to come back to her house if she didn't kill him, concern or no concern. He hadn't needed to take such good care of her, though, in order to keep her alive. She frowned. He could have handcuffed her in the basement and tossed down bread and water. She pushed aside the brewing confusion—she had bigger problems right now than trying to figure out the Harvester's motivation.

He steered her downstairs to the kitchen, and she didn't argue when he pointed to one of the chairs at the table and went to work on breakfast.

Even if she did kill him, it sounded like his cousin was well on his way to finding her, which meant she still couldn't come back to her house.

The thought made her a bit sad. She loved this house—alone in the woods, with the beautiful forest in summer, and a fantastic view of the valley below in the fall and winter. Even if she was lonely sometimes.

His laptop beeped from its spot on the counter, and he turned away from the stove to look at it. His expression hardened in a flash. "Damn."

Andi didn't like that look. "What?"

"Stavros."

A shiver snaked its way up her spine, and she folded her arms over her chest. "Not so happy with you?"

"He's already on his way back. He'll be here by tonight."

She shot to her feet. Dealing with one Harvester at a time was a challenge, but she couldn't possibly handle two. Not now. Thalia's words rang in her head. *Danger is coming from more than one direction.* Well, hell.

Kallan caught her gaze. "We can't wait until tomorrow, Andrea."

She shook her head, panic freezing her lungs, then swelling and rising into her throat so it nearly choked her.

"All right. Breakfast, and then we need to go." He stirred something in the pot and then shut off the burner.

Andi didn't want breakfast. She just wanted to move. Her

stomach churned uneasily, and her head started to thump in time with her heart.

He put a bowl on the table in front of her and touched her shoulder. "You need to eat."

She glanced down at the bowl, filled with steaming oatmeal, sprinkled with cinnamon and raisins, and felt a lump in her throat. "I'm not hungry."

"You'll need it later." He pushed her shoulder gently, and she sank back onto the chair.

He sat beside her, tucking into his own breakfast.

After a moment, she picked up her spoon and stuck it into the oatmeal. He was right, damn him.

"Andrea."

She looked up at his gentle tone.

"Will you trust me not to let him get you?"

How could she trust a man destined to kill her?

As if he read the question on her face, his jaw clenched. "I promise, *agaph*, he won't kill you. I won't let him."

His vow rang out in the still room, and for some reason, it made her panic subside just a little. She let out a shaky breath and lifted some oatmeal to her mouth.

Kallan finished his own breakfast quickly, then set about rinsing dishes. When she'd finally finished hers, he pulled her to her feet and set his hands on her shoulders. Her face was pale and set, her blue gaze shuttered. "Can you start bringing up supplies from downstairs? No more than we can carry."

She nodded, and he released her. Her silence worried him. As had the question plain in her eyes earlier.

She didn't trust him. She *couldn't* trust him.

Of course she couldn't. He existed just to kill her, as had his ancestors existed to kill hers.

That was before his heart had let her in.

He knew he couldn't tell her how he felt. Not yet. She'd never believe him if he blurted it out now. It was far too soon.

But after they'd gotten through this…

He frowned at the bowl he was rinsing. How would they get through this?

He shut off the water and put the dirty dishes into her dishwasher, then turned in time to see her drop an armload of water bottles onto the table. He went down to the basement with her for the second trip, gathering more water while she picked through some food boxes. Dehydrated pouches of stuff. MREs meant for serious hikers. Or survivalists.

He caught her gaze over the water, and a ghost of a smile touched her mouth. "Just in case?" He'd assumed the boxes were just being used for storing other things as many people tended to keep in their basements.

She nodded. "You never know when you might need to disappear into the woods." She grabbed a sturdy-looking backpack too, and tossed it at him.

He just caught it, watching her pick up another.

Upstairs, they sorted through the supplies spread over the table, dividing them between the two packs. "We need First Aid supplies, dry clothes."

She nodded. "I have a kit upstairs. Bug spray, sunscreen."

He watched the sway of her hips as she went up the steps, too distracted by their planning to fully enjoy the view. This was how one had to live when one was hunted.

It sucked.

He unpacked his own small backpack, then repacked it inside the bigger pack. When she dropped more things onto the table, he caught her wrist. "I'm sorry, Andrea."

She blinked up at him, her expression somber. "It's the way it's always been between our families." She lifted one shoulder in a half shrug.

He couldn't argue. "I'm sorry I brought Stavros to your door."

Her gaze dropped to the table. "Sounds like he would have found his way here eventually anyway."

The stubborn woman wouldn't let him apologize. He tugged her closer, startling her, and planted a hard kiss on her mouth. When he set her back, her wide eyes had darkened slightly. He wanted to kiss her again but resisted the urge. "We need to move."

She nodded, still staring up at him for a second, before she turned to the small mound of clothing she'd dropped onto the table. She methodically rolled socks and shirts before stuffing them into the pack, did the same with a pair of jeans and a jacket. There wasn't much room left in her backpack.

Nor in his, he noted.

"If I promise not to use it on you, can I have my dagger back?"

He gave her a measuring look, marking the stress lines around her eyes, the rigid set of her shoulders.

She met his gaze full-on. "I promise."

He nodded slowly. "You may need it."

A frown line appeared between her dark brows.

His cousin was persistent, after all, and Stavros wouldn't let Kallan stand in his way. He'd let no one stand in his way when he set his sights on something.

Perhaps he should have let his cousin come yesterday when she could have turned him to stone, solving one part of their problem. It wouldn't have solved the issues between them, but it would have gotten Stavros out of their way.

Andrea looked around the room, then into the living room. "I need one more thing."

He turned to watch her go up the stairs before he moved to the chest she kept along the living room wall. He touched the latch so the lock gave, then pulled out her dagger, as well as his own weapons. And her silverware. He grinned at the look on her face when she got to the foot of the steps again.

"Well." She stared while he put her knife block back on the counter and dropped the forks and knives back into the drawer.

"The lack of silverware would look odd if anyone came in."

Her mouth flattened. "You think he'll search the house?"

"I would, if it were me." He saw no sense in lying to her. Not now. Especially since Stavros was the most dangerous of his cousins.

She swallowed, then nodded briskly. "I suppose so."

He dropped his gaze to her hand, where a small box peeked out between her thumb and finger. "What's that?"

"My grandmother's necklace. I wouldn't want to lose it. If I can't come back."

Kallan felt his chest squeeze as she tucked the box into her backpack along with her cell phone and its charger. He knew he wasn't personally responsible for the war their families waged. It had been going on for centuries and centuries. But he felt responsible for leading his cousin here. Perhaps his digging into the myths and lore had alerted Stavros to her whereabouts. He had no way of knowing.

She stuck her wallet into the pack too, then zipped it up. "I think that's it."

"You'll need to put on boots, I think." He cleared his throat.

She toed off her sneakers and bent to grab the hiking boots beside the back door where he'd put them after that first night. His gaze caught on the curve of her behind, and his breath snagged in his chest.

Now is not *the time.* Still, he watched the play of her muscles in the close-fitting denim as she put her boots on.

"Can you think of anything else you want to take along?" He needed a distraction.

Andrea shook her head. "I think we're set." Her jaw was tight, and her eyes were clear. Resolute.

He took a quick breath and held out her dagger.

Their fingers brushed when she took it from him, sending heat rushing up his arm. And hers, judging by the way her eyes darkened and widened. She turned away, sticking the dagger into the sheath he knew was inside her right boot, then straightened.

"Ready?"

She nodded. "Let's go."

Kallan helped her get her backpack onto her shoulders, then hoisted his own before letting them out of the house. "Which way?"

She lifted her chin toward the far corner of the house, away from the trail they'd taken once already.

And he followed her, noting her purposeful stride as they headed into the shadows of the towering trees. He hoped this turned out better than all the other encounters between Harvesters and Medusas over the last generations.

But he couldn't say for sure, which made him nervous. Edgy.

Andi kept up her steady pace as they trekked farther into the forest. The sounds of the birds and chattering squirrels kept them company, as they had for the past two hours. He didn't try to carry on a conversation with her while they walked. He was clearly accustomed to physical activity.

Which meant she'd have a harder time than she'd anticipated in ditching him.

Not that she'd imagined it would be easy.

Nothing could possibly be easy about this. Her luck clearly didn't run in that direction.

She paused to take a sip of water from the bottle she'd tucked into the side of her backpack, and he stopped beside her. Warmth spread up her spine, and she frowned into the bottle she held. *Stop it.* He was not potential mate material, no matter how happy her hormones were when he was near.

"All right?" He took a quick drink from his own water, his arm brushing hers as he did so.

She shifted her weight onto her other foot, away from him. "Fine."

He met her gaze.

Her pulse skipped.

"I know you don't want to trust me, but you can. On this, you can."

It sounded like a vow, she thought, panic making her heart beat faster. She didn't want to believe him.

But on this one thing, she realized she did. Of course she did. Even though she hadn't wanted to, she'd trusted him not to kill her after they'd made their bargain for the scissors. He'd earned it.

She swallowed, her mouth dry, and lifted her water bottle to her lips again, giving herself a distraction from the intensity in his green eyes.

He sighed, then took another drink.

Andi closed her eyes briefly, girding herself, and capped her bottle. The next stretch would be more of a challenge. Maybe this would be where her luck changed.

Or not.

Two hours later, she panted softly, her heart pounding hard as she put one hand on the nearest tree trunk and dropped her head to pour the rest of her lukewarm water over the back of her neck.

Straight up the side of the mountain, and he was still not doing more than breathing hard, the bastard.

She felt her backpack shift, and glanced to the side.

"Getting you another drink." He tugged a bottle out and then rezipped her pack.

She mumbled her thanks and chugged down half the bottle in one go. Then turned in time to see his throat working as he swallowed the last of his bottle. His skin glistened with sweat, muscles beneath shifting and making her want to touch. With her fingers, her tongue.

She inhaled slowly and looked away again. It seemed she was stuck with him. At least for now.

He touched her arm, and she lifted her gaze. "Do you want a break?"

She shook her head. "Not if we want to get there before dark."

He frowned. "What if I think you need a break?"

Andi felt a little surge of annoyance. "You're not my father."

"Thank Goddess," he muttered, brushing away a drop of perspiration from her temple.

She blushed.

"Andrea, I'm just trying to point out, and obviously badly, you had a really rough day yesterday, and maybe you should take it a little easier than you have so far today."

"I'm sorry." She took a drink from the fresh bottle. "I haven't had to run for my life before, and I'm not used to requiring help, and apparently, neither is sitting well."

Kallan smiled a little, and his fingers slid down to the

corner of her mouth. "Apology accepted." He leaned down and kissed the tip of her nose lightly, startling her.

She resisted the urge to shift her head so their mouths would meet. Instead, she put her bottles away and adjusted her pack on her shoulders. "The next leg should be easier."

He gave her a knowing smile, but kept his mouth shut.

And she found herself smiling back.

Stupid.

But her smile didn't fade as quickly this time.

As she walked, more slowly now, she let her mind drift to what it would be like to actually have a real relationship again. If she could ignore the fact he'd come to kill her, there were other aspects of the past few days she could get used to. Like having someone to talk to who didn't think she was a complete nutcase. Like having someone who not only believed in the myths that shaped her life, but had also been influenced by them. Like the smoking-hot sex.

She fanned herself a little.

"You all right?"

Heat climbed her throat. "Still cooling down from that last segment," she called back over her shoulder. "Jackass," she added under her breath.

She resolved to think of nothing but getting to safety for now. Getting distracted by wishing for things she knew she could never have wouldn't keep her safe from Kallan's cousin.

Andi froze in mid-stride, her heart thundering in her chest suddenly, and it wasn't from exertion this time. Her gaze stuck on the dark, shiny creature lying across their path, and her pulse pounded in her ears.

His hands landed on her shoulders. "What?"

"S-snake," she whispered.

"Are you kidding?" He moved to stand beside her, and

looked into her face. "You're serious," he said after a couple seconds, a grin tugging at his mouth. He glanced to the trail ahead and started to laugh. "It's only a garter snake."

Andi ground her teeth together, heat climbing her neck to her face, but not in a good way now. Just because that damned Athena had cursed her to sprout snakes on her head every month didn't mean she liked them.

He laughed until she wanted to hit him. Or better yet, turn him to stone. Too bad she wasn't PMSing anymore.

Not looking at Kallan, she folded her arms and waited for the snake to finish slithering across the path.

Still chuckling, he gestured to the trail ahead. "All clear."

She hated him. Sticking her chin in the air, she marched past him, barely resisting the urge to smack him as she went. She consoled herself with that mental image for a few minutes, of punching him square in the nose. Or mouth. Maybe knocking the smug grin off his face. Drawing blood would be good. She curled her fingers into fists at her sides as she went, only vaguely aware of him close on her heels.

After a while, though, she grew more aware of his near-ness, as the forest darkened around them. His heat was within reach, if she stopped and stretched out her arm. Not that she would. Especially not now.

"How about some lunch?"

She jerked herself back to the present and glanced over her shoulder at him. "There's a good spot just ahead," she said after a second.

He grunted a reply, but said nothing more, simply striding along behind her.

As they neared the small clearing, Andi slowed her pace, shrugging her pack off her shoulders, and then sank onto the flat boulder there.

Kallan dropped his pack next to her feet and sat on a

fallen tree a foot away. "How much of the mountain is yours?"

She gave him a measured look as she dug an energy bar from her backpack. "Most of it. I'd have thought you would know."

He rested his elbow on his knee and his chin in his hand, green gaze steady on her face. "I wasn't worried about the size of your property, just in how to reach you."

That didn't make her feel better. She tore open the wrapper and took a bite of the granola mixture.

"I didn't anticipate we'd need somewhere to flee to."

She stopped chewing and met his gaze.

"I should have anticipated it."

"Why would you? You thought you were coming to kill me and steal something. You had no way to know your job would be far more complicated than any Harvester ever knew." She swallowed the food and took a big swallow of water to wash it down, where it sat in her stomach like a lump of lead. She took another drink, but it didn't help.

"I thought I was coming to kill a monster," he corrected her, touching her knee with his water bottle before he sat up straighter and took a drink. "I didn't anticipate you."

She wasn't sure if that was a compliment or not, so she didn't reply.

"How far, Andrea?"

She glanced at the path behind them. If she'd taken him the more direct route, they'd nearly be there already. As it was, she'd dragged him up the rocky side of the mountain to the hottest part of the day, then on a slight detour to the west. From here, they still had miles to go.

She hoped she hadn't delayed them too much. Or that his cousin hadn't traveled faster than Kallan had guessed.

"Around two hours." If they were really fast.

He looked skyward, where the sun had dropped slightly, and was now no longer directly overhead.

Andi looked at her watch, surprised to see it was after two. She'd dallied too long.

"Is there a direct route from here to there?"

She glanced up, startled, and found a hint of amusement in his gaze. He knew, damn him. He *knew* she'd taken a roundabout route. "Yes." It wouldn't be easy, but it would be direct.

He nodded, then dug into his own backpack for an energy bar—which he inhaled. "You should finish yours," he said around his last bite.

She forced herself to eat the rest, but it tasted like dirt. She drank her water slowly, then put the wrapper and empty bottles into her pack. She grabbed two fresh bottles and tucked them into the outer pockets where she could reach them easily.

Kallan took her pack, and she let him help her into it. His hands rested on her shoulders for a moment, and his warm breath slid over the top of her head. "I don't mind," he said softly. Then a quick kiss brushed her hair before he straightened up and away.

She inhaled shakily, her pulse stuttering. She wanted badly to trust him, but there was that small problem of him planning to kill her—to expose her family to the world as monsters.

realized he could hear water that was louder than the stream below. The falls. "Can we go faster?" If Stavros had arrived early, he might already be in the forest, and on their trail. Kallan wanted to have her safely away before dark, when it would be harder for his cousin to track them. But he did wonder *how* the cave was protected exactly. That might prove problematic.

She squared her shoulders. "Of course." She picked up her pace a little, and he smiled at her back.

Of course she could. She'd never admit weakness. Not to him. Not *even* to him. Maybe especially not to him.

"*Agaph.*"

She stumbled, then righted herself, her wide, wary eyes turning back toward him.

"I think I'm falling in love with you."

Shock widened her eyes more. "What?"

He caught her upper arms. "I said I'm falling in love with you." He bent and pressed a hard kiss on her mouth, ignoring the heat rising up in him. "I can hear the water. How far?"

She stared at him for a moment, as if she hadn't heard the question, then gave her head a slight shake. "Maybe half a mile. You'll have to swim." She pulled away and started walking again.

He huffed out a hard breath and followed her. She didn't believe him. Why should she? He hadn't given her much to believe in since his arrival, except his intent to kill her and find a way to take the amulet.

Of course, it was hardly his fault either, given the history of their families. He kept his eyes on her backpack as she strode along, as she stepped over fallen branches and moss-covered rocks. Her step was sure, if slower than it had been several hours ago.

She finally came to a stop a few minutes later, hands on her hips as she surveyed a wide pool with water tumbling into it from the falls overhead. At the opposite end, the pool spilled into a burbling creek.

Kallan stopped beside her, their arms brushing. "How deep is it?"

"Deep." She studied the water, then looked at the rocks high above. "You'll have to stay close, and make sure your pack is sealed tightly. They're waterproof, but only if you've closed everything properly."

He touched her shoulder. "I will. Can you keep it protected once we're inside?"

She met his gaze, her own grim, and he noted the exhaustion shadowing her eyes. "I can. I will." She looked away, her throat working.

Unease tickled his spine, lifting all the hair at the back of his neck, making him look around. Stavros was coming. "Let's go."

She adjusted her backpack and waded into the water.

He followed, then dove with her at the center of the pool. They swam down, underneath the rushing water, down farther still, before they finally surfaced behind the falls. About six feet over their heads was an opening.

He boosted her to the first foothold of rock, and she climbed up, disappeared into the blackness. He hurried up after her, then dropped his pack inside the cave as water sluiced from his face and hair.

Andrea had abandoned her own backpack about four feet farther in and was brushing water from her face as she looked around. "I have supplies in the back," she said at last, glancing at him over her shoulder. "Not enough to last forever, but enough for a few days."

He considered. Stavros was not the best tracker in the world, but he'd be able to follow some of their trail. If they were lucky, he'd lose his way up the steep rocky cliff and retreat down to the house. But he may just call in reinforcements. And if he called in a cousin who was a tracker, then they were in trouble, because Stavros would know where they were long before he reached the end of the trail due to his own particular talent.

Kallan didn't want to consider that yet. "You need to get dry."

"I think a fire first." She pulled a small flashlight from inside her pack and then made her way deeper into the cave. He followed the narrow beam of light, which bobbed along the cavern walls, smiling a little to himself at the wet footprints she left behind as his eyes adjusted to the near-dark of the cave.

Andrea had stopped, squatting down in front of a set of small shelves, and pulled out a camp stove.

He lifted one eyebrow when she held it out.

"I like to be prepared." Her tone was a little defensive, making him smile.

He took the stove, then the lighter she offered next. While he waited, she found a lantern too, and lit it. Immediately, the small alcove leaped into light and shadow. The contents of the shelves were revealed as more MREs and dehydrated food pouches, bottled water, camping gear. "Very prepared," he murmured.

She pushed to her feet. "Are you making fun of me?"

He shook his head and felt water drip down the back of his neck. "Just making an observation." He waited while she shimmied past him, and she seemed very careful not to touch him as she went. Kallan followed her out into the main area of the cave again, where she set the lantern on a ledge midway up the wall.

She faced him, hands clenching and unclenching at her sides, her eyes troubled.

"Go ahead." He'd been waiting. Ever since he'd opened his foolish mouth along the trail.

She caught her lower lip in her teeth, a tiny frown lining her brow. "You should get dry too," she whispered at last.

When she turned away, grabbing her pack and retreating to the smaller chamber at the back, he felt some of the stress leave his shoulders but his stomach knotted painfully. Trying to figure out his next move, he dragged his wet shirt off over his head, then bent to unknot the wet laces of his boots.

It would never work. He knew it. If anyone had suggested to him that he'd fall for the Medusa, he would have laughed at them and then punched them bloody.

From the rear of the cave, he heard the same wet shushing noises of clothing hitting the stone floor, and he clenched his jaw, trying not to imagine her wet and naked. And failing.

"Andrea?"

Sudden silence.

"How many sleeping bags do you have back there?" He had to know.

The soft sounds resumed, this time more quietly so he assumed she was quickly pulling on dry clothes. "One. But there are extra blankets." The reply was unsteady, as if she might be imagining the same things he was.

One sleeping bag. Of course. He shut his eyes for a second. As he went to his backpack, he unbuttoned his cargo pants, then tugged out dry clothing. His fingers were clumsy on the heavy material, made clumsier by the enticing images floating behind his eyes.

He shucked his wet pants and moved toward the front of the cave to dress.

A choked sound from Andrea made him freeze as he stuck his foot into his dry cargo pants. And every nerve in him hummed to life, zinging electricity to his groin.

Slowly, he straightened and turned just far enough to see Andrea still as a statue only a couple yards away. Her wide eyes were dark with surprise and something else. Against her dry shirt, her nipples were tight, making his mouth water. She'd pulled on a loose pair of knit pants that rode low on her hips, exposing several inches of belly between them and the hem of her shirt, and her feet were still bare.

Kallan dragged his gaze back to her face, noting the color tinting her cheeks, the way her lips were parted and the quick lift of her breasts with her breathing. "Turn around, Andrea." She might want him, but he knew she still didn't trust him.

Her gaze drifted lower, over his chest and arm, lower still to his bare hip. He was suddenly very glad he hadn't turned fully to face her, or she'd really be getting an eyeful now.

"Andrea." He made his tone harder now, and her wide eyes lifted slowly again to his face.

And she took a step toward him.

He sucked in a quick breath. "Stop."

She hesitated, then took another step.

His body ached, and he ground his teeth together for a heartbeat, just long enough for her to reduce the distance between them by another foot or so. "Don't."

She came to a stop within arm's reach, and he could see in the diffused light coming through the falls the desire darkening her blue eyes. "I want to."

His fingers tightened reflexively on the canvas pants in his hand. He wanted her to, also. "I don't want you to regret this."

She lifted her right hand to touch his back, and he rasped in a breath, feeling his muscles bunch under her fingers. "You feel good." She dragged her fingertips down along his spine, then lower, over his buttocks.

Kallan dropped the cargo pants and spun, catching her hand. "Think, Andrea." *Goddess, please.*

Her fingers twitched in his, and he could hear her quick breathing. She held his gaze for a long moment, then lifted her free hand.

He groaned when her palm skimmed over his belly. He didn't mean to, but it slipped out before he could stop it. And when her cool fingers slid lower, wrapping around him, he forgot why he should be dissuading her.

"Kiss me," she whispered, her breath warm on his chest. "Please."

He bent to her blindly, catching her mouth and devouring her. His heart banged against his ribs, and his cock jerked into her touch. He couldn't resist her.

He freed her other hand and slipped his fingers around her back, pulling her closer. She felt so damned good, even with the thin layer of cotton blocking him from direct contact with her skin. He lifted his other hand, dragging her shirt up to capture her breast—unbound now, its tip taut and tempting. He rasped his thumb over it, back and forth, until she arched into his touch, a soft sound escaping her.

"Andrea." He breathed against her mouth, forcing his eyes open.

Her eyelids fluttered open, and she slid the tip of her tongue along his lower lip.

"Tease." He kissed her again, hard, then lifted his head. "Are you sure?"

In answer, she tightened her grip around his erection, then

dragged her hand down to the base of him before stroking up to the tip.

His hips rocked into her caress of their own volition.

Kallan released her breast and scooped her up, swallowing back a curse when the move forced her to relinquish her grip. He carried her back into the interior of the cave, and set her on her feet long enough to grab the sleeping bag. "Help me with this."

She unzipped it, and they spread it over the rough floor together. "I think we need a blanket too," she murmured, rising again to rummage through a shelf until she came up with what she wanted.

Once the blanket was spread over the sleeping bag, he caught her wrist and drew her toward him again. "Are you sure?" he repeated over the hammering of his heart.

She put her mouth in the center of his chest, planting a gentle kiss there, then lifted her gaze to meet his. "Yes."

He tugged her shirt up again—and off—then fumbled with the drawstring on her pants, before he dropped them, too, so she was as naked as he. "So pretty." He stroked the back of his fingers over the puckered tip of her breast.

She shut her eyes for a second, her breath catching.

Kallan smiled when her eyes opened. "Lie down." If he helped her, he'd undoubtedly be too rough and immediately drive himself deep into her warmth. And she wasn't ready yet. Not yet.

She dropped to her knees and held out one hand to him. He knelt in front of her, easing her closer, closer, close enough for her tight nipples to brush his chest.

"Sweet Goddess," he breathed.

She smiled a little at that, then moved nearer, so her plump breasts flattened against him.

He tried to ignore the way his erection pulsed between their bellies. They had time. There was no rush.

But Andrea opened her mouth along his collarbone and dragged her lips over his skin, her tongue flicking out occasionally, while her fingers stroked his shoulder, his arm, his back.

He eased them to their sides on the blankets, sliding his own hand down her back to her hip, then between her thighs. Oh Goddess, she was wet already. Slick and hot. He dipped one finger inside her, loving that her hips rocked toward his caress. Her fingers tightened on his back at the same time.

He smiled as he feathered kisses over her forehead, her temples, her cheeks, meandering a path to her mouth, which was open and waiting when he finally arrived.

As determined as he was to take his time, to explore every inch he hadn't gotten to taste and touch, her fingers moved more urgently over him, tempting him. Teasing him. When she stroked his erection again, using her thumb to brush over the sensitive tip, he thrust three fingers deep into her wet sheath, driving a moan from her throat.

Her muscles clenched around him, and her fingers instinctively tightened around his erection, making his brain start to malfunction.

After he eased his fingers out of her to tease her clit, her sharp cry urged him to repeat the caress, over and over, until she trembled beside him, on the verge of release.

"Please," she gasped, her fingers frantic on him.

He still wanted to take his time, to kiss his way down past her beautiful breasts to her belly, to the hot flesh he was currently teasing. But he could no longer think that hard. Instinct ruled him, and instinct demanded he be inside her. *Now.*

He rolled her to her back, pushing her thighs wide with his knees.

"Please, Kallan."

His name on her lips only made him more determined to get inside her. To hear it again. To drive her as far out of her mind as she'd driven him. He caught her wrist and dislodged her fingers from his throbbing erection, then lifted her hips into his thrust.

Her cry was primal, as was his groan, when his body settled deep inside hers—so deep he could go no further.

Holy Goddess. He caught her mouth, keeping his hips still over hers for a moment. He felt complete with her. A silly notion, one he would only have attributed to silly romantics. But now…

Andrea's fingers dragged through his wet hair, and he nipped at her lower lip. "Are you all right?" He kissed one corner of her mouth, then the other.

She nodded, a hint of a smile curving her lips. "But you need to move."

Masculine pride welled in his chest, and he shifted his hips against hers, so the top of his cock rubbed her clit. "Like that?" he asked over her gasp.

"Gods, yes, and more." She dragged him down to kiss her properly.

Kallan let her, while he began a slow withdrawal, feeling her trembling inner muscles clasp his cock as he did so, then just as slowly, pushed back into her. His heart swelled to compete with his erection, near to bursting.

"I love you," he breathed, rocking in and out of her.

Andrea murmured something alongside of his throat, her fingers digging into his back, his ass, as her hips lifted into each thrust.

He quickened his pace just slightly, and soft cries met his lips when he caught her mouth.

Her hips lunged to meet his, and he felt her body tightening, quivering around him, under him. "Kallan."

Just his name, but it was enough.

He thrust harder and faster, somewhere his mind registering the sounds of her pleasure as his body took over from his brain. When her release broke, it sent him over the edge of his own orgasm. He collapsed over her and realized he was whispering, over and over, "I love you, Andrea, I love you."

He opened his eyes in time to see a tear slide from the corner of her closed eyes, and his thundering heart constricted painfully.

Goddess, what had he gotten himself into?

Andi felt tiny shivers still skate over her bare skin, the occasional shudder from Kallan, and the warmth from the camp stove not too far from their blankets.

She'd given in to instinct, just this once. It didn't seem like such a good idea now. After. But it had seemed just the right thing earlier, when she'd seen him at the front of her cave, changing from the wet pants to dry. When desire had exploded in her middle. He was absolutely beautiful, all sculpted muscle and hard angles, with those green eyes that shifted from bright to dark with desire in a flash.

And he'd said he loved her.

Her breath caught in her chest, and her eyes opened, staring at the stone ceiling.

He couldn't possibly.

She frowned, then shivered when his warm breath touched the side of her throat.

They were enemies. Their families had been enemies for

several thousand years. Would remain enemies until the end of time.

He couldn't love her.

She shut her eyes again. But hearing the words was a nice thing, she admitted to herself. It had been years since she'd heard them from anyone besides her parents or a cousin or aunt. And, if she were honest, she might never hear them from anyone else, given the situation they were in.

Kallan rolled to his side, keeping her tucked against him, and tugged the top blanket up to cover them both. "Are you all right?" He kissed her forehead.

She nodded, keeping her eyes shut. Gods, how on earth had she wound up here?

"Are you sure? You had a rough two days, then we trekked all over your mountain today. You're not sore?"

"I'm fine," she whispered, wishing she didn't still feel heat simmering in her belly somewhere near where their bodies remained joined.

He touched her chin, and she lifted her face reluctantly. His green eyes were still dark as they searched hers. Apparently, he saw too much, because his lips flattened a little. "I didn't want you to regret it."

"I don't." She was a little surprised to find that was true. "I just…" She inhaled slowly. "I don't know how this happened."

A wicked smile flashed over his face. "The usual way. If you need a refresher, I'll be happy to demonstrate."

She laughed in spite of the confusion bubbling in her veins. "I think you just did."

He eased his hips slowly backward, wincing all the while. "I think you need a better demonstration."

She sucked in a quick breath.

"I had other intentions for you. Plans for slow and easy,

kissing every inch of you." His gaze slid down to the tight peaks of her breasts. "I think I need to remedy that."

Andi felt the flush slide up from her chest to her face. "Every inch?" she squeaked. "But I haven't had a shower since this morning."

He slid his mouth across hers, from one corner to the other. "The falls are a little too rough for that, I think." He kissed his way down her neck to her shoulder. "Besides, right now, you smell like sex. It smells good."

Heat flashed through her, turning her belly into a molten pit of need again. She realized she'd lifted her shoulder into his caresses and tried to lie back, but then his lips skimmed over the top swell of her breast, meandering around and around the tight tip. She shifted, but he avoided her nipple, instead licking his way to her other breast and treating it to the same delicious torture.

"Yes, every inch," he breathed just before he sucked her aching nipple into his mouth.

She couldn't help arching into his touch, or the soft sound that escaped her. "Every inch?" she managed again, sliding her hands up his back and into the tangle of his long hair.

"Every. Luscious. One," he agreed, nipping at her swollen breast between each word.

"Oh Gods." It was barely a breath.

He chuckled, and commenced the tasting.

When he'd finished a very long time later, the daylight no longer shone through the falls. Andrea finally breathed evenly, though he knew she was still wide awake. Kallan wanted to sleep. But under his hand, he could feel just how alert she really was—the muscles in her back not tense yet, but ready to go any second.

"What's wrong?" He slid his hand down her spine.

"He's coming."

He considered that, letting his senses open a little. "Not close yet. Maybe he's waiting until morning to try to find the house." He shifted a little, settling her nearer, and she let him, but she didn't relax.

He hadn't really intended to tell her how he felt earlier, but she'd looked so defeated as they hiked through her woods, and he couldn't stop the words when they burst out. Nor could he have kept them contained earlier while he was making love to her.

She dragged one hand up his side. "We won't be able to stay here indefinitely. I never really planned it to be a permanent hideaway."

He stared up at the stone ceiling. "Are you prepared to go out of the country?"

She lifted her head at last and propped her chin on his chest. "I might be."

Of course she had papers ready. His Medusa was smart. Kallan smiled a little. "How do you feel about Scotland this time of year?"

Andrea frowned. "Scotland?"

"You've never been, have you?"

She shook her head. "Do we need a visa?"

"If we do, I can take care of it. You've got a passport, right?"

"I've got a couple." Pink touched her cheeks at the admission.

He felt his lips curve again.

"Why Scotland?"

"No ties. It could be anywhere you've never been."

He watched her as she considered that, as she realized the

truth of his words. Her blue gaze shifted back to his face. "I hate to run."

He understood. Really. But he wanted her out of Stavros's reach.

"This is my home. My *life*. I'd rather stay here and just kill him."

"Bloodthirsty." He realized he'd called her that the first night, and evidently, so did she, as her blush deepened.

"If it was just you, you'd stay and fight."

He wanted to lie. "Yes," he said at last, opting for honesty.

"You haven't tried to take the amulet either. No more ideas?"

He sighed. "No."

She rolled off him, presenting her back. "What do you see?"

A lot of gorgeous skin, he realized, his mouth watering.

"The tattoo, Harvester," she said, and he imagined from her tone that she was smiling a little.

He dragged his gaze down her spine, then studied the design. The flowers were bright and numerous with the snake slithering among them, winding itself around the cup's stem. He skimmed one fingertip along the flowers at the top, then lower, to the bowl of the chalice. Heat flared.

She sucked in a quick breath. "Why does it do that?"

"I've no idea." He hadn't been able to find anything about why it would do that, anywhere, in any of his research. Probably because no one else knew the truth about Medusa's Goblet. He stroked along the rim, feeling her skin warm under his touch, then slid his finger down the stem to the base. Heat all along the way. But as soon as he touched the flowers or the snake, nothing.

"I'm sure she never intended you to be able to take it."

"I'm sure she didn't." Which meant his family had been set an impossible task thousands of years ago. He frowned, rubbing over the bowl of the cup again and the heat intensified. It still felt like her warm, satiny skin under his touch though.

He slid his fingers away, curling around her hip to draw her back against him. "I don't know." He kissed the back of her head.

"If you can't take it, you still have the other part of your job to do."

Kallan's fingers tightened on her hip just a little, and his heartbeat quickened. He couldn't kill her.

Which meant his cousins would not only do the job if they managed to track her down, but they'd have to remove him from the equation as well.

He shut his eyes. This situation was a complete no-win.

Andi sat a couple feet away from the camp stove later, watching the pot filled with rehydrated stew begin to thicken and bubble. Kallan stood at the cave entrance, wearing only his boots and unbuttoned cargo pants. His black hair was rumpled and his jaw hard as he stared out into the dark waterfall. He'd been increasingly edgy since the discussion about the amulet, and she'd decided it might be best to keep her mouth shut for a little while.

His current anger seemed to stem from her reminder that he was supposed to kill her, not from his inability to take the cup.

Not that she wanted to die.

She frowned and stirred the stew, realizing her stomach was gurgling with hunger pangs.

Dying didn't frighten her as much, though, as his declaration earlier. She went cold, then hot just recalling it.

He loved her.

Good Gods, how had that happened?

Or was it just a distraction?

Scary as the idea was, she didn't think he'd been lying when he said it. Not the first time, nor any of the other times he'd repeated it when they were rolling across the blankets and sleeping bag earlier.

Her heart pounded harder. Aside from her family, no one had ever said that to her.

She stirred the stew briskly, trying to distract herself.

But she looked again at the front of the cavern, where Kallan still stood with one arm braced against the rock. A muscle jumped in his tight jaw.

She dragged her gaze away from his face to the wide shoulders and strong muscles visible in his back and arms.

"You need to know I'll die before I let him kill you," he said, startling her.

Andi blinked, and he turned his head toward her, his green eyes as hard as his jaw. Her heart jumped up into her throat. Gods, he was serious. A hot splatter of stew hit the back of her hand, and she jerked her spoon away from the small pot to turn the burner off, forcing herself to look away from him.

"Maybe you should be practical," she started.

"Maybe you should think about trusting me a little," he cut in, swinging around to fully face her.

The front view was as distracting as the back, she realized, absently noting the crisp dark hair spattered over his wide, muscular chest and narrowing onto his flat belly, to that unfastened button…

She pulled her gaze back to his face when he stepped away from the cave opening.

"I got you safely away before Stavros could kill you. I just spent the last two days taking care of you." His nostrils flared. "I don't know how you've managed by yourself all these years."

A lump pushed her heart down out of her throat, making her nose and eyes sting.

"If I haven't earned a little trust after the last two days, I don't see how you can ever trust anyone."

That was low. She dropped her spoon into the pan and pushed to her feet. "That wasn't very nice."

"It doesn't look like your family rushes to help you out every month."

She couldn't argue, as it was true, but that didn't lessen the sting.

"So when did anyone take care of you last, Andrea? Besides me?"

"Not since I was thirteen," she yelled. "Then it wasn't so bad, until Annis died. Now I take care of myself." Her vision blurred a little, and she blinked hard.

Kallan moved toward her, his mouth a flat line, his green eyes flaring sparks. "But you trust them anyway?"

"They're my family." It really was that simple. If she truly needed them, one of them would come.

"They've abandoned you to the Harvesters." His shout echoed in the cavern.

To her horror, a tear slid down her cheek, but she didn't wipe it away. "They need to be safe too," she whispered.

"So the sacrifice of one isn't a big deal if the rest are safe?" His tone was still rock-hard, though lower in volume.

Andi didn't want to think about it that way. His view of the whole situation was so distorted.

Wasn't it?

"As long as none of us get the amulet, it's okay to lose the Medusa every once in a while?" He touched her cheek, wiping away the tear there.

Another fell, and she wasn't sure if she was angrier at him or herself. Or her family.

He pulled her into his arms suddenly, and she let him, hiding her face against his chest. Another tear fell, and she shut her eyes. "You're wrong," she whispered around the lump in her throat.

He grunted but didn't say anything else, rubbing one big hand up and down her spine, spreading warmth she hadn't realized she needed.

Her racing heart gradually eased back to a normal speed as he held her, and she inhaled shakily. Under her cheek, his chest was wet. That could *not* be from her, she thought, sniffling a little. "Are you ready for supper?" she asked after another moment.

He took a slow, deep breath, then let it out just as slowly. "Think about what I said, Andrea. Please." He kissed the top of her head and loosened his hold on her.

She nodded, not meeting his eyes, and turned back to their dinner, which they ate in silence. She did a quick clean-up afterward, then paced the chamber. "We'll need to take turns being on watch tonight," she said finally. "I'll take the first shift."

Kallan remained in the middle of the nest of blankets where he'd sat to eat his stew, and his green gaze missed nothing when she faced him from the back of the room. "Do we have another way out of here? In case?"

She tipped her head toward the back of the cave.

He pushed to his feet and followed her into the smaller chamber.

Andi took a quick breath, then eased the shelving unit away from the wall a few inches to uncover a hole. It was big enough for her to get through, but she suddenly realized *he* might have a problem.

Evidently, so did he, judging by the frown on his face. He squatted down to study it. "That's it?" He touched the rock on one side. It didn't look as though the passage was wide enough for him.

"'Fraid so." Cold settled in her belly. If she had to escape that way, she didn't want to leave him behind to face his angry cousin.

"I'll manage," he said shortly, shoving to his feet. "Hopefully we won't have to use it." He helped her push the shelves back into place. "Your protections, they're strong?"

She nodded. She'd given them a boost before they'd clambered up behind the waterfall, and she was certain they'd hold.

"Stavros has a different talent," Kallan said slowly, putting his hands on her shoulders and rubbing gently.

She swallowed. "You mean he has to worry about whether he's locked his keys in the car?" The joke fell flat, and the cold in her belly seemed to expand.

"Every Harvester has a different ability."

Her mouth went dry. "What is his?" she asked, though she was very afraid of the answer.

"He can sense magic."

Like her protections. Her knees went watery. He'd know exactly where she'd done her spells around the property boundaries.

And he'd find the cave, protected as it was.

She met Kallan's gaze and didn't feel at all reassured.

"He can also undo whatever was done."

Her knees gave out, and she dropped to the floor, staring up at him.

He crouched down in front of her. "It will take him a little while. He can't just undo something automatically. It'll take a while to figure out all the steps, but eventually he'll find what he needs." He rubbed her shoulders again. "The best thing we have going for us right now is that tracking isn't his specialty. As long as he's alone, it's going to take him some time to search the property."

Andi shut her eyes, feeling worse by the second.

"If he's brought one of my cousins who is skilled as a tracker, we're in trouble."

CHAPTER SEVEN

Kallan hated having to tell her all that, as her face had gone a shade paler with each revelation. But she needed to understand what they faced. She needed to know if she wanted to survive.

But she swallowed after a moment, and she opened her eyes, the blue dark. "All right." She pushed to her feet, brushing aside his hands and moving to the mouth of the cave. "I'll be right back."

He watched her pick her way down the rocks to the small ledge behind the falls, waited as she knelt and chanted something he couldn't hear over the water. But he could feel the surge of energy as she did whatever it was she was doing. Likely adding to the protection on the cave for the night.

But so much magic would be a beacon to Stavros once he was close enough.

He bowed his head, racking his brain for something else to slow his cousin down and coming up empty. Stavros was too smart to fall for another lie about his location.

Andrea clambered back inside and let him catch her wrist to pull her upright.

"We have to be gone before he gets here," he said gently.

She nodded.

"And you'll have to undo everything when we go. Otherwise, it'll still draw him."

She nodded again. "Fine."

"Do you have any preferences for where we go next?"

"Wherever you want."

He frowned. "Really?" There were a lot of places they could go that wouldn't be flagged automatically and immediately as possibilities by his cousin.

But she was being awfully agreeable.

Kallan studied her face more closely. "For how long?" He had a sneaking suspicion…

"Until I can take care of your cousin myself."

He shook his head, smiling. "No." Still, he gathered her close, despite her slight resistance. "It wouldn't be safe for you."

"Nothing much is safe for me right now." She lifted her face so he could see the anger flaring in her eyes. "I just want to go home, to my house."

He held her gaze for a moment. "You know you can't."

"No, not right now."

"Not as long as you're the Medusa," he corrected her. "If Stavros has found your house, you can bet it won't be left unattended until he's convinced someone else is now the Medusa." He slid his hands to her lower back, easing one under the hem of her shirt so he could stroke the spot where her tattoo started. "As long as you carry the amulet, you're a target."

"Then you'd better kill me, because I won't spend my life running." She pushed away from him, striding around him to pace the room.

He couldn't do that. She knew it too, damn her. He

dragged one hand through his hair and swung away to look out into the darkness. He'd never run before, from anything. But he would run, at least temporarily, to keep her safe from Stavros.

He just needed her to trust him a little. Enough to keep her safe. That would be a good start.

Andi took a sip of water as she sat in the mouth of the cave hours later, listening to the falls. Occasionally night sounds reached her—an owl hooting, several deer leaping into the stream.

Behind her, Kallan lay in silence, but she knew he wasn't sleeping. He was far too alert, too tense for that.

She was completely exhausted, but she didn't want to sleep.

"You should lie down."

She shut her eyes. It was tempting. To lie down beside him and rest. But she couldn't. Not when there was a man hunting her—maybe even in her home or on her mountain now, stalking her like she was an animal.

"Andrea."

She glanced at him. "I'm fine. You should get some sleep while you can."

He sighed, but didn't reply.

She knew he didn't sleep, though. Not for a long, long time. She stared out into the dark, trying not to think of the things he'd said to her. The accusation he'd made about her family earlier. That one hurt. The other declaration scared the hell out of her.

It also made her heart beat faster with pleasure.

That was not a good thing. She couldn't have a man in love with her who intended to kill her.

Then again, that same man had also promised he'd die to protect her. He'd already lied to his family to keep her safe.

Kallan Tassos was a lot more complicated than she would have guessed.

Hours later, her brain had simply given up on trying to figure out the tangled mess of her life when she felt his hand on her shoulder. "My turn."

She didn't argue this time, getting slowly to her feet and stretching. He kissed the top of her head.

"Get some sleep, *meli*. I'll keep watch." His hand slid down her back, and he nudged her toward the sleeping bag.

Andi kicked off her boots and rolled into the blankets, which were still warm from his body. She inhaled deeply, his scent making her smile a little. He smelled good. She fell asleep thinking that.

When she woke, there was faint light outlining the cave opening where Kallan stood, every muscle tense.

"Is he coming?" She threw back the blankets and grabbed her boots.

"He's somewhere on the mountain. And he's got company." He glanced over his shoulder at her, but it was still too dark to see his expression.

Her heart pounded crazily in her chest, making it hard to breathe evenly. She fumbled with the laces on her boots for a few seconds, then got to her feet. "How long?"

"If they follow our trail from yesterday, five hours or so. If they follow Stavros's eye for magic, much less." He moved away from the entrance. "Either way, we need to be gone long before he finds this place."

She nodded, folding blankets with trembling hands.

"Andrea." He caught her wrists as she wrestled the sleeping bag into submission.

She looked up and found his eyes dark with concern, but his jaw hard with determination.

"We'll be fine."

She swallowed and nodded. "Okay." She had to trust him on this—that he would get her to safety and not hand her over to his cousin who wouldn't care if they got the amulet or not before he wiped her off the face of the earth.

After all, he hadn't killed her over the past few days when it would have been extremely easy.

She paused in her folding at that thought.

The Harvester hadn't killed her.

She glanced up and found him back at the cavern opening again, the line of his shoulders stiff. She'd trust him in this. She *had* to.

She got everything put away, hoping she could come back sometime soon. Or just sometime. She stood staring at her shelves of supplies and felt a lump try to clog her throat.

She swallowed it down and grabbed some MREs to add to her backpack, turning away. "We'll need more water for today."

"Do you mind packing while I keep an eye on things?" He looked at her over his shoulder.

"No." She felt better with something to occupy her mind, and repacking her backpack kept her busy for almost five minutes. Then she gathered more water bottles for Kallan, though she didn't root through his pack. Instead, she set them down beside his backpack and moved to the doorway, touching his back lightly. "I'll watch while you do your pack."

He kissed her, hard and fast, and left her blinking stupidly at the stone wall when he moved away.

Andi inhaled and forced her gaze to the water streaming

in front of the cave, noting the brightening of the sky outside. The birdsongs multiplied and amplified around them.

It only took him a couple minutes to replenish his back-pack, and then he stood beside her, his body warm. "We should eat before we head out. But nothing requiring a fire, I think."

She agreed, heading to the back of the cave again to find something.

They ate in silence, both watching the lightening sky outside, tension making the air around them heavy. When she'd finished her energy bar, she glanced up to find him watching her.

"Do you trust me for this?"

She nodded, noting the way his jaw relaxed slightly at her response. Her pulse beat faster.

"All right. Then let's go." He touched her cheek lightly and moved away to grab the packs.

They climbed down, and Andi knelt on the ledge to undo her protections on the cave, her head bowed and eyes shut. While she was at it, she sent a quick plea to the Gods that she'd be able to return here again safely.

They swam away from the cave in the opposite direction from where they'd arrived yesterday, and climbed—dripping—onto the other bank, careful to step only on the rocks and not into the soft earth. The less evidence they left behind for his cousin to find, the better.

Kallan glanced at his watch several hours later. They'd been heading down the other side of the mountain, away from Andrea's house, and she hadn't relaxed at all the entire way. In fact, he'd bet that if she weren't wearing her backpack, her shoulders would be hunched up with the tension in her. He strode along behind her, just a step or two, periodically opening his senses to see if Stavros was getting closer.

Not gaining on them yet.

When they reached the foot of the mountain, they had to figure out where to go from there.

He'd been joking last night when he mentioned Scotland, but he'd been thinking about it for a while now as they walked. Neither of them had any ties there, and it might be a safe place temporarily.

Andrea stopped suddenly and he caught her arms to stop himself before he knocked her over.

"What's wrong?"

She shook her head. "I thought I heard something."

He cocked his head to one side to listen. He heard nothing but the chattering of the squirrels and birds in the trees. He opened his senses further and felt his heart skip a beat. "He's closer." Maybe nearly to the cave. Where their trail would stop, at least for a while. Stavros would need one of the cousins who was expert at tracking—rather than just simply good—to pick it up again. Kallan hoped Stavros hadn't brought Pietro or Giles.

She shook her head. "Maybe my imagination is just working overtime."

"Perhaps." He patted her arms before releasing her. "How long to the road?"

"Half an hour, tops."

Maybe it had been a car she'd heard.

She started walking again, then stopped when a bobcat leaped from a low branch onto the old trail they were hiking.

Heart pounding, Kallan caught her arms, watching the cat watch them. It was only a few yards away, and if it decided they looked like something worthy of a taste, he needed to get her behind him. She lifted one hand to cover his, staying him.

The cat's dark eyes remained on them, unblinking for a very long moment, and then the animal jumped into the brush on the other side of the trail.

Andrea smiled up at him, then began walking again. He let out a breath he hadn't realized he was holding and started after her.

It took less than thirty minutes to reach the road, but there was no traffic. Getting a ride might be difficult.

Kallan surveyed the area, then dug his map out of one of the pockets on his pants. If they went east here, it would be good for losing Stavros, but not very helpful in a more permanent escape. If they went west, though, they were more likely to find a ride. And stay in Stavros's hunting ground.

A low hum reached his ears a second before Andrea turned to him, anxiety shadowing her eyes. He shook his head. "It's good." Not one of his cousins.

Her expression relaxed slightly, but she reached for his hand anyway.

Surprised, he linked their fingers and smiled down at her. A minute later, a truck rumbled around the bend, slowing when Kallan put up his free hand.

An old man sat behind the wheel of the dusty pickup, a battered baseball cap perched on the back of his head, and he rolled his window down. "You kids need a ride?"

"Where are you heading?"

"Ellsworth."

"That would be great. We were supposed to meet friends, but I think we must have missed them." He gave her fingers a light squeeze.

"Climb on in." The man gestured to the passenger door.

Kallan led the way around the front of the truck, shedding his backpack, then took Andrea's to put into the back before he helped her up into the cab. When they were both settled, he leaned forward. "I'm Phil." He ignored the startled glance Andrea shot him at his introduction. "I really appreciate the ride."

The old man took his right hand off the wheel and stretched it toward Kallan. "Ted. It's a long way to anywhere from here, Phil."

Kallan shook his hand. "It is. We met our friends yesterday to hike onto the mountain, and after we broke camp, they got ahead of us. I guess they figure we made it back to town, but we landed on the wrong side of the hill."

Ted laughed. "It happens, even to the most experienced of us at least once."

Kallan relaxed, chatting with the man about hiking and then the conversation moved on to more general topics, and the drive to Ellsworth was quickly over. Ted dropped them downtown at a spot where Kallan told him they could walk to their friends' apartment. They hefted their packs.

Andrea let out a long, slow breath and closed her eyes. "That was interesting, Phil." When she opened her eyes, she showed faint amusement mingled with worry.

He winked at her. "We got to town, which is where we needed to be, and none of my cousins are nearby. Now we'll get a car and head for Boston."

"Boston?" She let him lace their fingers and started walking at his side.

"International airport, *agaph*." He gave her fingers a squeeze. "You did bring a passport, right?"

"One or two." She bit her lip. "Where are we going?"

His phone vibrated in his pocket, and he ignored it. "I'll let you know in a little while." He steered her toward the rental car office he knew was only a couple blocks away.

She didn't protest though he could see the questions in

her eyes, and he wished he had some way to reassure her this would all work out.

He couldn't, though. Not as long as she was the Medusa. As far as he knew, there was only one way for that to change, and he was in no hurry now for *that* to occur.

Within twenty minutes, he'd rented a car with one of his alternate identities, and they were on their way south, out of Ellsworth.

Andrea sank back against the passenger seat, closing her eyes. "Are we safe for a little while?"

"Yes." He knew for sure Stavros was nowhere near them. He needed to make sure it stayed that way.

She sighed and relaxed a little more.

"Get a nap. We'll be on the road awhile." He touched her cheek lightly, and she opened her eyes, rolling her head against the headrest to look at him. "I know you didn't sleep enough last night," he said. His pocket vibrated again.

She smiled faintly. "Neither did you."

"I'll be fine. Close your eyes again, *meli*." He stroked her cheek, then put his hand back on the steering wheel.

She obeyed him. He knew exactly when she fell asleep— just twenty minutes out of Ellsworth. He relaxed then, but only a little. When his phone vibrated again, he sighed. He was sure it was Ari or Stavros, but didn't bother to look. He'd have to pick up a new phone before they flew out of Boston, and they'd need a suitcase. They could hardly get on an international flight without some luggage, and he knew the airline would never let them have their weapons in a carry-on.

That was one good thing about getting on a flight some- where, he mused as he drove. No one else would have a weapon there either, so his Medusa was safe for a while.

And she *was* his Medusa. He was equally sure of that,

whether she believed him or not. Perhaps he would be able to persuade her once they got to their destination.

And maybe he could figure out a way to keep her safe permanently.

Andi woke when the car beneath her slowed, and she jerked upright in her seat.

"It's all right. I'm just going to grab us some food." Kallan gave her a little smile.

She exhaled slowly. "Okay." She dragged her fingers over her head automatically, then remembered she hardly had any hair left to straighten. For now, anyway. Her hair grew back quickly, she'd discovered. Just in time to have to cut it again.

She sat up straighter. He was steering the car onto an exit ramp from the highway. "What time is it?" She fumbled to turn her watch face toward her.

"Suppertime. You slept through lunch." He touched her wrist. "And I'm starving. We'll stop, grab some supper, take a look at the flights leaving Boston, buy me a new cell phone, and continue on to the airport."

She nodded, trying to make her brain wake up and function properly. "Where do you suppose your cousin is?"

"Probably back at your house, at least temporarily."

She didn't like the sound of that. At least she hadn't left anything with contact information for any of her family that would get anyone else hurt. "Do you think I can use your computer later? To send an email to my family."

"Of course." He hadn't even hesitated.

She liked that more than she should. She looked out the side window at the blur of buildings they passed. "Where are we?"

"York. What are you hungry for?"

Her stomach rumbled, and she blushed. "It doesn't matter."

He was smiling when she glanced over again. "How do you feel about Chinese?"

"Sounds great."

He steered the car into a strip of shops and restaurants, and she inhaled deeply. Already, she could smell the food, making her stomach growl more loudly. Two doors down from the Chinese restaurant was an electronics store, and she nodded to herself. Kill two birds with one stone.

Kallan touched her knee. "Are you all right?"

She turned to look at him. "I'm better. Thank you."

His smile widened. "How do you feel about shopping?"

She wrinkled her nose. "Depends on what we're shopping for."

"We're going to need a little luggage for our trip."

She considered that as he climbed out of the car. "I guess it would look funny to get on a plane without anything," she said when he pulled her door open.

"Very. And we don't want anyone to remember us for anything like that." He caught her hand to pull her up and out of the vehicle. "So we're going to get dinner, a new phone and a few things for traveling." He kissed her lightly. "Sound like a plan?"

Andi nodded, her lips tingling just from the brief contact.

"Good." He bent into the backseat to pull his laptop from his backpack and then guided her into the restaurant. After they'd placed their orders, they found a table in the corner, where he booted up the computer and pulled up a travel site.

She watched his fingers tapping over the keys and recalled those fingers sliding over her. Heat rushed to her cheeks, and she forced her gaze away from his hands, instead looking at the computer screen. "Scotland? You were serious?"

He nodded as he entered some info in the query boxes. "I am now."

She pondered for a moment while he purchased tickets. "Why?" Not that a little planning time was bad. But so far?

"You have no ties there, right?"

She shook her head.

"Neither do I. It's not the first place anyone is going to look for either of us, and that should buy us some time to figure a way out of this." He lifted his gaze from the computer screen to meet hers. "And I *will* find a way."

The determination in his tone made butterflies flutter to life in her belly.

His expression softened a little, and her heart beat faster as he leaned nearer.

"Number sixty-four!"

Andi jumped at the shout. "I think that's us," she said, her mouth still tingling in anticipation of his kiss.

"I think it is." He kissed her, quick and hard. "Would you grab it while I pull up the other site?"

She pushed to her feet, pulse hammering in her ears. Excitement and nervousness rushed along her veins, both from his kiss and from wondering what he would find on his family's site regarding their search. The thought made the excitement fade away as she gathered their dinner onto a tray.

Kallan's jaw was tight when she got back to the table, though he tried to relax when she returned.

"That good, huh?" She set the tray down and started serving the food.

He moved the laptop over so there was room for everything on the table. "Sit, *meli*."

She dropped onto the seat beside him.

"Stavros is on the hunt, but he's got no idea where to go right now." He caught her hand in both of his, and she realized her fingers were cold. "I'll post, tell them I'm in the midwestern part of the country, say I missed you in Ohio and found some new leads to follow." He held her gaze, his bright and steady. "We are getting out of the country tonight."

She nodded, her appetite diminished.

"You need to eat anyway," he said gently, as if her thoughts were written on her forehead. "I don't think they're serving dinner on the overnight flight." He kissed her knuckles. "Then we can shop and you can try to bankrupt me."

His teasing made her smile a little, but she looked at all the food spread in front of them, not in the mood for any of it.

Being on the run sucked, even if the sexiest man alive was with you.

After they'd eaten and Andrea had sent off a cryptic email to a cousin and one to her mother, Kallan led the way through several shops, starting with the electronics store where he found himself a new phone they could use overseas and that his family wouldn't be able to reach him on, until they were adequately supplied with things to get them out of the country. A new suitcase, a couple changes of clothing—plus a new outfit for each to wear now so they didn't have to travel in the same clothes they'd swum and trekked down the side of the mountain in—some toiletries, and things to occupy them on the plane, if either of them could keep from passing out with exhaustion. He knew he'd have to catch a little sleep eventually, but not until they were airborne. Then back to the car, where they emptied their backpacks into the suitcase as well, including their weapons.

Andrea smiled as she tucked her dagger into one of the

inner pockets on the suitcase. "It's a shame they won't let me carry that on the plane."

He laughed, making her smile deepen. "It's probably better for everyone they don't." He tucked his own knives into another pocket. "We should have gotten a carry-on, too."

She shook her head. "No need. You have your smaller pack with the laptop. That's plenty, plus there'll be room for the books and magazines now that everything else is out of it." She zipped the suitcase. "I think we're set. Are we still good?"

He checked his watch. "Perfect."

They climbed into the front seat of the car, and he steered back onto the highway, where they made really good time all the way to Boston. For once, getting into the airport was quick and easy, though he didn't relax his guard. There was always the off-chance one of his cousins might be flying in or out from somewhere else. It wasn't until they were on the plane, winging their way to Scotland, that he breathed a little easier.

Andrea sat with her head back against her seat, her eyes shut, but he knew she wasn't sleeping.

"We're clear for now." He covered her hand on the armrest.

"I know. It's exhausting, being so tense all the time." Her head shifted toward him on the headrest, and she opened her eyes. "Makes me want to go back in time to about a week ago and then just stop time."

Sharp pain pinched at his chest. A week ago, he hadn't gone to her house yet. He didn't want to go back to not knowing her. Not now.

CHAPTER EIGHT

Andrea slept at last, her fingers relaxing in his. He watched her for a while in the plane's dimly lit cabin, the way her lashes fluttered every now and then against her cheeks, her chest rising and falling evenly beneath the blanket he'd put over her earlier.

She'd tried to read a magazine, but couldn't focus, so he'd taken it from her and tucked it away in the backpack and asked about her mountain. That relaxed her a little, and eventually, she'd simply stopped talking, exhaustion finally catching up with her.

Kallan tightened his hold on her fingers just a bit. There had to be a way to keep her safe from the rest of his family.

It was clear there was no way for his family to take the amulet, and right now he didn't care. He just wanted the extended Tassos family not to be hunting her. At the moment, the only way he could think to stop that was for her to drop completely off the map, which they were doing.

Maybe once his own brain had rested a little, he could come up with something else.

He smiled, closing his eyes. Just a nap. He never slept well on airplanes.

This time was an exception. He woke only when Andrea nudged his elbow with hers.

He opened bleary eyes to find her shifting her seat into the upright position. "What?"

"We're landing soon."

He sat up straighter too, rubbing one hand over his jaw, rough with stubble.

"You snore."

He lifted one eyebrow and turned to meet her gaze. "I do not."

She was trying not to smile, and failing. "When you sleep sitting up, you do." She dropped her gaze to the blanket in her lap.

He leaned in for a quick, hard kiss, and her smile was nowhere to be seen when he sat back. "I need to shave."

Her gaze slid over his face, darkening faintly. "You look fine."

"'Fine'?"

Her gaze lifted to his. "Better than fine," she whispered, her fingers rising to touch his chin.

Heat spread from the spot, and he caught her hand in his to pull it away from his face, before he forgot they were in a public place. "We're finding a hotel close to the airport, then we can both sleep. *After.*"

Hot color washed up her cheeks, and she bit her lower lip as she glanced away.

Kallan took a deep breath. "Now quit tempting me," he teased gruffly, dragging one hand through his hair. "Scotland is beautiful."

"You've been before?"

"A couple times, but not nearly long enough." He untangled her fingers so he could lace them with his, enjoying her warmth. "The mountains are incredible, and so are the islands."

"Where will we go?" Curiosity lit her eyes as she turned a little in her seat so she could face him.

"We can wander until we find a spot we like." It actually wasn't a bad idea. He considered that. "We could head up the west coast, visit some castles and islands along the way. Or hike in the mountains."

Andrea smiled faintly. "Like a real vacation." Her expression was dreamy, as if she too were considering it.

"Yes. When was the last time you had one of those?"

Her smile faded. "Not since high school, with my family." *Before she became the Medusa.* Though unspoken, the words still hung between them.

He gave her fingers a gentle squeeze. "Then you're overdue."

"I don't want to run from them for the rest of my life." Her sharp gaze focused on his. "I can't."

"I won't let him get you." His fingers tightened even more on hers.

She took a measured breath. "I know."

She didn't look convinced, he realized. Or maybe he just wanted there to be something else in her face.

Andrea swallowed, then gave him a tiny smile. "So, vacation. I want to see everything."

Kallan forced a smile for her. "I'll see what I can do about that." He'd do anything to keep her, but he wasn't sure his chances were very good right now.

She leaned over the armrest and their joined hands to kiss him, lightly. "Thank you."

He stared down at her head when she sat back and shut her eyes. He knew she was thanking him for more than the vacation. But she still didn't fully trust him. Not in every-thing. Not yet.

Andi didn't say much as they gathered their things from baggage claim in Glasgow, or while Kallan rented a car. When he saw the tiny vehicle they'd been assigned, his green eyes widened with something like dismay, and she laughed. His gaze narrowed on her face.

"Just wait." The promise in his voice didn't threaten violence. Only pleasure, and lots of it.

She couldn't wait.

He did not, however, check them into a hotel near the airport, instead steering the subcompact car out of the city and into the hills to the north. They drove through several smaller towns and villages, until they came to the coast, which she'd seen only briefly from the plane earlier that morning.

It was beautiful.

She had her face nearly pressed against the window, trying to see everything—the rocky shore, the lush green of the hillside sloping down to the darker rocks, the cottages dotting the landscape. It took her a moment to realize he'd stopped the car, as her attention was focused on the dark blue-gray waves rushing up onto the rocks.

She blinked and turned to look at him.

He grinned at her. "What?"

She shot a glance past him to the low, sprawling building on the other side of the car. "Where are we?"

"Your bed awaits, Sleeping Beauty." His tone was husky with promise and laughter.

Andi shivered, then turned her attention more fully to the inn as the discreet sign hung from the side of it proclaimed.

MacInnes's Inn, to be more accurate.

She shoved her door open and clambered out, inhaling deeply of the salty, fresh air. "Oh Gods, it's amazing." She met his gaze over the top of the car. "Wow."

He grinned even wider. "I know." He shut his door and tilted his head toward the building. "Let's get checked in. Then you can take a walk if you want."

She met him at the back of the car and caught his extended hand, twining their fingers. Warmth spread up her arm at the contact, and she took a breath of the cool, crisp air to distract herself.

Inside, the inn's front room had gleaming, dark wood floors and trim, and a fire blazing in the monstrous fireplace at the opposite wall. And a petite old woman stood behind a counter that reached nearly to her shoulders, glasses perched on her nose and a welcoming smile on her lips.

Andi smiled back, unable to help herself. "Hi."

"Good mornin'." The woman held her gaze a moment before lifting it to Kallan's face. "I'm guessin' you just drove in from the airport."

He nodded. "Yes, ma'am."

Approval lit her eyes. "I have a lovely quiet room on the shore side available."

"We'll take it."

"Come, let's deal with the formalities. Can I get you a cup of tea, dear?" She gestured to the chairs at the other end of the lobby. "I can pour you one while he takes care of the paperwork."

"I'd love one." Andi watched the old woman nod before walking out from behind the counter to a kitchenette on the left. When she returned a moment later, she carried a steaming pot on a tray and several cups and other things arranged on it as well. "Can I take that?"

"A poor hostess I'd be." The old woman snorted delicately. "No, you just sit. I'm Gert, by the way."

"It's nice to meet you, Gert," Kallan said when Andi opened her mouth to reply. "I'm Scott and this is Laura."

She shut her mouth. She'd been just about to introduce herself as Andi, rather than the name on her passport. Her heart beat faster at the realization.

"Ah, nice to meet you both." Gert set the tray down on the low table in between several chairs and a sofa. "Sit, sit."

Andi sat, feeling her knees wobble a little. Kallan squeezed her fingers gently, as if he knew. She smiled up at him, shakily.

His own smile was gentle, understanding shining in his green eyes. Along with other things. Desire. Promise.

"How long are you visiting with us, then?"

Andi jumped slightly, blushing.

Kallan sat. "Here or in this beautiful country?"

Gert's smile was knowing. "Both."

"We're taking our first vacation," he offered, putting their joined hands on his thigh and stroking his thumb along the back of Andi's. "We were thinking of a night or two here, if we could, before we make our way up the coast."

"You'll have been on the overnight flight, then, won't you?"

"Yes, ma'am."

"Tired, too. Should I call you to wake you before supper?"

"That would be great." He shot a heated glance at Andi, who sucked in a quick breath.

She tuned out the rest of the conversation, unable to focus now. She accepted the cup of hot tea from Gert and sipped at it cautiously. It was delicious, but not as delicious as the feel of his hard muscles beneath her hand. She drank, though, to keep from saying anything she shouldn't. It occurred to her that it might be difficult to remember to lie.

She hadn't thought of that when they started this flight from Kallan's cousin.

Just about the time she'd emptied her cup, Kallan was pulling her to her feet. "I'll get our bags, sweetheart," he murmured, "if you want to head to the room."

She met his gaze. The walk on the shore could definitely wait. "All right." She stretched up on tiptoe to brush his mouth with hers, feeling a surge of satisfaction when his eyes darkened rapidly with need. He released her hand slowly, then hurried outside.

"So Laura, what do you want to see most?" Gert went back to the counter with the papers she'd had Kallan fill out.

"I'm not sure. I told him I want to see everything." She smiled self-consciously.

The old woman smiled again. "I like that idea myself. I don't think I've seen it all yet, and I've lived here my whole life." She pulled a key from a hook behind her. "There you are, dear. All the way at the end of the long hallway there, on the left."

"Thank you." Andi took the key. "Can I help with the tray?"

Gert waved her off. "You're nearly asleep on your feet. I'll get it. You get some sleep so you can properly appreciate all this beauty around you."

Slowly, Andi walked back down the hallway until she reached the end. The door was glossy, dark wood, and she touched it lightly before putting the key into the lock. It took a little effort to get it to turn, and then she swung the door open onto a big, bright room dominated by an enormous bed.

She blushed.

"Hey." Kallan's greeting was soft, but still made her jump. "Nice."

She stepped aside so he could carry in their suitcase and backpacks.

He dropped them in front of the open closet and pushed the room door shut, then latched it and fastened the chain. "Now, let's see." He turned back to her, his eyes bright with intent.

Andi stood on the spot, part of her wanting to run from the overwhelming need rushing through her, and the other part wanting to let him have his way with her.

She'd been reading too many of the older, early romance novels, if she was having thoughts like that, she mused, hearing her pulse pound in her ears. No one said things like "have his way with her".

But she thought she might like it if he did.

"Are you tired?"

She thought about it. "Yes. And no."

His lips curved slightly. "Really?"

"Thank you." Before her brain was useless, she needed to remind herself of one more thing.

He tilted his head. "For what?"

"For reminding me who I am here."

His expression cleared. "It would have been really hard to explain to that lovely old lady why the name on your passport doesn't match the name you gave her." He smiled, squaring his shoulders. "Did you want to take that walk on the shore now?"

She shook her head. "No. Let's go to bed." Her tone was husky, even to her own ears, and his eyes darkened in response.

"So you are tired, after all." He tugged his shirt free of his jeans, whipped it over his head and took a step toward her.

Her gaze slid down over his chest, lingering, then back up to his face. "Not exactly." She yanked off her own shirt, gratified to see his stunned expression when the garment went flying across the room. She took a step toward him then, and it was his turn to swallow, hard.

She put her hands on his chest, skimmed lightly over the muscles there, before detouring to his sides, then up to his shoulders.

"Andrea."

She smiled. "Yes, Kallan?"

His throat worked, and she heard his breath catch when she rubbed her palms down over his hard little nipples. "What are you doing?"

"Touching." She stretched up to drift a kiss on his parted lips, then dragged her open mouth along his stubbled jaw to his throat. Under her hands, his heart pounded faster. "Tasting." She nipped at his shoulder next, then flicked her tongue over the same spot.

His breathing went ragged.

"Are you tired, Kallan?" She leaned closer to press her aching breasts against his chest, and stifled a sigh of relief.

He captured her waist and lifted her to him, his mouth demanding when it caught hers. Along her belly, she felt his arousal, hard and hot. Her own body echoed the latter, dampening her panties.

She slid one arm around his neck, tangling her fingers in his loose hair while the kiss went on and on.

"*Agaph*," he rasped against her lips.

In reply, she wrapped her legs around his waist, making him groan when she rocked into him. "Tell me what that means," she breathed.

"Love." One of his hands slid down under her, holding

her more securely. Temptingly close to where she wanted him to touch, but not near enough.

Andi nipped at his lower lip, which got his attention. He reared back just a little, so she could see the flush riding his cheekbones and how his green eyes looked like rich velvet. "Let's go to bed," she whispered. She punctuated that with a roll of her hips that rubbed her clit against his erection, teasing them both.

He apparently didn't disagree, turning to carry her in that direction.

She didn't want to release him when he eased her onto her back, but he muttered along her lips that they needed to lose their shoes. Reluctantly, she unwrapped her legs from around his waist, and he rewarded her by sliding his hand higher, pressing hard just where she most wanted it. She arched up into the caress, a rough sound escaping her with the pleasure coursing along her veins.

He made her forget.

He made her forget he'd brought danger to her home. Made her forget they were on the run so she could stay alive.

Mostly, he made her forget that their families were enemies and she shouldn't want him. Should never have touched him except in battle.

And right now, she didn't care about any of that. She just wanted him to keep doing what he was doing.

Kallan finally lifted his head reluctantly, releasing her mouth and dropping to his heels on the floor beside the bed, between her open legs. She didn't move, her breath coming fast, lifting her breasts. Her lace and silk bra didn't cover nearly as much as it revealed, which was good and bad for him.

Good because it was a hell of a view.

Bad because it made him even more desperate to get her naked, and he really wanted to slow down.

He took a quick breath, then another, and shifted his focus to the laces on her sneakers. His fingers were clumsy, shaking, and it took him several tries to get the first one undone. The second was easier, and he peeled away her socks next, smiling when she flinched as he hit a ticklish spot. He dropped back onto his ass and ripped his own sneakers off, ignoring the laces, then his socks.

Then he got to his feet, the wood floor cool under his toes, but that was no distraction from the lovely view before him. The pretty, useless scrap of bra revealed her tight, dark nipples, making his mouth water. Lower, her thighs were still parted, tempting him.

He gave in to the temptation, unbuttoning her jeans. "Lift up." He unzipped them too, and when she lifted her hips, tugged them down, leaving her with only panties that matched the bra, the lacy front revealing crisp black curls and damp silk lower. He dropped to his knees again in front of her and leaned in, inhaling the spicy scent of her arousal.

"Kallan." She touched the top of his head.

"Right here." He pushed her thighs wider and licked the inside of one.

A soft puff of breath escaped her, and her belly quivered.

He smiled and slid his fingers higher, stroking her through the panties. "I haven't got to do this yet," he murmured. "Have to correct that." He eased inside the silk to her wet folds, making her hips jerk toward him. "Mm, yes." He nibbled along her inner thigh, closer. Closer.

Pressed his fingers into her liquid heat and heard her moan.

His cock ached unbearably inside his jeans.

Not yet.

He stroked her until she writhed on the bed, then he tugged the wet silk aside to put his mouth on her, and she cried out.

The release startled him, it rushed through her so quickly, almost before he was ready for it. Certainly before she was ready for it. Her pleas for more, for him to stop, for him to come inside her, made his pulse beat harder in his head—in his groin. But he still teased them both, tasting her desire with his tongue, sliding his fingers deep to stroke over a spot that made her shudder anew.

When she was on the verge of coming again, he took a final lick of her clit, then sat back on his heels. His gaze slid over her, from her wet, flushed sex up to her swollen breasts —the taut peaks he desperately wanted to taste still encased in silk and lace—to her face, pink with pleasure.

She was beautiful.

She was *his*.

He unfastened his jeans and shucked them as he rose so he could step out of them, freeing his erection.

Andrea opened her eyes, dark as night, and smiled up at him, her lower lip trembling.

"You're not naked yet," he said unnecessarily, tugging at her panties.

"Don't rip them. We didn't bring that many." Her smile widened.

"You don't need them." Still, he didn't tear them as his first instinct demanded, but eased them off her, then pushed her thighs wider. "Come." He tugged her upright so he could undo the back clasp of her bra and slide it off her as well. Then he dropped her flat on her back again, making her laugh, and shifted her further onto the bed so he could crawl over her.

He stretched over her, stifling a groan at the feel of her

wet sex so close to his cock, hyper-aware of the slide of her silky skin under him—thighs, belly, breasts soft along his muscles—until he'd pressed her into the mattress. "Are you ready for me?"

Her eyes lit with challenge. "Are you ready for me?" Her hands came up to his shoulders, gripping him tightly as her legs rose to wrap around his waist.

The move brought his erection lower, into full contact with her wet folds.

He took a shaky breath.

Her smile turned sly, and she shifted her hips so the tip of him slid into her.

He groaned. She felt so damned good, he needed to sink deep. But he wanted to tease her a little more, to show her how much she meant to him.

Andrea caught his face between her hands. "Come inside me, Kallan. Please." Her playful smile was gone, replaced by something else. Something he couldn't identify.

He eased a little deeper, feeling her inner muscles grip him tight before relaxing enough for him to slide further, until he was fully seated. His breath left him in a rush, and he felt her shudder around him.

He bent to kiss her lightly, and her eyes shut for a second before fluttering open. "I love you, *meli*."

She smiled, and something sparked in her eyes before she closed them, arching beneath him. "You feel so good." Her fingers slid back into his hair. "Kiss me."

He obliged her, kissing her over and over, lightly and deeply, until they shared their breath, until he realized their hips were rocking together steadily, until he couldn't stop the impending explosion of orgasm rushing to meet him. Meet them.

And when it broke, it left them both limp and gasping for breath.

Kallan recovered himself enough after a few minutes to roll to his side, keeping her tight in his arms. He was slick with sweat, and her head was damp too. Sliding his fingers along her nape, he realized her hair was already longer than it had been several days ago after she'd chopped it off.

Andrea kissed his shoulder, still panting for breath. "Wow."

He smiled at the wall on the other side of the bed, distinctly pleased with himself.

She eased back far enough to look up into his face, and she shook her head.

"What?" He slid his other hand down along her spine, feeling goosebumps dance over her skin.

"Men." But she said it with a smile as she burrowed closer.

"*Agaph*." He caught her chin, tilting her face toward his.

Her smile softened. "What?"

"You're cold. We should get under these covers and actually take a nap."

She winked at him as she clenched her inner muscles around him, and his body came roaring back to life. "I'm not tired yet."

Kallan swallowed. "Is that so?"

"Yes." She pushed at his shoulders so he rolled onto his back.

The view was very nice from this angle. He pulled her lower so he could nuzzle his way to one of her nipples, making her breath come in irregular gasps again. "We'll have to fix that."

"Oh, please do," she murmured, arching into his mouth while her hips circled over his.

This time when they tumbled over the edge, she dozed almost immediately.

Leaving Kallan to wonder just what he'd seen in her eyes earlier.

He didn't want to hope, but he couldn't help it.

Clearly, she trusted him enough to keep her safe. And she trusted him with her body.

Maybe she'd trust him with her heart as well. Eventually.

He shut his eyes for a moment, his pulse skipping a few beats.

It wouldn't solve their biggest problem, though.

His eyes opened again and frowned at the wall. No way were any of his cousins getting their hands on his Medusa.

The problem was he couldn't see any way of stopping them.

Andi woke much later, feeling better than she had in days. Rested. Secure. Warm.

The latter was probably due to the very large man wrapped around her beneath the blankets.

Okay, so the first two were also probably due to him.

She inhaled deeply, enjoying the spicy scent of him. Of them.

She shouldn't feel safe in the arms of the man who'd come to kill her.

She opened her eyes slowly, her gaze landing on the curtained windows. The drapes weren't closed the whole way, so the afternoon sun peeked into the room.

She wished she could talk to one of her cousins. Even her mother might have some insight if she got desperate enough for an outside perspective.

Kallan's big hand closed on her nape, drawing her nearer. "You awake?"

She smiled into his shoulder. "No."

"Hm. Too bad." His other hand slid lower, and curled around her hip before easing between her thighs.

A rush of heat burst in her middle, distracting her from her current worries.

"Are you sure you're not awake?" His fingertip inched inside her.

"Mm. I'm not sure." She kissed his shoulder.

His chest moved with a silent laugh. "I guess I'll have to wake you up then." He withdrew his finger, and she bit her lip to keep from protesting. Then he shifted closer, replacing his finger with his scalding erection.

She moaned as he pressed inside her, dropping her head back against the pillow.

"Yes?"

"Definitely."

He nuzzled her throat as he slid deeper, and she lifted one leg to wrap it around his waist, easing his way. "Waking up yet?" he murmured.

She laughed, arching into the hand cupping her breast. "Possibly."

His stubbled cheek rasped along her collarbone as he bent to her nipple. "Let me know when you're really awake." His teeth scraped over the sensitive bit of flesh, and he proceeded to rouse her to a fever pitch. Then he began all over again. This time, when the wave broke, she wept.

Kallan rolled onto his back and gathered her closer. To try to calm her, he rubbed one hand along her spine, and the other cupped her head against his chest. "*Agaph*, what is it?"

She shook her head, crying harder. "I don't know." It was a little frightening, this surge of emotion, and she fought it.

He kissed the top of her head, murmuring to her again.

Eventually, she managed to stop crying, and lay spent atop him.

Andi put her head up a little, trying to make her bleary eyes focus. He grabbed the tissue box from the nightstand without a word, for which she was extremely grateful. She pulled out a handful and dried her face, and his chest.

"Shall we shower and take that walk on the shore now?" he asked after a few minutes.

She nodded, a damned lump clogging her throat.

He eased to a sitting position, with her still straddling his hips, and cupped her face.

"I'm a mess." And with a rusty-sounding voice, she realized, trying to lower her face.

He smiled, holding her in place. "You're still my beautiful Medusa." He kissed the tip of her nose. "But if we go to dinner with you all red-nosed this way, Gert is likely to think our honeymoon is over already."

She smiled at his teasing, but her pulse raced faster with fear.

And she realized what must be wrong with her. Her hormones were still out of whack. That had to be it.

Uncertain, she eased off him and got to her feet, sliding her hand over the top of her head, where her hair was mussed and damp with sweat. It was probably sticking up everywhere, she mused, avoiding the mirror on the dresser.

Just residual hormones.

"Aristotle Tassos."

The elderly man started, jumping from his chair so the papers he held fluttered to the floor beside his desk.

Athena remained standing in the doorway to his office,

watching his olive skin pale before he dropped to his knees, bowing his head.

"My Lady." His voice shook.

"Your nephew has taken the Medusa away, Aristotle. How could a Tassos do that?" She glared, noting his silver hair was thinning far more than the last time She'd deigned to visit him.

"My Lady?" He straightened slightly, though not far enough to actually look directly at Her. "My nephews burn to kill the Medusa."

"Not Kallan." She watched his mouth drop open. "He has helped her escape." She narrowed Her gaze on his stunned face. "How could you not know this about him?"

Her Harvester shook his head slowly. "I am so sorry, My Lady. I assure You I will find him. And her."

"I am sure you will. I expect you will." She set Her hands on Her hips. "Do not fail Me, Aristotle. It has been many years since your family has fulfilled its duty. It may be very bad for you and yours if you fail again."

Aristotle nodded, bowing, his face flushed a ruddy color. Embarrassed, She was sure, by the reminder of the failures of recent years. *Good.* He and his should be humiliated to have been outwitted by the Medusas of the past several generations.

"I would hate to have to return to see you on this matter again, Aristotle," She said, gentling Her tone just a little. "I understand you are loyal to Me, even if one of your number is no longer."

His mouth tightened. "I will make sure we get her this time, My Lady."

Athena nodded. "I will be monitoring your progress."

She was gone before Aristotle looked up.

CHAPTER NINE

A ndrea watched Kallan's fingers skim over the keyboard of his laptop, as he logged into his family's site to enter his latest false clues.

She got to her feet and wandered around their room. They'd already unpacked their toiletries when they showered before their first walk, so she could see toothpaste and brushes littering the counter in the bathroom when she passed the open door. The open suitcase lay on the chair beside the dresser, with its meager contents revealed: two days' worth of clothing, her backpack, and—still tucked into the inner pockets— their cache of weapons. She'd checked. Surreptitiously, of course, when she was taking out fresh clothing, but her blade still rested in the suitcase where she'd packed it yesterday.

She felt a twinge of guilt at having felt the need to check for it. But the dagger had been her constant companion for many years. Every girl born into her family received a similar weapon when she had her first period, a rite of passage for the Medusa's descendants, one of the first they all shared.

"Do you need to send anyone email?"

She started, turning to see Kallan offering his laptop to her. "No," she said after a moment. "Not for a few days."

He nodded and closed it down. Then he turned an intent green gaze back onto her.

Her heart beat faster.

"Do you want to talk about earlier?" He got to his feet, and she jumped, then took a deep breath when he put his laptop away.

She flushed. "Not really."

He set his hands on his narrow hips when he straightened up, studying her for several long moments. "I think I'd like to."

She swallowed, her mouth dry. "Leftover hormones." She jerked one shoulder in a shrug.

"Still? You think so?" He lifted one hand to push his hair away from his face, making her think she'd like to do that too —to slide her fingers through his hair.

She caught herself and frowned. "Yes, I do." That was all it was. "And stress. It's been a rough week."

He nodded slowly, once. "If you say so." He moved toward her, but she held her ground this time, despite her racing pulse and the little voice in her head urging her to move.

He stopped a foot away. "Do you trust me, Andrea?"

She blinked. "Yes." She hadn't had to think about it. Clearly, she trusted him now. He'd spirited her across the ocean to avoid the cousins intent on murdering her. If that didn't mean she could trust him, she didn't know what did.

He looked satisfied with her answer, faint tension lines disappearing from around his mouth. "Ready for bed?"

She frowned when he moved around her to go into the bathroom. *What the hell was that about?* When she got to the open door, he was brushing his teeth. He glanced over and winked at her.

She'd missed something, obviously.

She was still pondering it when he came out of the smaller room. He brushed a kiss on her cheek as he unbuttoned his jeans, then stopped moving. She heard the faint buzz of his old cell phone vibrating, and watched his expression harden.

He took the phone from his pocket and looked at the screen, his mouth flattening.

Her mouth went even drier. "Stavros?"

He nodded, then pushed the talk button, holding his free finger to his lips in a signal for her to be quiet.

Andi didn't need to be told twice. In this case, she didn't need to be told once.

"Hello, Stavros. How is your hunt going? Any luck in Maine?"

She walked unsteadily to the foot of the bed and sank onto the mussed blankets, her heart galloping.

"Too bad. I'm sorry you missed me in Ohio. I thought we'd have her for sure." Though he kept his tone light, his expression was hard. He stretched out his free hand to stroke over the top of her head. "Team up? Why? We cover more ground this way, moving over separate areas. Besides, I thought you believed your lead was the one?"

She shut her eyes and bent her head, her stomach roiling and making her glad she hadn't eaten much for supper.

"Really? Uncle Ari's idea?" His tone was strained now, and when she looked up again, tension lined his face. "I'll think about it and see what I can come up with here, in the meantime. Did you see Anatole's message yesterday? He's in Mexico, thinks he's on the right trail." His knuckles were white on the phone.

Andi took a quick breath, lifting one hand to cover his where it had fallen to her shoulder.

He flashed her a quick, forced smile. "All right. I'll talk to you in a few days." He thumbed the off button and tossed the phone into the open suitcase across the room, then dropped his head back and shut his eyes.

"I'm sorry," she whispered, pushing to her feet and wrapping her arms around him. Under her cheek, his cotton shirt was warm, and beneath that, his heartbeat rushed along— thump-thump, thump-thump.

He folded his own arms around her and exhaled slowly. "Not your fault."

It was her fault, even though she knew it was simply an accident of birth for them both.

"Get naked, Andrea." As he spoke, he pulled at the back of her sweater, tugging it off her shoulders.

She eased back and let the sweater drop from her arms. His expression shifted from worry to desire in a flash. Her blood thickened in her veins, making the need pulse harder, almost painfully, through her body.

He tugged his shirt over his head, then unzipped his jeans and let them fall to the floor.

His body was beautiful, she thought, watching as his erection swelled and rose toward her. His thighs went taut as he braced himself when her hand lifted to touch him. Just a glancing brush of her fingers on his skin.

She unbuttoned her shirt and yanked it free of her jeans, then tossed it aside so she could touch him again, this time wrapping her fingers around the thick, tempting shaft.

"Andrea."

She smiled, and wrapped her other hand around him too, squeezing.

"Oh, Goddess." His hips jerked toward her.

She slid her hands down to the base of his erection, then back up, rubbing one thumb over the tip of him.

He caught her hips and yanked her close, his mouth descending to cover hers roughly.

Andi let him take over, not disappointed to find him eager and demanding, his hands urging her to swift arousal and finally release. They barely made it to the bed before the explosion claimed them both.

This time when he whispered, "I love you, *meli*," she didn't even flinch. She smiled into his throat and held him closer.

Kallan sat on a rough boulder next to the shore the next day, watching Andrea wander closer to the water. She looked absolutely relaxed, delighted with the small pebbles she'd paused to examine more closely.

His call from Stavros last night still troubled him. His cousin was furious he'd missed Andrea in Maine. Livid that he'd gone to Ohio on Great-Uncle Ari's say-so and found nothing. And he was absolutely the angriest that Kallan could ever remember that Kallan was brushing him off.

Stavros would be even more determined now to find her. He had never taken defeat gracefully, not even when they were kids skipping rocks on a lake, or when they were a little older and participating in the training exercises that were tradition for boys in their family.

His cell phone vibrated in his pocket. He should just leave the damned thing in the suitcase and check his messages once a day and only carry the new phone in case he actually needed to make a call. For some reason, he'd put the old one back in his pocket. Habit.

Andrea glanced up when he pulled the phone out, and her smile faded.

Stavros again.

He stuffed the phone away and pushed to his feet.

She stood still, a wet rock in her hand, when he got to her. "How would you like to see Inverness?" he asked.

"When?"

He brushed a smudge of dark, grainy sand from her cheek. "Tomorrow."

She nodded silently.

He wrapped his arms around her and stared at the rolling waves. Running wasn't something he'd ever expected to do. He'd never run away from anything before. Ever.

But he'd run to the ends of the earth to keep Andrea out of harm's way.

Andi didn't mind traveling into the Highlands. She hadn't ever imagined she'd get to visit Scotland. She certainly hadn't thought she'd be seeing it with a man who was so incredibly attentive to her, in and out of bed. Or with a man who whispered "I love you" on a regular basis.

She definitely hadn't imagined she'd get a warm, tingly feeling in her middle every time he said it.

That made her a little nervous. More than a little nervous, to be very honest.

She was afraid she was starting to believe. To believe the man who'd come to kill her was in love with her. That they could have a future.

And if she believed that—that she might have something she'd stopped dreaming about years ago, something now within her grasp—the risk of losing her life would be much,

much more difficult to accept than when she'd expected to spend the rest of her life alone.

They were walking hand-in-hand on Culloden battlefield when Kallan suddenly went still, his entire body stiffening. His fingers around hers tightened almost painfully.

"Phone?"

He shook his head. "We need to go." Without another word, he turned her back toward the parking area and hustled her into the car before speeding onto the road. They'd driven half an hour in the wrong direction before he relaxed enough so his knuckles weren't white on the steering wheel.

Andi's stomach had knotted on itself about a hundred times in the past thirty minutes, and she wondered what the hell was going on.

"I don't know who it was, or even exactly where, but one of my cousins was nearby. Too close," he said at last, uncurling one hand from the wheel to reach over and give her leg a gentle squeeze. "I don't think he realized we were there, and he's definitely not following us."

She took a shallow breath—feeling some of the tension banding her chest ease—then another, deeper breath. "Now what?"

"Back to Inverness. For now." He gave her a reassuring smile. "You want to play with the GPS?"

It took her several tries to punch in the right address for their hotel, so the GPS would give them the correct route back to the city. Even when Kallan caught one of her hands in his, her fingers still shook.

Being on the run sucked.

Being on the run and knowing that one's pursuers could stumble on one anywhere in the world sucked even more.

She bit her lower lip as she stared out the car's side window. She knew believing was no good. Not when his family could find her anywhere in the world. She had no future, with or without Kallan.

"It's okay, Andrea."

"No, it's really not." She realized her fingernails were digging into her palm and uncurled the fist she'd made subconsciously with her free hand. Crescent-shaped marks remained when she looked. "Can all of the Harvesters sense one another?"

"No."

She looked over at him, her hand dropping back into her lap. "No?"

A muscle in his jaw ticked. "No. There are a few of us that I'm aware of, but it's not something we tend to share."

"Why not?"

He inhaled slowly, steering the car onto the road the GPS indicated. "Because some of my cousins don't like when another gets into their territory, or their hunting grounds."

"Like Stavros?"

"Like Stavros."

"He doesn't have that ability?"

He shook his head.

Andi pondered that while he drove along narrow, winding roads.

"What are you thinking?" he asked.

"Maybe we should have stayed in Maine."

He shot her a disbelieving look. "And let him kill you?"

"That isn't what I meant." She frowned. "If he didn't know you were there, he might have given up when he couldn't find me."

"Andrea, even if he couldn't sense the protection spell you had on the cave, you don't know my cousin. He doesn't give up. He's still there, traipsing through your forest trying to figure out where you went." Frustration laced his tone.

She flexed her fingers in his grip, wiggling them until she could link them with his. "But that doesn't mean he would find me. I'm not as helpless as you seem to think."

Kallan clenched his jaw even tighter. "I don't think you're helpless. If you went to that cave without me, however, all your magic would have brought him right to you. If he had come there three days sooner, and I hadn't been there, you wouldn't have been able to fight him off. He'd have killed you, and you wouldn't have been able to stop him." His grip on her hand was almost painful now.

Andi tugged on her fingers, trying to free them, but he didn't release her. "I wouldn't have gone easily. And if he'd come then, most likely, *he'd* be dead now."

She could actually *hear* his teeth grinding together, and the faint sound alarmed her slightly. "That does not make me feel better," he said after a moment. "We have to find a way out of this without you winding up dead."

She stopped trying to pull her hand away and let out a slow breath. "I don't want to argue with you, Kallan." She just wanted to stop the threat to her life.

"Let's check out of the hotel and head north."

She blinked at the abrupt change of subject. "O-o-okay."

He lifted their joined hands to his mouth and kissed her knuckles. "I'm sorry. I don't want to argue with you either."

She nodded when he glanced over at her again. "We'll have to go back, though, you know."

Something flashed through his eyes, too quickly for her to decipher. "We'll see. Maybe we ought to find out everything we can about the amulet."

She settled deeper into her seat. "Like if there's any way to get it besides cutting it out of my back?" Pain pricked at the center of her chest.

"That wasn't what I meant. Are you trying to pick another fight?"

She shut her eyes. "No. I just hate feeling like this. Like I can't do anything to put an end to this. Like one way or another, it's going to end badly." She heard the GPS recite new instructions. "Like I'm wasting time." Now that she'd had time to think, now that her flight instinct had eased from their initial escape from her home, her stand-and-fight instinct had come back with a vengeance.

The car jerked to a stop in the middle of the road, and she turned to look at Kallan, startled.

The expression on his face was shuttered, but she saw the flash of anger and pain in his eyes clearly this time. Her heart beat faster.

"'Wasting time'? Exactly what does that mean?"

Her chest tightened. "I didn't mean with you," she whispered. "I meant in trying to escape the inevitable."

His expression didn't change. "Which is what?"

"Someone in your family is going to wind up killing me, Kallan." The pain in her chest squeezed tighter, making breathing more difficult. "I'm not looking forward to it, but I'm afraid there's nothing I can do to avoid it forever. So why run? I'd rather face it fighting than running like a coward."

His eyes darkened, but he remained silent for a moment. "I see," he said at last, setting the car in motion. That was all.

Andi felt the lump in her throat swelling, and closed her eyes, leaning against the headrest and turning her face toward the window. Her eyes and nose stung, and she was afraid she was going to burst into noisy tears any second. She concentrated on inhaling and exhaling slowly, though it didn't stop the stinging. She felt a tear burn its way down her cheek, but she left it alone rather than wipe it away and let him know she was crying again like some leaky human hormone overload. Her damned hormones should be back to normal by now.

It was some time before the car came to a complete stop, after the city went blurring past her, and he turned the engine off.

By then, a whole lot of tears had slipped down her face, but she refused to make a sound to give herself away.

One of his fingers glided over her wet cheek, and she inhaled unsteadily, trying to swallow back a sob.

"I didn't mean to make you cry again, Andrea."

She couldn't open her mouth, or that sob was going to make its escape, and it had friends crowding behind it. Lots of friends. Instead, she turned her face further toward the side window.

He cupped her chin, pausing when his fingers encountered more wetness on the other side of her face, then turned her toward him.

"Ah, *agaph*," he whispered, leaning close enough to rest his forehead against hers. "Don't cry."

"I'm not," she managed, the sob turning to a hiccup.

"I can see that." Despite his light tone, he didn't smile, his green eyes somber.

"Still hormones."

He nodded. "If you say so." He wiped tears from her cheeks, his touch gentle.

Andi gulped in some air, desperate not to cry in front of him again. Not like she had the other day. She couldn't remember the last time she'd cried that way. And to do it twice in a span of only a couple of days? She'd *never* done that. Not even when she first became the Medusa.

He kissed her lightly. "You trust me, right?"

She nodded, unwilling to speak again and completely lose control.

"Trust me to keep you safe from my family." His thumb stroked under her eye, gathering fresh tears and swiping them away. "They will never get through me to you."

She shut her eyes and felt more wetness slide down her face. "Damn, why can't I stop crying?" A sob rushed past her lips.

He released her seatbelt and pulled her into his arms. "It's all right, *meli*." He kissed her temple, then shifted so her head rested on his shoulder. "I promise, it's all right."

Her breath kept coming in jerky little gasps, and her chest hurt from trying so hard not to cry.

"Let go, Andrea. You'll feel better after."

She shook her head, but burrowed her face into his shirt.

One of his big hands rubbed slow circles up and down her spine. "I love you, *agaph*." He kissed the top of her head. "Even when you fight with me."

It was the sweetest thing anyone had ever said to her.

The sobs burst past her lips now, and all she could do was hang on for the duration.

Kallan held on tight, letting her cry until there was nothing left. He murmured into her hair, rubbed her back. And closed his own eyes, wishing he could absorb some of her pain.

Wishing she could let down the last of her barriers and let him into her heart.

He had a terrible feeling that was the source of her pain. And there wasn't a damned thing he could do about it. Except wait and see.

He wasn't very good at waiting.

When she finally stopped crying, she lay against his shoulder, hiding. He let her for a while, stroking her hair and her shoulder, while he inhaled her sweet scent. After a few more minutes, she sat up, reluctance etched in the lines of her face, with her red nose and eyes swollen from crying.

She was still gorgeous.

He bent to kiss her lightly, and tasted the salt from her tears. "Do you want to stay here while I get our things and check us out of the hotel?"

She shook her head. "No, I want to wash my face. I'm a wreck." She swiped the back of one hand over a damp cheek. "And you need a dry shirt." She didn't meet his gaze as she touched the wet splotch.

"You can cry all over me, *meli*," he said lightly. "I don't mind."

"I don't usually cry." She shot him a brief, embarrassed glance. "I don't know why I'm so weepy all of a sudden."

He didn't offer his own opinion on that one. "I don't mind," he repeated. "But if you insist, we should go in now and get our things together."

She let him steer her through the lobby to the old-fashioned elevator, and then along the hallway to their room. For a minute, she stood at the window overlooking the street and river below, staring at the castle on the opposite bank. "I used to wish I could live in a castle," she said at last. "When I was a little girl. I always thought we'd be safe in a castle. That the Harvesters could never get my family if we lived in one." She glanced back over her shoulder at him. "Pretty stupid, huh?" She pushed off the window frame and moved toward the open suitcase.

"No, it's not stupid." He caught her hand when she reached for an unfolded shirt. "If I thought a castle would keep them out, I'd find one for you."

A little smile curved her mouth. "You're very sweet. For a Harvester." Her smile deepened.

He growled and yanked her closer so he could kiss her

hard, then released her. "Go on. You wanted to wash your face. I'll get this." He gave her a gentle push toward the bathroom.

He heard water running, then splashing for a minute. He folded a pair of jeans into the suitcase.

"Kallan?"

"Yes?" He added the shirt she'd reached for, then her sweater.

"Thank you. For being patient." She peered around the doorway, her brow creased by faint worry lines. "I promise I'm not usually so high maintenance."

He dropped the sweater into the case and went to her. He tipped her chin up, studying her reddened eyes—not as swollen now—her nose which was still red, and her mouth, which was also puffy. And held her gaze while he kissed her. Then he released her and went back to the packing, his heart pounding hard.

For a few seconds, she remained where she stood, looking dazed, then she went back into the bathroom, where he heard more water running.

He grinned into the messy suitcase like an idiot.

They had missed the last ferry crossing for the day by half an hour. Andi bit her lip as Kallan's eyes spit green fire. She wondered if he was willing the boat to return for them.

She touched his back gingerly.

He looked down at her, his expression only softening a little.

"There's a very cute inn about five minutes back the way we came. We can spend the night there and be back for the first ferry tomorrow." She rubbed her fingers in a circle on the back of his shoulder. "Relax."

He let out a long, slow breath. "I'm sorry."

She lifted one brow as she tipped her head to the side. "We're on vacation, right? No schedules." She wished she could really think of this as a vacation and not just a life-or-death flight across the world. But maybe the reminder was what he needed right now.

"Yes, vacation." His hard mouth softened, and his gaze dropped to her lips. "I think the inn sounds like a good idea. Maybe we can find a place to walk along the shore."

"But no swimming. That water is too cold," she teased.

His expression lightened further. "And you with no bathing suit." His gaze slid lower, eyes darkening.

Andi swallowed. *Well.*

"Let's go get a room." He wrapped his arm around her shoulders and herded her back to the car.

Anticipation made her shiver as he followed the winding coast road back the way they'd come. When he winked at her while checking them into the little inn, she decided to just enjoy the time here. To enjoy Kallan. While she had the chance.

They carted their things into the room, which was farthest from the lobby, in the back of the inn, and with a door of its own leading directly onto the rocky shore. Andi opened that one and stared out at the gray waves for a long time, smiling at the birds that dove low over the rocks and water, calling to one another. She wondered how her deer were faring with her gone. Or if the moose had made an appearance in the last few days.

"Shall we take a walk?" Kallan's big hand settled at her nape, thumb sliding along the side of her throat and making her shiver, warmth oozing along her veins and distracting her from her thoughts.

"Okay." She gave him a smile over her shoulder before

she moved away, outside, where she dashed over rocks, between clumps of scrubby grass that waved in the breeze.

Behind her, she heard his heavier footfalls, and she laughed, running faster.

He caught her before she reached the water, his hands grabbing her waist and swinging her into the air so she shrieked with laughter.

When he set her on her feet, a dangerous light glinted in his eyes, and she felt her pulse leap in anticipation.

She backed away a step, then another, and he stalked her, his steps eating up more space than hers did. Another step and her heel caught on a rock.

Kallan grabbed her before she fell on her ass into the water, then hoisted her over his shoulder while she giggled, pounding on his back.

"Put me down."

He patted her butt just hard enough to make her belly flutter in anticipation. "Soon enough." He strode over the rocks, away from the inn.

"Where are we going?" She put her head up to see the inn getting smaller.

"For a walk." He squeezed her rear.

Her pulse jumped crazily, and she swallowed back a squeak. "Where to?"

"When we get there, you'll see." Another firm pat on her butt, followed by a squeeze—lower this time, high on the back of her thigh.

Her panties were damp already, she realized, closing her eyes. "Oh Gods," she whispered.

His long legs carried them around a curve of shore until the inn was out of sight, and they were in a sheltered cove. When he stopped walking and eased her off his shoulder, letting her slide down the front of him, she inhaled unsteadily.

His erection teased her, nudging at her belly as her feet hit the ground.

"Have you ever made love out in the open?" he asked gruffly, keeping her in the circle of his arms.

She shook her head. Her brain obliged her, though, by creating all kinds of enticing images of doing just that with Kallan.

A faint smile curved his lips. "Are you game?"

In reply, she stretched up on tiptoe to kiss him.

Instead of letting her tease him, his mouth opened over hers, his tongue plunging into her warmth as he lifted her nearer, pressing his cock into the space between her thighs.

She wrapped one leg around his waist, felt how wet her panties were and rocked her hips against him.

He grunted, yanking her shirt free of her jeans, then slid his hand up to catch her breast. He teased the puckered tip until she moaned into his kiss.

It was as if the wild setting had set loose something primitive in them both. They couldn't get their clothing off quickly enough, couldn't bear to stop kissing to breathe, couldn't stop touching, couldn't touch enough, and when he thrust up into her wet sheath, they both cried out.

She clung to his shoulders, arching her hips against his while her head dropped back. He took the opportunity to drag his open mouth along the column of her throat—nipping, then soothing with lips and tongue.

And all the while, their hips swayed, together, then away, harder and faster, until they both came apart. Andi realized that scream she'd just heard had come from her own throat, and his shout of triumph made her body clench tighter around his.

He nuzzled his way along her collarbone, breathing hard.

"Are you all right, *meli*?" He licked over the spot where her pulse beat crazily at the hollow of her throat.

"Fabulous. You?"

She felt his grin against her neck. "The same."

She gave her inner muscles one last clench around him, and enjoyed his drawn out groan that raised goosebumps on her skin.

"Tease." He dragged the edge of his teeth along the side of her throat.

"Not apologizing." She threaded her fingers into his hair, feeling how damp with sweat it was at his nape.

He slid one hand along her back, touching each knob of her spine as he went, before slipping over toward her hip.

Heat burst along her back, and she realized he'd touched the cup in her tattoo. "Ow."

His fingers moved away. "Sorry." He kissed the side of her neck, then lifted his head. "Are you hungry?"

She cupped his face, stroking her thumb along his stubbled jaw. "You know, I'm suddenly starving."

"I hate to do this." He held her hips, then lifted her up, off him.

She liked his wince as it matched her own. When he set her on her feet, she took a moment to steady herself as he moved away a little. Her legs still quivered with the aftershocks of pleasure.

"Andrea."

She glanced over her shoulder and found him standing a foot away with his jeans in one hand, his gaze on her lower back, eyes wide with surprise. "What?" She looked over her shoulder, twisting to see what he was looking at and failing.

"The cup. It's changed colors."

"What?"

"It's silver."

She shook her head. "It's gold. It's been gold since it came to me."

His dark head moved from side to side, very slowly. "Definitely not gold now."

She grabbed her clothing, tugged on her jeans and shirt, then balled her undergarments in one hand while she slipped her feet into her shoes. She needed to see.

Kallan stepped into his jeans and picked up his own shirt before he stepped into his sneakers. "Come. I'll show you." He held out one hand to her.

She took his hand, and they hurried back to the inn. While he closed the door, she almost ran into the bathroom. She unfastened her jeans with shaking fingers, shoved them down and pulled the back of her shirt up.

The cup was silver, though the edges still had a faintly gold tint to them.

She stared at her tattoo.

What the hell did that mean?

Kallan stepped into the room and met her shocked gaze in the mirror. Seeing the question in her eyes, he shook his head.

Andi touched the cup with one finger. It felt exactly the same as it always had. Nothing else about the tattoo had changed, except the color.

"I need to email my cousin," she said, noting her voice was unsteady, probably to match the galloping of her heart in her chest. "Or one of my aunts."

Concern darkened his eyes. "Let me boot up." He hesitated a moment longer in the doorway, watching her as she turned her gaze back to the tattoo, before he left the smaller room.

She stared at her reflection, studying the rest of her tattoo. The snake still coiled around the goblet, its scales shiny green and black. The flowers still surrounded both, the bright reds and pinks unchanged.

She didn't understand why the color had changed. Or how.

Tearing her gaze from the mirror, she tugged her jeans back up and fastened them with shaky fingers, and let her shirt fall back into place, concentrating the whole time on breathing steadily.

Kallan was waiting in the other room with his laptop on the foot of the bed.

She pulled up her email server, tapping her fingers over the keys to compose an email to Aunt Lydia. She stopped typing after she finished her initial greeting. How was she supposed to explain this without telling her aunt about Kallan? She started to type again hesitantly, then deleted everything she'd written. Back to the beginning.

He sat down behind her, rubbing her shoulders so she realized how much tension had gathered in them in just a few minutes. "Take a breath, *agaph*." His warm breath ruffled the hair over her ear.

She did, then another, feeling some of the tension leave her between the breathing and his massage. "Okay." She shut her eyes for a second, then refocused on the computer screen. Simple was usually best. "Dear Aunt Lydia, I hope you're doing well. I wonder if you've heard any lore that might explain a color change in part of my tattoo. I've learned recently the cup in my tattoo is an amulet." She paused, wondering how that would sound.

"You don't need to go into detail, *meli*," he said quietly. "If she knows or has ever heard anything, you won't have to explain it all."

He was right, of course. She shot him a quick smile and went back to her email. "The cup has always been gold, but recently changed to silver, and I'm wondering if you can tell me anything about what that means." She bit her lip, rereading what she'd written. It would have to do. She signed it and hit the send button with a still-trembling finger.

Kallan wrapped his arms around her, drawing her back against his bare chest.

She shut her eyes and enjoyed the warmth he shared with her. The last of her shaking eased. "She won't see it till later." She opened her eyes, twisting to look up him.

"Is there anyone else who might know?"

She considered that for a moment, then slowly shook her head. "Aunt Lydia has been sort of the family matriarch since her mother died. If anyone knows, it'll be her."

"Then we should get our supper before they stop serving food." He kissed her lightly.

Andi pushed to her feet, though her appetite had fled.

He touched her chin when he rose. "We'll figure it out."

She wanted to believe him. But it was just one more thing on top of so many things that were wrong in her life right now.

It seemed the only good thing she had was Kallan.

That thought startled her as she walked with him out of their room.

The man who'd come to kill her was now the best thing she had in her life.

How screwed up was that?

CHAPTER TEN

Kallan didn't try to settle Andrea down as she paced their room. Not after the first attempt, anyway.

She kept looking at the computer as if willing her aunt to reply to her email. And it wasn't working.

He glanced at the clock on the bedside table—one-thirty. A.M. Andrea should be exhausted by now after the day they'd had. But he could feel the nervous energy stirring around her, flowing from her into the room.

It was starting to make *him* feel unsettled. Add to that his own lingering unease about their brush at Culloden with one of his cousins... He wished he knew who it had been, and why they were there. It had to be a coincidence, but he didn't like it.

When her email program finally chimed out that she had mail, she practically jumped onto the bed.

He stifled a smile, sitting up from his spot against the headboard to look.

Dearest Andi,

I'm doing just fine here. And I have to guess you're doing the same wherever it is you've got off to. That relieves me greatly.

As for your earlier question, I'm afraid I don't have any concrete answers for you, only guesses and none based on close personal experience or even family rumors.

The cup has been discussed as Medusa's Goblet, a possible amulet, for many years, but no one has come right out and said so, at least not that I've heard about. Silly, if you ask me. Our Mother clearly knew what she was doing when she crafted her protection for us all those years ago. I have never heard of it changing colors before, though I can offer you some suggestions as to the meaning. Keep in mind, these are just supposition on my part.

The color could change as an indication of danger, though I'd imagine it might have changed color before now if that were the case. So I think you can rule that out.

I suppose it could change color after one has it in one's possession a certain amount of time. Again, I've never heard of this happening, so who really knows? Annis never mentioned the cup at all after the initial discussion of her tattoo. I feel certain, however, that she would have said some-thing if it had ever changed colors while she was alive, because she was horrified enough when she got it. I don't believe 'tenure' would change the color.

It could also change color because of some emotional change in you. Extreme stress might contribute to a color change, as could something like a tragic loss in your life. It may even change color if you were to fall in love, though you would first have to meet a man for that to occur.

I can tell you it isn't because you've gotten pregnant, as the only Medusa to ever give birth was our Mother. (And, again, you'd have to meet a man first.) I highly doubt anything minor could cause such a change, so anything little, like a slight illness or injury is unlikely the cause. I really have to believe that only something momentous would cause such a change.

I could continue to make guesses, darling Andi, but I have to admit to true ignorance. I simply do not know. Please try not to worry too much over it. Take very good care of yourself and stay safe. Please let me know if I can do anything to aid you.

Much love,

Lydia

Andrea's shoulders slumped a little when she got to the end. "Well, it was worth a try."

Kallan clenched his jaw to keep from saying the things rushing through his mind right now. Foremost was the voice wondering what color the cup would turn if she ever admitted her growing feelings for him. If she let that last wall tumble down. Because he had an idea that was the cause of the color change, just as her aunt had suggested.

She let out a long breath, rubbing her forehead. "I'm sorry I've been such a wreck tonight." She looked over at him. "I didn't mean to snap at you earlier, either." She touched his forearm, sending curls of warmth along his veins.

He forced himself to relax and push thoughts of the chalice out of his head for now. "I think I can take it," he said lightly.

She studied his face for a few seconds. "You're tired. So am I." She skimmed her fingers up his arm, almost absently. "We should get to sleep so we can catch the ferry in the morning."

He wouldn't disagree. Being on an island in the north Atlantic with no other Harvesters would make him feel a lot more relaxed. He shut down the laptop. "Did you set the alarm yet?" Best to keep this light now. She was still very disappointed with her aunt's response.

She turned away to do so, her shirt riding up as she stretched over the bed to the alarm clock. All he could see were the flowers, but he knew the rest of her tattoo was there. Changed.

And he was certain he knew why.

Unfortunately, he didn't know what to do about it. Or how that change could keep her safe from his family.

When she climbed into bed a few minutes later in nothing but her panties, he gathered her close and shut off the light, his brain too busy processing possibilities for him to sleep.

Andi noticed Kallan's brooding over breakfast, but didn't say anything. She'd done enough of her own brooding last night that she thought he was entitled to a little if he wanted. She peered into her teacup, swirling the residual leaves around in the tiny bit of liquid left. Maybe the tea leaves could help her. She smiled to herself as she finished the drink, then flipped the cup upside down on her saucer. She hadn't read tea leaves since she was a teenager. It had always been more fun than anything else, but she knew some of her aunts took it very seriously.

He shot her a questioning glance.

She lifted one shoulder and picked up her fork to stuff a bit of fluffy scrambled eggs into her mouth while she waited for the cup to fully drain.

"We have forty-five minutes till the ferry goes," he said after he finished a piece of sausage. "Is there anything you want to do in the meantime?" He held her gaze.

Heat slid into her belly at the intensity in his green eyes.

"It's too bad we checked out of the inn already," she murmured.

He smiled for the first time all morning, and she relaxed a little. "Who needs a room for that?" He winked and stuck his fork into the fried potatoes on his plate.

She laughed, then flipped her teacup right-side up, peering into the scattered, soggy leaves.

A goblet shape was clear near the opposite rim. She tried to make her suddenly racing heart slow down. The amulet. But what did it mean here?

She frowned, taking a slow breath as she rotated the cup a little. Most of the tiny leaves had settled randomly, not forming any sort of shapes, though she did see a little scythe near the bottom of the cup—obviously a reference to the Harvesters in her life. When she'd turned the cup to the other side, a heart shape was also rather definite.

She shot a glance at Kallan, who was busy stuffing in his breakfast and seeming not to notice her consternation.

She forced herself not to frown, studying the formations. What relation did the cup and her heart have? Or the cup, the scythe and her heart?

She set the cup down and shifted her gaze to the window at her left, staring at the gray waves rolling onto the rocky shore and the matching gray sky. She couldn't come up with anything that made any sort of sense. She let her mind drift, her focus shifting to the swooping birds over the water and hopping along on the rocks.

Still nothing.

She sighed and propped her chin on her hand.

"What's wrong with your tea leaves, *agaph*?" He lifted his glass of orange juice to take a sip.

"Nothing." Still, heat washed up her throat to her cheeks.

He picked up her cup before she realized his intent, and

peered at the wet leaves stuck to the inside. "Mm, the amulet." He slanted her a somber glance.

Her pulse beat too fast again.

He turned his attention back to her cup, rotating it first one way, then the other. Then his eyebrows shot up, and he lifted his gaze back to her face, which felt as if it were bright red. "Hm."

She shut her eyes for a second. She knew she was going to regret asking, but the words rushed out before she could stop them. "What 'hm'?" She looked at his shoulder instead of his face.

"Your heart."

Reluctantly, she met his gaze again. "What about it?"

He shook his head, but it was clear he had some idea.

Andi hesitated. She didn't know if she really wanted to hear it. No matter how tangled her own thoughts on the matter were, his were sure to be pointed and likely going in a direction she didn't want to follow.

Kallan set her cup on the saucer. "Are you ready?"

She lifted one brow, watching him fold his napkin beside his plate and push his chair back. "Really? That's it?"

He shrugged. "You clearly don't want to hear it."

She shoved her own chair back, frowning up at him now. "When has that ever stopped you before?"

A grim smile curved his lips. "Maybe I've learned a lesson or two along the way." He put some money on the table and stuck out his hand.

Andi stared at his fingers for a few seconds, torn. She knew she might not want to hear his thoughts on the tea leaves. But she wasn't sure she liked this either. Was she a coward for leaving it alone, or smart for not starting the discussion? How badly did she want to know his opinion?

Badly enough to hear something unpleasant? Or should she not open that box of arguments? At least, not right now.

She put her hand in his, slowly, feeling only slightly better when his fingers wrapped around hers. His jaw was set when she looked up, and she had the awful feeling she'd just made the wrong choice.

The ferry left on time, and the crossing was rather smooth, considering the choppy waves Andi glimpsed from her seat inside. Kallan sat in silence for much of the trip, reading brochures he'd picked up at the ferry office, his expression calm. But every once in a while, when she snuck a peek at him, a muscle in his jaw jumped in aggravation.

She sighed and let her forehead rest against the cool glass. "Tell me." She knew she was going to regret this as much as not asking. She shifted her gaze so she could see him from the corner of her eye.

His head shot up, his green eyes focusing on her. "What?"

"Tell me. About the tea leaves." She swallowed at the intensity in his gaze.

"Just a theory." He jerked one shoulder, but his expression was far from casual.

"Let's hear it." It shouldn't be like pulling teeth, getting him to share this. Should it? Maybe he was still pissed she hadn't wanted to hear it back at the inn's restaurant.

He considered her for several long moments, as if gauging her sincerity. "I think it meant the future of the amulet is tied to your heart. To your emotions."

She winced. "You don't think it just meant if anything happens to stop the beating of my heart, like the little scythe at the bottom, the cup goes bye-bye, on to the next Medusa?"

It made the most sense, she mused, as she'd been thinking of little else since they left the restaurant.

He shook his head. "No. I think it means your future is tied to both, but mostly to your heart."

He was holding something back. She narrowed her eyes as she watched him. "And?"

He sighed. "Isn't that enough?"

"You're not done with that thought."

"How do you know?"

She smiled a little. "We've spent how many days together now, twenty-four-seven? I think I might know a little bit about you by now."

His expression relaxed a little. "What do you think you've learned about me?"

She tipped her head to one side, still studying him. "You're thoughtful. I'm sure you planned every step out before you came to my house. Then when your plans went to hell, you didn't just rush into something else, but stopped to consider the best course of action in the face of new facts."

His beginning smile disappeared.

Andi's smile widened. "I'm sure you've never lied to your family before, as you're uncomfortable doing it now, despite the new situation."

He remained stubbornly silent.

"You are generous. Funny. Easily annoyed by my smart-ass comments." She felt her smile slip a little. "And you're determined to do the right thing, no matter what it's going to cost you, now that you know things you didn't know before we met."

"You forgot the most important thing," he said hoarsely, setting his handful of brochures down on top of his backpack.

She swallowed.

He caught her free hand and tugged, pulling her toward

him. "You forgot that I'm in love with you, Andrea," he whispered, lacing their fingers so their palms met, and her pulse quickened. "You didn't mention that because I love you, I've entered a whole new, uncharted world." His grip on her hand tightened a little. "I will die before they get to you."

She let him pull her around the small table and into his lap. Under her ear, his heart pounded, matching the racing of her own. His arms settled her nearer, and he rested his cheek atop her head.

She'd also neglected to mention she was hurting him, knowing he loved her and being unable to trust him enough to open her own heart.

Her eyes flew open. *That* was what he'd realized when he looked into her cup earlier.

"It's all right, *agaph*." His warm breath caressed her scalp, ruffling through her hair.

It wasn't. She knew it. But she didn't know what to do about it.

She slid her arms around his waist and inhaled shakily.

As if he knew what she was thinking, he rocked her slowly in his seat, one hand stroking over her back, spreading warmth along her spine.

Her eyes burned, but she refused to give in to the tears this time.

She'd forgotten how complicated relationships were. And she'd certainly never had one *this* complicated.

Kallan didn't know what to say to lighten the mood in the car after they got off the ferry. Andrea was pale and silent, her eyes haunted as she stared out the window. He steered the car into Kirkwall and found the hotel he'd decided on after studying the brochures on the ferry. It was too early to check in, though, so he drove past it and out of the little town again, along its narrow streets and past ancient buildings.

The island wasn't that big, so their chances of getting lost were slim. He followed a meandering road until they reached a stone circle. A bus was loading up a tour group when he parked, and Andrea turned her blank gaze from the side window to the hill ahead of them. Her eyes cleared a little.

"Brodgar," he said gruffly. "I've always wanted to see it."

She shot him a quick smile, pushing open her door.

He met her at the back of the car and caught her hand in his. Her fingers were cold, even before they stepped into the brisk wind.

When they got to the edge of the circle, she stopped, inhaling deeply as her eyes shut. "There's so much power here," she said softly.

He could feel it too, even though spotting magic wasn't his specialty. The site was so old—surely a lot of power had been raised here over the centuries. Looking straight across the circle, he could see a loch in the distance, and a small patch of clear blue sky above it, the sunlight there contrasting sharply with the dark gray clouds over their heads.

Andrea tugged on his hand, and he let her lead the way into the circle. A ripple of energy danced over his skin as they stepped inside it, and she laughed with sheer joy. Kallan relaxed a bit more, enjoying the pleasure in her face. The wind whipped through his hair, tugging at the ends of hers too, making him realize how quickly it was growing. It had nearly gotten back to the length it was when she'd cut it off. Already.

She put her hand flat on one of the stones and closed her eyes, the remaining tension leaving her body. "This is gorgeous."

She was gorgeous. A lump clogged his throat for a moment, and he didn't reply, just watched her.

"So much energy, so much old magic. I bet Stavros would hate it here." Her lips curved in a faint smile. "He'd never be able to undo all this."

She was right about that. But he didn't want to think about his cousin right now. Instead, he bent and dropped a kiss onto her forehead.

They walked the entire circle, pausing to touch a stone, or simply to look at the vistas in the distance. And sometimes just to stand in each other's arms.

It was peaceful, and Kallan decided he could stay there for the rest of the day. Maybe forever.

Until the next bus full of tourists arrived.

Andrea shot him a look of mingled regret and amusement when the first group stepped into the heather, breaking the silence they'd enjoyed. "Guess that's that," she whispered.

He agreed and steered her back to the car, and then drove back toward town and the hotel.

Once they checked in, it was after lunchtime, so they walked hand-in-hand among the shops and restaurants in town until they found a place to eat. Andrea hummed her pleasure over her soup and sandwich, and he was happy there was some color in her cheeks again, even if it had just come from the wind whipping their faces as they walked.

His phone vibrated against his leg while they relaxed after their meal.

"You may as well answer it," she said with a rueful smile. "He'll just keep calling."

One look at the screen told him it was indeed his cousin again. He thumbed the phone on. "Yes, Stavros?"

"Have you found her?"

"No." His mouth tightened, and he made an effort to relax

it. Andrea's fingers brushed over his hair. "My leads out here have dried up."

Stavros cursed. "I know she was here."

"Where are you?"

"Still in Maine, Goddess dammit."

His heart thudded painfully inside his chest. "What about Anatole's lead in Mexico?"

"It's a dead-end, of course. I don't know where she went. I could use your help."

For his cousin to admit he needed assistance, he must be frustrated beyond all endurance. "You know tracking isn't my specialty. You should call Vasily." His mouth was dry, and he used his free hand to pick up his water glass.

"He's here with me, and even he can't find her trail. She just vanished, the cursed bitch."

Kallan's mind flashed an image of his cousin as he would look right now, his hard face flushed with anger, his short dark hair sticking up everywhere from him having dragged his fingers through it a thousand times, and determination shining out of his dark eyes. Kallan's pulse drummed in his ears.

"I'm sorry. If Vasily can't find her trail, I'm of no use to you, Stavros." He took a quick sip of water and put the glass back on the table before he spilled it.

Andrea's blue gaze was sober as she patted his arm before sliding her fingers down, then wrapped both her hands around his.

He smiled at her. "We'll pick up another lead," he said to his cousin, trying to sound as if he meant it.

Stavros cursed again. "I want to kill her. This one is *mine*."

Wrong, she's mine! Kallan realized his fingers were clenching into a fist inside Andrea's hand, and he forced himself to uncurl them. She pressed her lips together, worry lining her forehead.

"I'll call you in a day or two," Stavros said after a second, making Kallan realize he hadn't replied to his cousin's last statement. "Perhaps one of us will find something in the meantime. Or Uncle Ari may hear something to help us."

Kallan muttered his agreement, then turned the phone off and stuffed it back into his pocket.

Andrea leaned into him, and he freed his hand from hers and wrapped his arm around her shoulders. "You know if you just let me go back in a couple of weeks, I can take care of him myself," she said against his throat.

He forced a laugh. "Best not even to think about him. He's across the ocean, and we're safe here. *You're* safe here." He kissed the top of her head. "Come, let's go. We haven't seen all these shops yet, and I saw a distillery up the road." He released her reluctantly and pushed to his feet.

If he had to handcuff her to himself again, he'd keep her here—safe from his family. As long as he could.

Andi saw the worry shadowing his eyes over the next few days as they crisscrossed the island, visiting burial chambers and prehistoric villages and just sitting along the shore watching the roiling gray of the ocean. Every time he touched her, she felt the underlying concern.

Even now as they settled into the hotel room for the night, his shoulders were bunched with tension. He stood looking out the window facing the street in front of the hotel. Full dark hadn't fallen with the longer summer days, so dim light still shone.

She sighed silently, rubbing her forehead with one hand.

All the tension—his and hers—was making her crazy. "Get naked, Harvester."

His head turned in her direction, and his focus sharpened on her. "What?"

She smiled. "I said get naked." She gestured to his clothing. "I have plans for you."

He pushed off the window frame and unfolded his arms, one hand going to his hip. "Really?"

She crossed the room to him and yanked his shirt free of the waist of his pants, then tugged it up until he had to help her get it off over his head. When he emerged, his eyes had darkened to a lovely forest green. "That's a start," she muttered, sliding her hands up from his flat belly to his shoulders. She pressed a kiss into the middle of his chest, then tugged at the belt around his waist.

"What sort of plans did you have in mind?" he asked conversationally, his hands resting lightly on her shoulders.

"Naked, sweaty plans." She finally wrestled the belt into submission, then wrenched the button open and pulled down his zipper. Inside the cargo pants, his body was swiftly reacting to her actions, hardening.

"I see." He didn't argue as she knelt to untie his boots and cooperated when she indicated he should step out of them and his pants, leaving him naked in front of her.

She paused there for a moment, letting her gaze slide up the length of his strong legs, to the erection jutting out in invitation. She responded to the invitation by lightly stroking up from root to tip, teasing him. Then she pushed to her feet and continued her exploration, fingertips gliding over his skin, along his belly, to the small, dark nipples among crisp black hair.

His cheeks were flushed with desire when she finally stretched up to kiss him.

Kallan's hands came to rest on her shoulders. "Do these plans involve you getting naked at some point too?" he asked, his tone strained.

"Eventually," she agreed, dragging her open mouth along his cheek to his earlobe.

A startled groan passed his lips.

She smiled and leaned closer so his erection rubbed against her belly. She could feel his heat even through her clothing. Or maybe that was her own body warming up in response.

In any case, she enjoyed it immensely, and curled her fingers around him, squeezing gently. He made a soft sound of pleasure, so she repeated the movement, a little harder this time.

His hips shifted toward her.

She bit his earlobe, feeling the way his breath caught in his chest, then slid her tongue over the spot to soothe him.

Then she stepped back, releasing him. "You need to be flat on the bed so I can reach you." She moved away and tugged down the blankets. "Come here." She gestured to the crisp white sheet covering the mattress.

He took a shuddering breath before he obeyed her. She was pleased to see his erection had thickened even more, the tip glistening. The sight had heat and wetness rushing to dampen her panties.

While he stretched out on his back, she toed off her boots and socks, then clambered onto the bed to straddle his calves. She stroked her hands up his legs, feeling his muscles tense and relax beneath her fingers, tensing once more when she reached mid-thigh. Then she slid her fingers back down to his calves.

A shaky breath rushed out of his mouth, and he laughed. "Tease."

"Don't worry, Harvester," she said with a smile. "You'll get what you want. Eventually."

"It's the 'eventually' that concerns me." Still he stretched his hands up to rest them behind his head. "I'm supposing I can't touch you yet. Since you're still dressed."

She considered, then nodded. "Not yet." She ignored the tingling in her breasts and the tight nipples pressing against her shirt. She could wait. A little while.

She dragged that little while out as long as she could, teasing him and herself for an eon before she finally took him inside her aching body, desperate for release.

Each thrust was quicker, shorter than the one before it, neither of them fully in control now. When the pleasure bloomed, exploded, she stifled her scream in his shoulder, while his hands settled at her hips, jerking her closer, closer, as if he'd pull her right inside himself if he could.

And some small, still-functioning part of her brain rejoiced in that. Rejoiced in the knowledge that she would let him do it and stay there forever, happily.

Her eyes popped open, and she jerked her head up in alarm.

Kallan turned his face to catch her mouth.

Holy Gods, she was falling in love with him. Andi shut her eyes again and let him kiss her. Her body shook, and not from the force of her release this time, but from the new knowledge rushing around her head.

He folded her into his arms, rolling to his side, bodies still intimately connected. He was shaking, too, she realized, sliding one hand up his wet back. His whole body. Maybe he wouldn't notice she was also trembling all over.

Yeah, right.

He lifted his head an inch or so, and she opened her eyes reluctantly. "I love you, *meli*," he said softly.

She smiled up at him, feeling the now-familiar sting in her eyes, and her lower lip wobbled.

She couldn't tell him what she was feeling. Not yet. It was too new. Too scary.

Too dangerous.

CHAPTER ELEVEN

Kallan kept his eyes shut in the morning, listening to Andrea's even breathing. Feeling it puff warmly against his chest where she slept. Dim light showed around the edge of the curtains when he peeked, so he knew it was time to get up.

But he wanted to stay right where he was.

The emotion shining in her eyes last night had made his heart jump right up into his throat. He didn't know if she realized yet or not. He hoped it wasn't his own emotion that made him think it. Made him desperate to believe it.

It couldn't be.

He inhaled her scent, the spice and sweetness. His Medusa.

He smiled into her hair.

The way she'd looked at him had made him feel like he could do anything, including keep her safe for the rest of their lives. Preferably very long lives.

Except she kept insisting they had to go back. Sure, he knew when they left that they couldn't run forever. But with every day that passed, he knew he had to seriously consider returning soon. There was no other option, really, for either of them. He didn't like it, wasn't ready to admit it to her. To fight his family to save her. He'd been trained all his life to fight—to kill. He just hadn't known he was being trained to kill the woman he would love, not the monster his great-uncle claimed.

She stirred against him, one of her legs sliding over his knee.

He ignored the way his body came to life at her sleepy caress.

"You're very alert already," she mumbled against his skin.

He smiled, sliding his hand over her skin. "Just thinking we should check out today."

She lifted her head, her blue eyes focusing on his face. "We have company?"

He shook his head. "Just feels like it's time."

She propped her chin on his chest, considering his words. "Okay." She stretched up to kiss him lightly.

He caught the back of her head when she would have moved away, his mouth open over hers to take another kiss, deeper.

When he released her lips, she opened her eyes, dazed.

"Well." She cleared her throat and inhaled unsteadily.

He grinned, pleased with himself.

She rolled out of bed, and he followed her with his eyes. Then sat up, his heart pounding painfully inside his chest. "Andrea."

She turned around, her discarded clothing dangling from one hand.

"The cup isn't silver anymore." He motioned for her to turn around again.

It definitely wasn't silver, at least not most of it. The

edges that had been tinged with gold were silvery, but the body of the cup was now pink—very pale pink.

He shoved the blankets aside and got to his feet, moving to stand behind her. Turned on the nearest light so he could look more closely.

"What color is it now?" She twisted to look at him over her shoulder.

"Pink."

"Pink?" She frowned. "What does it mean?"

He shook his head. Maybe he'd been wrong about the cause of the color change. Maybe it really didn't have anything to do with her emotions. Maybe it was something else.

Maybe she wasn't really in love with him.

His heart pounded still harder, trying to escape its prison. That wasn't it. He knew she felt something for him. Something strong.

But that didn't explain the amulet's color change, apparently.

He touched it, lightly. Heat still flared at his touch, making her flinch.

He wished he understood how the original Medusa had created it. Then he'd know exactly what was going on now. Maybe.

Andrea turned to face him, her wrinkled clothing a shield, concern furrowing her forehead. "What now?"

He shook his head, his brain spinning too fast to catch a rational thought. "We should get moving," he said at last, touching the crease between her brows. "We'll figure it out."

That was another of those promises he knew he shouldn't make, but couldn't help making anyway.

Like that he'd keep her safe from his family.

He took a deep breath and followed her into the bathroom

to shower. They could decipher whatever was causing the goblet to change colors. It just might take some time.

After all, two weeks ago, he hadn't even known the amulet was embedded in the Medusa's skin.

He also hadn't known he'd fall head over heels in love with her.

He smiled when she glanced over at him from the sink. "Good morning, *meli*," he said lightly.

She snorted. "Yeah." Shaking her head, she stepped into the shower.

Goddess help him, he thought as he stepped in too.

Andi enjoyed the ferry ride back to the mainland much better than their trip to Orkney. She stood with Kallan at the rail to watch the island shrinking behind them, then moved to the front to see the mainland come into view.

"We can come back." He slid one hand around her waist.

Assuming his cousin didn't kill her first. She bit her lip to keep the words in. He didn't appreciate her reminding him of the danger following them. She let him pull her into his side, turning her mind to the color change of the amulet.

The first change had been startling enough. But to find it had changed again…well, that was pretty incredible.

She thought of Aunt Lydia's email. Danger was a reasonable guess. Except the immediate danger had passed, at least for now.

Extreme stress was a fair guess, but if that were the case, it should have changed color before she and Kallan had even left her house. Which ruled out stress.

It couldn't have been the time she'd had it in her possession, certainly not if it had never changed before and now had changed twice in a matter of days.

She tapped her fingers on the smooth rail, pondering the water far below them.

Which really only left the emotional angle.

And she didn't want to ponder that one right now.

But to be fair, she took a deep breath of the salty air and went ahead anyway.

She knew her emotions were a tangled mess where Kallan was concerned. It was hard to know even where to start. She knew there was that whole captive syndrome where the person being held by someone else came to believe the captor was the most important in their life.

That didn't fit here, she admitted. There had been attraction even before she'd discovered his real identity, and being in close quarters only enhanced it, despite the brutal reality of their positions and situation.

She clutched the railing tighter and closed her eyes. She didn't want to delve too deeply into the emotions swirling so close to the surface—not now. But she could admit to the emotional upheaval being the most likely cause of the amulet's color change.

But what did it mean?

She'd never heard of anyone falling in love after becoming the Medusa and the curse moving on to its next victim, though the curse never fell on anyone who had already fallen in love.

And she just wasn't ready to admit to actually being in love with him. Not yet. Not without being sure. And how in the hell could she be sure when she'd never been in love before?

Frustrated, she sighed and pushed off the railing.

"Penny for them."

She smiled reluctantly up at Kallan. "They're not worth

that much." She turned to face him, sliding her hands up to his shoulders. "Where are we going?"

"I was thinking Edinburgh." He put his other arm around her too, holding her closer.

She felt safe in that circle, she realized.

There was no Harvester, no Medusa. Just she and Kallan. The man who'd already saved her life rather than taking it as was his duty.

Andi's heart swelled. She ignored that for now. "Have you been there?"

"Briefly. But there's much more to see than I did when I was there years ago." His gaze was somber on her face, as if he knew she was withholding something vital.

She lifted onto tiptoe and kissed him lightly. "I've been thinking about the color changing," she admitted.

He nodded. "I knew it was something important. And?"

She hesitated. "I'm pretty sure I've ruled out some of Aunt Lydia's possibilities."

He waited.

Her pulse beat too quickly in her head. "I'm leaning toward the emotional angle." Panic welled in her middle, setting loose a herd of giant butterflies.

He wisely kept his mouth shut.

She swallowed, uncertain just what to say next. But she knew it was important she say something. It had to be the *right* something. While she thought, she rubbed her thumb in a small circle at his collarbone. Under her hand, she felt the steady beat of his heart. She swallowed again, aware of the silence growing.

"I don't want to mess this up," she whispered, blinking against a sudden burn.

His fingers tightened at her waist, and his bright eyes darkened slightly.

She studied him for a long moment, then cleared her throat. "You're not what I expected a Harvester to be—any more, I guess, than I'm what you were expecting." She bit her lip. "I do trust you, Kallan. I...I think I might be falling in love with you." Her voice dropped off to a whisper.

He yanked her against him, resting his face on top of her head when she hid her face in his throat. Against her breast, his heart thundered under his ribs now, too.

She realized she was shaking, and held on tighter to him, shutting her eyes. Honestly, she'd never had so many urges to cry in all her life as in the last two weeks with this man. And they weren't all bad.

Andi kissed his neck, feeling his pulse jump beneath her lips.

He caught her chin and forced her face up.

Heat washed up her cheeks, matching the stinging heat in her eyes.

He smiled at her, his intense gaze shiny. "Come kiss me, *agaph.*"

She obliged him, lifting to his mouth.

This was a new sort of kiss, she mused while her brain still functioned. Oh, there was plenty of heat and need in the mix, but so much emotion... She shivered nearer to him under the onslaught.

The relief coursing along her veins made her feel so much better, she realized as he drove off the boat and onto dry land. She'd admitted to the feelings inside and nothing bad had happened. Besides, Kallan had already seen her at her worst. If they could get through that, they could get through anything.

Except for cousins.

Her smile faded at that thought.

Because even if she was in love with Kallan and he with

her, his family still wanted her dead, and she *would* face them eventually.

That might be a bigger problem than they could overcome.

They found a tiny inn heading south, about a mile from a castle he promised they could visit. *Later.*

Excitement still rushed along his veins from her revelation on the boat. Kallan couldn't believe she'd really admitted to her feelings.

Perhaps not a huge declaration, but this was a really big step for her. It was only a matter of time.

He hoped.

He led the way through the inn to their room for the night, nearly dragging her which made her giggle.

He loved that sound.

He loved everything about her. And he planned to show her in just a few minutes.

He wrestled with the key for a moment, muttering curses under his breath when it didn't turn at first. Her giggling changed to full-on laughter by the time he turned the knob and dragged her inside the room.

Up against the wall behind the closed door.

Her laughter cut off suddenly, the air knocked out of her when he wedged one knee between her thighs.

"Oh Gods," she choked out, her hips lifting toward his.

He caught her mouth with his roughly, his hands dragging her shirt up, and out of his way.

This was no gentle thing as he'd planned, but a maelstrom of emotion and desire.

They fumbled with each other's clothing, barely out of them before he lifted her again and thrust deep. Her cry was muffled against his mouth, her fingers digging into his shoulders as she wrapped her legs around his waist.

The whirlwind rushed through them in only minutes, leaving them panting and sweaty along the wall.

Andrea started giggling again.

Kallan grinned into her hair, struggling to catch his breath. "Yes?"

"Wow." She still trembled with aftershocks, and with the uncontrollable giggles.

Before he knew it, he was laughing with her, and they'd tumbled to the floor, tangled together.

A long time later, while she hiccupped with residual giggles, he slid his hand over the top of her damp head, drawing her nearer. "Goddess, I love you," he managed.

"I love you too," she whispered, then froze in his arms.

Kallan grinned anew and leaned away far enough to see the horror-struck expression on her face. That just made him grin wider. "I know." He kissed her hard and fast and pulled her closer.

It took several minutes more for her to relax against him again, but at last, she sighed and the tight muscles in her neck eased under his fingers.

Now if he could figure out how to get rid of the threat his cousins posed, they could spend the rest of their lives together.

He shut his eyes, feeling some of that tension gathering in him now. That was a tall order.

Andi sat at the tiny round table in the tea shop, staring at the targes on the shelf around the top of the wall, at the other tourists crowding the room. Kallan sat opposite her, looking very male in this very feminine sort of place. Except for those shields.

"What's wrong?" His tone was patient, as it had been for the last few days whenever she'd withdrawn.

She frowned at the targe with the nasty four-inch spike sticking out from its center. "I hate running away." The idea never went away, especially now since she seemed to have made up her mind to deal with her other emotions.

Kallan touched the back of her hand on the table.

She met his eyes, guilt tightening in her belly. He'd done so much to keep her safe, and she felt ungrateful at the same time she knew she had to go back and stand her ground.

He tipped his head to one side, and her gaze caught on his shiny hair. It was longer now than when he'd first arrived at her house with his vacuum, and it felt amazing on her skin—as she'd been reminded last night when he knelt between her thighs in the very posh hotel room where they now stayed.

She gave herself a little shake. The memory was a distraction she didn't want right now, though heat had already started curling into her belly.

"You know why." Still patient.

"If it was just you, would you have gone halfway around the world?"

He frowned. "No."

She took a slow breath. "You would have stayed to fight, right?"

He opened his mouth.

"If you tell me it's because you're a man, I'm going to pour my tea over your head," she said, narrowing her eyes at him.

He shut his mouth.

Andi rubbed one hand over her forehead. "I don't want to argue with you, Kallan," she said after a moment. "But I need to go back. To defend myself. I'm the keeper of the goblet, so it has to be me."

"And if Stavros is still there?" His jaw clenched.

"If I time it just right, he won't be a threat anymore." She'd considered it. If they went back at exactly the right time and his cousin was still camped at her house, she could just turn him to stone.

"And the rest of them?"

Yeah, that part she hadn't worked out. She sighed and put her chin in one hand. "I know. And they won't all be courteous enough to come when I can make Harvester statues out of them."

One corner of his mouth lifted.

"But I can't spend the rest of my life running away, Kallan. I don't believe you can either."

His faint smile disappeared, and she knew she'd hit her mark.

She made her tone gentler. "We need a new plan."

He looked away, a muscle jumping in his cheek.

She turned her hand under his and caught his fingers with hers. His were warm and, after a second, he gave hers a squeeze and turned to face her.

"All right." He didn't look happy about it, though.

Her heartbeat slowed down a little bit.

"But we have to make sure it's going to keep you safe. Or I won't agree to it."

She nodded slowly, feeling an ache in her chest. "Okay."

He lifted her hand to his mouth and kissed her knuckles. "Can we drink our tea in peace now?" he asked gruffly.

Andi made her lips curve into a smile, hoping it reached her eyes. "Yes."

Kallan kept her hand in his while they finished their tea

and sandwiches, and she forced herself to focus on the present rather than the very uncertain future.

That would come soon enough.

Kallan kept his senses open as they wandered through the city over the next few days. Andrea had been quiet after he agreed to come up with a plan for her to return home to fight his family. Nothing he'd thought up so far would work, however. There were too many things he couldn't control.

Starting with his cousins.

Stavros had evidently given up on her returning to Maine, as his latest posts to the family site said he was traveling along the eastern coast, hoping to pick up a trail.

Kallan wasn't sure he believed that. Stavros was holed up somewhere coming up with his own plan. And Goddess help Kallan if Stavros had somehow discovered he was with Andrea.

He realized they'd stopped walking, and Andrea was looking into a store window. He smiled when he saw what had caught her eye: swords.

He leaned nearer. "You know those aren't sharp, right?"

She slanted him a dark glance. "Yet."

He laughed. "Which one has you so enthralled?"

She bit her lip, looking from one blade to another. "None in particular," she said finally, dragging her gaze back to his face. "I'm just thinking ahead."

"You really are a bloodthirsty woman, aren't you?" he murmured against her ear.

"You know it." She winked up at him and started walking again.

He let her drag him along, though now his mind turned to weapons. He had a stash of his own back in the States. Surely there was something in it she could use besides her dagger, which was intended for close combat, and he'd really rather she didn't get into that.

"Have you looked at the amulet lately?" he asked suddenly, stopping in the middle of the sidewalk.

She swung around to face him, startled. "No, why?"

"Just wondering what color it is now." He hadn't looked at it since her whispered declaration, when it was a blush pink.

She shrugged. "I wasn't really worried about it, I guess." A wry smile curved her lips. "Do you think it matters? As long as it's still there?"

He shook his head. "No, I suppose it doesn't." Though he thought he'd still like to know the reasons for the color shifts.

He thought he might take a peek later.

He was leaning in to kiss her when his inner sensor started shrieking an alarm. Another Harvester was nearby, *much* closer than when they'd been at Culloden.

He put his arm around her and started walking more quickly, guiding her away from their hotel.

Andrea didn't argue, though some of the color left her cheeks when she understood what was happening, and she moved faster too.

After several minutes of the other Harvester keeping pace with them, Kallan started jogging. Andrea let him lead the way, locking her fingers tight around his as they wove around tourists and locals alike for ten minutes. He felt his cousin getting closer, making Kallan break into a run, sweat sliding down his back. A few minutes later, their pursuer eased back, tempting Kallan to slow as well. He didn't, though his lungs ached and Andrea panted beside him. And in another moment, his cousin closed in again. Kallan sprinted faster, panic rushing along his veins as he dragged Andrea with him.

It took another ten minutes before his level of alarm dropped drastically, and he slowed his pace a bit so they could catch their breath. Whichever cousin happened to be in Edinburgh had stopped following them—though Kallan wondered now if it really was a coincidence that they'd had two brushes with his cousins. Or was it just one cousin? "He's not close anymore," he muttered. And he wondered why.

Still, he did a circuitous little walk around several more blocks before he steered Andrea away from the residential area they'd run into and flagged down the first cab he saw. Once they'd driven half a dozen blocks, the other Harvester wasn't near enough to sense at all.

When they walked back into their hotel room, Andrea dropped into a chair by the window and folded her arms on her chest. "We need to figure out a plan. Now."

He sat on the foot of the bed and covered his face with his hands, resting his elbows on his knees. She was right—running away sucked. And if running didn't get them away from his family, there wasn't any point in it.

But running back would get her killed.

"Let me see the amulet." He lifted his head.

She cocked an eyebrow, but pushed out of the seat and tugged her shirt out of the waist of her jeans, moving toward him.

He unbuttoned her jeans and eased the zipper down, then turned her around.

The cup was pure white.

He pushed her shirt up and her jeans down so he could see the entire tattoo.

Nothing else had changed, not the snake or the flowers. Just the damned cup.

He touched it, skimming his finger over the rim of it. Heat

flared immediately, and he pulled his finger away. Then touched the stem of the goblet. Same thing.

"I don't understand." He let her shirt fall down, covering the tattoo.

"What color is it now?" She moved away, to twist around in front of the mirror over the dresser. "Oh." Her eyes rounded. "Maybe I should email Aunt Lydia again. Maybe she's had time to do a little digging." She turned away from the mirror to meet his gaze.

"Perhaps." He knew there was nothing in the lore the Harvesters had collected over the centuries that mentioned the amulet changing colors. Always, it was gold.

Of course, none of their lore mentioned it residing in the Medusa's skin either.

He shook his head. It meant something. It had to. He just wasn't looking for the answer in the right place. Or perhaps he simply didn't have access to the right information.

Andrea pulled his laptop out of his bag and booted it up before she rearranged her clothing.

"Hey, I wasn't done," he teased.

She sent him a lingering look that made his pulse beat faster. "You'll have to wait, big boy. We have work to do."

It didn't take her long to fire off the email to her aunt, and then she started searching online for clues to amulets changing colors.

Hours. She spent hours searching and coming up empty. No one's mythology made any mention of this ever happening. By the time she gave up and rose to pace, her frustration had ratcheted up the tension in the room to a palpable level.

Kallan heard her email program chime for new mail and caught her wrist when she walked past him again. "Mail, *meli*."

She forced a smile for him, then sat, turning the laptop to face her. She tapped on the keys, bringing up her aunt's reply.

Dearest Andi,

How lovely to hear from you again. It's nice not to worry, and if you're filled with questions, then you must be in good health. That makes me very happy.

As for the amulet... I find it most interesting it has changed colors multiple times now. I'm not sure what the progression of colors means, however. I do not think, though, that the color change indicates any drop in the level of protection. Our Mother created it long ago and intended it to be permanent, so that shouldn't be a worry.

I truly wish I could be more helpful, dearest girl. Please stay safe and touch base with us when you can.

Much love,

Lydia.

Andrea dropped flat onto the bed, growling and glaring at the ceiling.

He moved the laptop away and stretched out on his side next to her. "It was a long shot," he reminded her.

She shut her eyes. "I know. But I keep hoping someone will know. I think we need to know why."

He agreed, but telling her that now wouldn't help, so he kept his mouth shut.

Instead, he lifted one hand to stroke away the worry lines on her brow. "Now what?"

"I need a break from the searching. Going about it blindly is no good. I need to think of some way to target it better." She opened her eyes and turned her head slightly to look at him. "Thank you."

He smiled. "You're welcome. Are you hungry? You've been at this forever, and I think it's after suppertime." It was hard to tell with the summer sun still shining brightly in the window.

She inhaled, considering. "I'm a little hungry." She met his gaze again, hers darkening. "I know a really good way to work up a fantastic appetite, though."

He laughed and leaned down to kiss the tip of her nose. "Really?"

"Yes. Would you like me to show you?" She rolled to face him, one hand sliding up the center of his chest.

Warmth slid along his veins, settling in his groin. "You might persuade me."

A very sexy smile curved her lips now, and she slipped her hand higher. "I thought I might."

He shut his eyes and let her have her way with him.

They could figure out the amulet later. Right now, his Medusa needed a distraction, and he was happy to provide it.

Andi stretched lazily the next morning, feeling Kallan curling closer, one big hand sliding over her hip. It had been several days since she'd told him they had to come up with a plan to return. Right now, she didn't feel as anxious about it. Not with the sexy man pressing closer to her, one of his strong thighs pushing against hers to let his heavy erection slide between her legs.

She inhaled sharply, electricity coursing through her.

"Yes, *meli*?" he rumbled against her nape.

She shook her head, canting her hips back toward his and wedging the broad tip of him into her damp folds.

"Mmm." He kissed her nape, then dragged his mouth along her throat to her earlobe. His hips rocked a tiny bit, forcing his erection slightly deeper inside her.

Andi tried to shift to allow him to slide all the way, but he stilled her with his hand on her hip.

"No rush," he breathed against her ear, his teeth scraping the sensitive lobe.

She disagreed. Reaching behind her, she curled her fingers around the base of him, smiling when he groaned, his hips rocking toward hers.

"Come inside me," she whispered, feeling the way her body grew slick in anticipation.

He rolled them over so she was on her belly, then dragged her hips up so he could thrust deep.

She cried out with the pleasure.

"Better, my impatient Medusa?" He nipped at her nape, then dragged his open mouth to her shoulder, giving her a sharp nip there as well.

She clenched her inner muscles around him in reply, smiling into the pillow at his guttural groan.

They moved lazily for a long time, only ragged moans and soft sighs floating in the air around them. Andi wanted to wake this way every day for the rest of her life.

Kallan reached around in front of her and pinched her clit —hard—sending pleasure spiraling through her.

"You cheat," she gasped, shaking underneath him.

He chuckled, then thrust harder on the next stroke. "No, I don't think so. Making you feel good makes me feel good."

She rocked back to meet him, her legs unsteady beneath her. "Hurry."

He didn't argue this time, his hips thrusting faster now, faster yet, until they both collapsed in the aftermath, drenched and trembling.

When his hand slid up her side some time later, she smiled. "We have to go back."

His fingers tightened on her briefly. "I know."

She rolled onto her back to face him.

The angles of his face were hard now, not relaxed as she imagined they must have been just a minute ago. "You should call Stavros and find out where he is."

The green of his eyes sparked. "It's too soon."

She knew what he meant. "I know. But if they're here and chasing us, there's no point in being here." She lifted one hand to stroke his hair away from his face. "We may as well go back and deal with them at home."

His gaze shifted away for a moment as he jaw clenched. "I don't want to lose you. Not when I can keep you safe."

"We'll face him together." She rubbed her thumb along his cheekbone.

He held her gaze for a long time, his searching. She could see the worry there, for her. Finally, he nodded once. "Fine."

"Soon."

He nodded again, and she wrapped her arms around him.

"We'll be fine." She hoped she wasn't lying.

CHAPTER TWELVE

Kallan left a message for Stavros in the morning, under Andrea's watchful eye. His gut was a tangle of knots, and he'd done nothing since yesterday but worry. He couldn't keep her safe if they went right to Stavros. If he let her wait until she was about to start PMSing, as she'd jokingly suggested, he could take her right to his cousin and let her do her worst. Except he didn't believe she was joking.

Still, that would only solve their problem until the next of his cousins tracked her down.

He frowned over the morning paper at her as she picked at her breakfast in a little restaurant they'd discovered several days ago.

Andrea stuck her fork into a mound of potatoes, then lifted up her teacup. "I've been thinking about the cup."

He folded the paper and set it to one side of his own plate. "Have you come up with anything?"

Her searching yesterday had still yielded nothing, and she'd given up before suppertime. "I don't know. I have some things I know from family tales." She wrapped her other hand around her teacup, as if her fingers were cold. "No descendant who has already fallen in love has ever received the curse. But I don't remember ever hearing about anyone falling in love after they've become the Medusa. Somehow, though, I think the color change might be related to that." She looked up from the dark liquid in her cup, her blue eyes troubled. "But I still have the goblet, which must mean that once you have the amulet, you're stuck with it until you die."

He scowled into his juice glass. He'd been hoping that was not the case. Selfish of him, maybe.

"But I haven't asked Aunt Lydia about that. So I need to ask her today."

He met her gaze, forcing his frown away. "All right. Can we wait to go back until you get your answer?"

She hesitated, then nodded slowly. "I guess so." She took a sip of her tea, not looking very happy about that development.

Kallan stifled a smile. "Where would you like to live?"

Her head came up, eyes wide. "What?"

"If we could live anywhere, where would you choose?"

She nibbled at her lower lip and set down her teacup. "I've never really thought about living anywhere else. I do like my mountain. I wouldn't mind traveling, though." She smiled a little.

He could live on her mountain with her. "So I should sell my house, huh?"

She swallowed hard. "Really?"

He nodded.

Her eyes went shiny, and she took an unsteady breath. "Wow."

He caught her hand where it lay on the table. "We can live anywhere you like." He'd go to the moon if she wanted.

A tear slipped down her cheek, and she swiped at it with her free hand, looking annoyed. "Damn tears. I swear I've never cried as much in my life as I have since you've been around."

He laughed, feeling more relaxed than he had since yesterday morning. "I don't mind, *meli*."

"*I* do." She smiled, though her eyes still shone with tears. "Let's get out of here. I need to email Aunt Lydia."

He put some money on the table and got to his feet, lacing his fingers with hers to lead the way back to the hotel. There, Andrea sent off an email to her aunt right away, plus answered one from her mother who wanted to be sure she was okay. Stavros hadn't called back, but it was early there, so Kallan wasn't surprised. Stavros wasn't an early riser, and if he was still livid over missing Andrea, he'd be drinking at night while he was searching for clues. Drinking heavily.

It was the one thing Great-Uncle Ari despised, and the one thing that made Stavros unlikely to succeed at his task.

The trouble was, he didn't drink enough to make him less dangerous when he was on the hunt.

Kallan pulled up the family site after Andrea was finished with her email. He wanted to check and see if anyone had posted anything about running into another Harvester in Scotland. Nothing. *Good.* That didn't mean whichever cousin he'd sensed didn't realize he was there—just that he hadn't mentioned it publicly.

He started paging through the family archive and came across the photo of the urn. "Andrea."

She crossed the room from where she'd been rinsing out underwear in the bathroom sink.

"You should see this." He turned the laptop toward her.

Her lips curved as she knelt beside the bed. "She's beautiful. I've never seen this before."

"You wouldn't have. It's in the Tassos family's private collection." His mouth twisted slightly.

She tilted her head to one side to study the urn more closely. "She's wearing the amulet."

"What?" He turned the screen back toward himself.

"On her thigh." She pointed.

His mouth dropped open. She was right. The Medusa had the gold goblet on the outside of her thigh, in plain sight. For centuries. He couldn't remember how many times he'd looked at this picture, but he'd never noticed the amulet before. He traced it with his fingertip, thinking. Over the years, he'd heard a lot of talk about the amulet, but he already knew his family didn't know it was embedded into the Medusa's skin as a tattoo.

How could they not know when the amulet had been in front of them all this time?

He considered that. How many years had it been since a Harvester had actually come across the Medusa? He couldn't remember anyone talking about it in his lifetime.

Andrea turned the laptop back in her direction so she could look at the photo again. "She really is beautiful," she whispered.

"So are you, *agaph*." He stroked his hand over her head. "I wanted you to see this before, but you were sleeping when I saw it last time."

"Even with the Goddess's full curse on her, she's just incredible. Strong and feminine at the same time. In spite of the curse. No wonder Athena was angry." A lopsided smile tugged at her lips. "I bet She was really pissed off when She found out about the amulet."

Kallan pondered that while she paged through some of the other artifacts. Athena would have been furious to have Her will thwarted. Which explained why the curse still carried on, most likely.

But that still didn't tell him for certain why the cup had

changed colors, or if there was a chance it might transfer to someone else now that Andrea had fallen in love with him.

And it didn't tell him how to keep her safe when they returned to the States in a few days.

Andi spent hours looking through the pictures of his family's collection, most of which centered around their ancestors, Medusa and Perseus. Fragments of pottery, decorative jugs and urns, platters and bowls, tiles. Only the one urn showed the amulet on the Medusa's leg, however, and she wondered why.

Maybe that was why the Harvesters had never realized the impossibility of their task. They assumed the cup was just a cup, not something the Medusa had adorned her body with while trying to protect her descendants.

She clicked onto another page, frowning at the tile with Perseus holding up the Medusa's severed head. In this particular painting, the Medusa was portrayed as hideously ugly, her tongue lolling out of her mouth, snakes still spitting from her head. Or maybe that was what happened to her in death.

Andi swallowed and shifted to her email program, her stomach tight with dread at that thought. Aunt Lydia had emailed back already.

She clicked on the reply and bent nearer to read.

Dearest Andi,

I'm so glad you're still well. It's best if I don't let my curiosity get the better of me and ask where you are. That way if anyone untoward should come calling, I can't answer any questions.

At that, Andi snorted, covering her mouth with one hand, and heard Kallan's footsteps approach.

Let's just say I hope you're having a little bit of fun wherever it is you are right now.

She should only know, Andi thought.

As to the amulet, well, you certainly have a lot of questions about that, don't you, my dear? I wish I had more answers for you.

It's been many years since a Medusa died from anything other than natural causes. Or accidental causes, in the case of poor Annis. I wish Celosia were less technologically challenged, as she would be the perfect person to answer this particular question, since she's the oldest one around now.

I don't remember hearing anything about a Medusa losing the curse after falling in love. But it's rather difficult to find a man who can overlook a woman whose gaze can turn him to stone once a month and with a head full of venomous snakes, isn't it?

In any case, I shall call Celosia and have a chat with her about this, then get back to you. I shall also refrain from asking if there is a man in the picture for you to be thinking of such a possibility. Safer all around, don't you think?

Please take care of yourself, darling girl.

Much love,

Lydia

Andi smiled to herself as she sat back.

"Well, that's a better response than 'no', isn't it?"

She glanced up at Kallan, who'd read over her shoulder. "Yes, it is."

"I'm looking forward to meeting your aunt." He touched her shoulder. "Would your mother know?"

Her smile faded. "I doubt it."

He studied her expression for a moment. "What happened?"

She swallowed. "Long, ugly, old story." She glanced away.

"I have time." He kicked off his sneakers and climbed onto the bed behind her. He tugged her back so she rested on his chest. "What did she do, Andrea?" He slid his arms around her waist, securing her there.

She put her hands on his thighs, sliding her fingers down to his knees, then back. "You'd think a woman who was born into this family would be a little more sympathetic when her own child got the cosmic 'tag, you're it', wouldn't you?"

He exhaled sharply, then kissed the top of her head. "She wasn't helpful?"

She laughed, but there wasn't much humor in the sound. Her chest ached just remembering. "Not so much." She realized her fingers were digging into his legs and forced herself to relax. "In her defense, I imagine she just never thought it would happen to her daughter. I don't know why. It happened to her cousin when they were just girls, younger than I was." She found a spot on one of his legs where the soft denim of his jeans was beginning to fray and picked at the threads for a moment. "When it was my turn, it was like she forgot. Maybe she *had* forgotten what it was like for Annis. We all grow up hearing the stories of the Harvesters, and the things that happen to the reigning Medusa. But when it actually happens to you, it's different. It's worse. And she never experienced it, so she didn't know." She realized she was making excuses for her mother and stopped. "She's tried since then. I haven't made up my mind to forgive her, though."

Kallan rocked her gently for a few moments. "If she's trying, maybe you should let her make it up to you."

"I'm thinking about it." She turned to rub her cheek on his shirt. "Thank you."

His lips grazed her forehead. "No problem, *meli*." He remained silent for a moment. "Are you hungry?"

"A little." She inhaled his scent, feeling better. Now if only she knew she could safely go home and not have his cousin waiting to kill her...

"Let's get some supper. Look at the castle with the lights on." Still, he didn't move.

"Okay." Andi smiled, relaxing fully.

"Or we can stay in and order room service." He inched one hand up from her waist to the underside of her breast.

So much for relaxed. All kinds of nerve endings came roaring to life.

She lifted her face to his, one eyebrow arched. "Really? You're not tired of staying in?"

He cupped her breast against his palm and lifted his thumb to circle her nipple. "With you? Never."

"Forget supper," she said, twisting in his hold to wrap her arms around his neck and drawing his mouth down to hers.

While it was lovely to stay in bed with Andrea—he'd do it for days if he could—Kallan decided in the morning he could no longer delay their return.

He didn't like it. Just thinking about it made his gut clench with fear and sweat pop out on his forehead.

But his Medusa was pretty well set on the idea. And she had a point: he didn't have it in him to run for the rest of his life. Not even to keep her safe. At some point, he would have to face down his cousin. Or cousins.

He shut his eyes again and settled her nearer as she slept. He just hated going into a situation without proper planning. He didn't know all the variables. Like how many of his cousins would be with Stavros? How long would it take Stavros to get back to Andrea's? Had he actually ever left?

Goddess, he hated thinking about all the things that could go wrong. And he absolutely despised the thought that he might lose her.

She rubbed her cheek against his shoulder, making the blankets slide down a little. "You're thinking way too loud for this early hour," she said sleepily. She moved closer, so she lay halfway on top of him.

He smiled reluctantly. "Really?"

He felt her own smile against his skin. "Really. So tomorrow?"

His smile vanished. "I suppose so."

"I wish Aunt Lydia had emailed me back. Even if Great-Aunt Celosia doesn't know the answer, it would be good to know that too. Either we have the information and try to figure out how to use it, or we don't and go in blind."

"You're amazingly lucid for someone who's just woken up." He kissed her head, breathing in the scent of her. Sweet and spicy.

"Dreams." One of her shoulders lifted. "And I thought about it enough before we slept last night. We've run into at least one of your cousins here in Scotland, which I believe can't be coincidental. Stavros hasn't called you back either. I don't like that."

He didn't either. It meant one of two things: Stavros was plotting and intended to keep his plans to himself, or he'd gone completely into the bottle and would be absolutely unpredictable and even more vicious. Neither was good.

"But we have to go. If we can run into them here, we're going to run into them everywhere." She turned to kiss his shoulder before she lifted her face. "Like it or not, Harvester. We have to go back."

Kallan kissed her lightly. "I know." He was already making tentative plans in his head. They'd need weapons, which meant they'd stop at his house, then make the drive to Maine from Baltimore.

"Stavros doesn't have any other super-secret abilities, does he? Besides the spotting magic and undoing it thing?" Concern shadowed her blue eyes.

"Not that I'm aware of. He also doesn't have the ability to sense another Harvester in the vicinity." He frowned, thinking of the unknown Harvester he'd felt here in the city and wondering if it were the same person who'd been at Culloden. If it was, how had they found him?

"What about the cousin who was with him?"

"Vasily? Tracking is it for him. He's very good at following ground trails, even over solid rock. But otherwise, he's not much use in a hunt." He considered that. Vasily surely couldn't track once a person had left the ground, could he? It wasn't something he'd ever asked before. Perhaps he should ask now.

"How many other talents are out there?"

He met her gaze, focusing. "More than I can count, probably."

The shadows in her eyes deepened. "Could someone have tracked us here?"

He hesitated. "It's possible, I suppose." He didn't want to lie to her. Not now. "We have people who are talented with computers who could, theoretically, dig into flight information. The false passports would slow them down a lot, but I can't promise it would stop them dead."

Andrea's mouth tightened. "I guess it's best to know." Her gaze shifted to his shoulder, and she looked as if she were thinking. Then her eyes cleared. "It doesn't matter. Aunt

Lydia will find out about the curse, and we'll deal with Stavros."

He smiled at her certainty. "I love you, *agaph*."

She smiled back. "Then you'd better feed me. I'm starving, and it's all your fault."

He laughed and rolled her off himself. "All right. Then we'll make flight plans and a list of things we need to deal with once we're back."

She sat up slowly, still smiling as she pushed the blankets down. "I think we need a huge breakfast today."

Kallan picked up his cargo pants from the suitcase and stepped into them. "Okay." He booted up the laptop and took his old cell from his pocket. Still nothing from Stavros.

Andrea tapped the keys on the computer to bring up her email, and then her smile disappeared. "Nothing." She sat back on her heels, looking as if someone had just snatched the last cookie from her.

"She'll email you, *meli*." He held out a lacy pair of panties. "I think these are yours."

A sly smile curved her lips. "You should be sure they are. You bought them, after all." She took them and rose from the bed.

"Turn around."

She rolled her eyes, but she turned.

The cup was now colorless. Rather, the outline was still there, but only the outline on bare, creamy skin, still surrounded by the snake and bright flowers.

"*Agaph*."

Her smile vanished. "What color is it now?" she asked, her voice a little unsteady.

"No color."

"What?" She hurried into the bathroom and turned so her back was toward the mirror, then craned her neck to look over her shoulder. "Oh my Gods." Her face whitened, and she leaned against the sink, staring at her reflection.

Kallan stood beside her, sliding one hand to her nape. "Are you all right?"

She shook her head. "I need to know what it means." She lifted her gaze to his face.

He pulled her close so she could put her face along his throat, and he felt her heart pounding at a crazy pace against his chest. "We'll find out." He intended to keep that promise, no matter what.

Andi didn't like the set of his mouth when she looked at him over supper in their room that night. They'd spent the day making their travel arrangements and plans for after they got back to the States. Now he was brooding again.

She almost felt like brooding herself. She still hadn't heard from Aunt Lydia, and had found herself checking the mirror every time she went into the bathroom to see what her tattoo looked like. It was ridiculous, she'd decided after the fifth time.

But the tension was growing already, and they hadn't even set foot back in the States yet. By the time they did, she'd be ready to go out of her mind.

"Have you worked with a sword before?"

She met his gaze over the table. "Not in years."

His mouth flattened.

"I'm good with my dagger."

One corner of his mouth twisted. "Unless someone gets your dagger hand wrenched up behind you."

She stuck her tongue out at him, gratified when his eyebrows shot up in surprise.

"We don't have time to spend training." He frowned into his plate.

Andi reached across the table and touched his forearm. "Stop."

He raised his gaze to hers.

"We can't plan for the unknown. There are going to be a lot of things we simply don't know when we go in. We'll have to improvise, even though I know that's not your specialty."

He shut his eyes, a hint of a smile tugging at one corner of his mouth. "All right. I get it."

"Do you?" She tightened her fingers on his arm. "You're going to have to relax, Kallan, or we'll be in trouble before anything even happens."

"When did you turn into a psychologist?"

She smiled a little. "Who hasn't picked up a little psychology reading all those myths over the years? All kinds of issues there—people ripe for some intensive therapy."

He took a deep breath and then let it out. "All right. Are you finished with your supper?"

She looked at her half-eaten meal. "Definitely."

He gathered up the dishes and set them outside their door. "Can we run through this one more time before you kill me?"

"Yes, but that's it for tonight." She sat back in her chair, watching him cross to the laptop still on the bed.

He settled on the mattress, and propped himself up with pillows against the headboard. "Tomorrow, our flight leaves at nine, so we have to be at the airport by seven-thirty."

"Check."

He shot her a sharp glance, and she smiled as she mimed zipping her lips shut so he would continue. "Assuming everything is on schedule there, we should be back in Boston before lunch, local time, and on our flight to D.C." He gave her a quick look to see if she was going to speak. When she didn't, a hint of a smile curved his mouth. "If all goes well, we'll be in Baltimore before suppertime, and can settle into my place overnight. Pick up some weapons. I still wish you were handy with a sword."

"You have guns?"

He frowned. "Yes."

"I can shoot." She pulled one foot up onto her seat and propped her chin on her knee.

"You don't have any guns in the house."

Of course he'd searched. "No. I don't own one, but I do shoot. I learned a few years ago, then decided having one in the house could be detrimental to my well-being if anyone from your family came calling when I was incapacitated."

"Good call," he murmured. "I'm not sure we want to drive across six states with guns in the car, though."

He had a point. She frowned, thinking. "We could ship them, couldn't we?"

"Ship them?"

"Yeah, overnight delivery or something."

He considered that. "We can check into it." He typed it onto the to-do list he'd saved earlier.

Andi waited.

"We need to be on the road the next day. I don't want to make the trip in one day, though. If we drive straight through, we'll be exhausted when we get there." He shook his head. "We'll still be dealing with the time change for a day or two. But we can't stay in Baltimore too long either, or someone is bound to notice I'm back in town."

"How many of your relatives live there?"

He lifted one shoulder. "At least ten or twelve have home bases nearby."

Yikes. That would be a problem. "Okay, so we don't stay in Baltimore." She waited.

"But Stavros could still be in Maine."

There it was. The one thing he kept going back to.

"And if he is, he's going to be dangerous."

She studied him. Tension lined his face, worry darkened his green eyes, his mouth flattened, and his inky hair was mussed from his hands dragging through it all day long while they'd worked this plan out. "If he is, we'll deal with him." She still would like to delay that particular leg of their journey just a little longer. Until PMS struck. Then Stavros wouldn't be an issue ever again.

Kallan held her gaze. "He's not going to be as easy to deal with as you think. He might not even be alone."

She put her foot back on the floor and pushed out of her chair. "We can deal with him, Harvester. Hell, look at us. The two of us shouldn't be here together. Our families have been enemies for centuries, and you came to me to kill me." She strode to the bed and faced him down. "We can do this."

He smiled unexpectedly and set the laptop onto the night-stand. "Come here, *agaph*." He held out one hand.

Andi put her hand in his and let him draw her onto his lap, where she settled comfortably.

His chest rose with a long inhalation, then—when he released it—his breath riffled through her hair. "You know he'll have to go through me to get to you."

"I know. But I know we can beat him. Just don't ask me how yet. I haven't worked out the details." She nestled nearer.

"I love you." He tipped her chin up so he could kiss her. Lightly. "Let me hold you for a while."

She relaxed against him, feeling warmth coursing through her that had nothing to do with desire, though that was there too. It always was—an undercurrent no matter what other thing they were doing or discussing. But this felt right. Just being with him this way.

She only hoped they had longer than the next two days to enjoy it.

Kallan tried to breathe evenly, to imagine the tension that pulled his shoulders tight flowing out with each breath, but it wasn't working. It hadn't worked twenty-four hours ago when they were still in Edinburgh. Not even that morning when Andrea had whispered some naughty ideas in his ear while they were flying over the Atlantic, though she had made him smile, which—he was sure—had been her real intention.

Stavros was still silent, which made Kallan very nervous. He'd wait till they were out of Maryland tomorrow before he called around to see if anybody had heard from his cousin.

Andrea's aunt still hadn't responded either, which made Andrea tense too, even though she tried to hide it. Right now, she was pacing his bedroom in Baltimore and shooting irritated glances at his open laptop every few minutes. While she was waiting, she'd done a quick load of laundry, found something for supper for them, and repacked their things into the backpacks and the suitcase.

He was stowing weapons into another case—swords and daggers, polishing and honing as he went to keep his mind semi-occupied. They'd decided earlier not to ship the guns, however. Andrea had looked a little disappointed, but agreed it wasn't their best option—guns were too noisy.

And if they changed their minds, they could pick something up along the way.

When his cell rang, they both jumped. He set down the

dagger he'd been sharpening and crossed the room to grab the phone off the dresser. Not Stavros. *Damn.* "Uncle Ari. How are you?"

"Have you heard from Stavros?"

Kallan shut his eyes. "Not in a few days." That was bad, if Stavros hadn't even checked in with Ari. On the other hand, perhaps it meant Stavros had holed up somewhere with a large supply of alcohol and wasn't waiting in Maine to ambush them.

"No one has heard from him. I'm worried."

The concern in the old man's voice was genuine, and Kallan felt a little guilty. "I left him a message a couple days ago, but he hasn't got back to me. Maybe he's busy hunting." He saw Andrea's eyebrows go up.

"I thought so, too, for the first day or two." Ari sighed. "I am afraid he's drinking."

Kallan frowned. That would be far too easy.

"I've called a handful of the cousins, but no one has seen him since Maine."

His stomach tightened into a fistful of knots. Even if he wasn't lying in wait somewhere and had started drinking, he was probably still in Maine, or nearby. Close enough that he could check in periodically to see if his quarry had returned.

"Would you let me know if you hear from him?"

He forced his attention back to his uncle. "Absolutely. I'll tell him to call you right away." He shook his head at Andrea when she gave him a questioning look.

"Thank you, Kallan. I knew I could count on you. How is your own hunt going?"

"It's not right now. I'm trying to track down a new lead, get back on the trail." His mouth was dry, and the guilt he'd felt earlier returned. In his entire life, he'd never lied to his family. Until Andrea. But he'd rather lie to the family patriarch now than lose her.

"Perhaps you should take a vacation. You've been on the road a long time. It might be you need a break. A pretty woman."

His heart stopped beating for a second before starting again, in double-time. Could Ari know? "A vacation?"

"Somewhere warm, maybe. You could visit your cousin Porfirio in Athens. Or meet up with Vasily in England. I think he was heading into Scotland."

Dear Goddess, they *did* know. "That sounds good. I haven't been to Greece in a while." He gestured to Andrea and shoved the dagger he'd been sharpening into the suitcase.

Eyes wide, she zipped it up and took it off the bed, then bent to pick up her backpack and sweater.

He put one finger to his lips and she nodded her understanding. He grabbed the other backpack and headed for the bedroom door.

Andrea followed him silently.

"Well, I should go. My waitress is coming with a dinner plate in her hand that looks like my meal," he lied, the guilt completely gone now.

"All right. When you get back into D.C., you should stop by to see me, Kallan. It has been too long."

"Sure. See you soon." He shut the phone off and stuffed it into his pocket. "Hurry. They know we were in Scotland."

He didn't have to say anything else. The color had fled her face when he glanced back over his shoulder at her. They walked quickly down the stairs to his basement garage and stuffed their bags into the trunk of his car. She didn't speak, just climbed into the passenger seat and buckled her seatbelt.

He started the car and hit the garage door opener at the same time, then pulled out swiftly and closed the garage behind them. "We'll have to rent a car somewhere. They know this is mine," he said after he'd driven a meandering route through the city for half an hour to make sure they weren't being followed, and finally hit an on-ramp to the highway.

"Philly. At the airport. There's long-term parking and car rental."

He shot her a tight smile. And the tag from their last flight was still on the suitcase, so they wouldn't stick out in the airport in case anyone was watching—as long as no one looked at the tag. "That's right. Very good idea." And Philadelphia wasn't too far away. "We can drive into New York and rent a different car there," he said after a moment. "Then if anyone does pick us up after Philly, we can lose them." He pulled his cell phone from his pocket. "Open the back of that."

She shot him a questioning glance in the light from the dashboard, but pried the battery cover off the back of his phone. "What am I looking for?"

"A tracking device."

Her eyes went round, and then she bit her lower lip, turning to the phone in her hand. She pulled out the battery pack, then poked and prodded at the rest of the phone's guts. "I don't see anything that looks like it doesn't belong," she said at last.

He frowned. "Can you pry off the rest of the cover?"

She didn't reply, instead turning her attention back to the plastic back of the phone and tugged until he heard it crack. She glanced at him apologetically.

"It doesn't matter. Just do it."

She broke the piece off. And there, stuck on the inside of the case was a small round disk with a tiny blinking light.

"Throw it out."

"You want me to litter?" Horror rounded her eyes.

"Andrea." Ordinarily, he wouldn't even think about it, but under the circumstances he didn't give a damn about the littering.

She shook her head and rolled the window down, just enough to let the small piece of plastic go flying into the night. The window slid back up.

"I'm sure he knew we were home too." Whoever had tracked him to Scotland would be able to track him back. He hoped they didn't realize who Andrea was.

His breath froze painfully in the middle of his chest. "The car." If his family had put a tracking device in his phone some time ago, they could easily have put one on the car any time while he was away from home.

She shut her eyes for a second, understanding him perfectly. "Definitely to Philly then," she murmured.

He nodded, pressing his foot harder on the gas pedal. The reading on the speedometer shot up to eighty-five.

"Don't get a speeding ticket. We just need to get there."

She was right. He knew that, but he just wanted out of the car. Safe from whoever was tracking them. Safe from his family.

The drive to the airport was quiet, punctuated only by occasional murmurs regarding exits in the proper direction. And in between, he wondered if the family patriarch kept such close tabs on all of the family, or just some. When they got to Philadelphia, he happily climbed out of the car in the long-term parking lot and gathered their things. Andrea took her backpack from him and shouldered it, her dark eyes somber. They remained silent on the shuttle to the airport, then blended in with the rest of the travelers as they made their way to the automobile rental counters.

Kallan whipped out another I.D. to take care of the car rental, forcing a smile for the woman behind the counter while the transaction ran through their computer system. "Thanks." He took the keys and paperwork from her and shepherded Andrea toward the shuttle for the rental car lot.

He relaxed only a tiny bit on the shuttle ride to the rental car, keeping an eye on everyone around them. Andrea's face was pale and lined with worry.

"Long flight, dear?"

He glanced over to see an old woman leaning toward Andrea.

She smiled at the woman. "It was, I'm afraid."

The woman studied her face and the backpack now in her lap. "Are you heading for one of the parks in the middle of the state, or to the Poconos?"

Andrea shook her head. "We're going to hike part of the Appalachian Trail."

He smiled his approval when she shot him a glance from the corner of her eye.

"Oh, we did that years ago, didn't we, dear?" The woman nudged her tired-looking husband with her elbow.

The man sighed and turned toward his wife. "Yes. A long time ago."

"It was lovely. You'll have a terrific time. But I hope you're going to get plenty of rest before you start hiking."

Andrea nodded.

"And be careful."

Kallan blinked, as did Andrea.

"You never know what sort of things you'll run into out there," the woman said more quietly, leaning nearer. "Human animals as well as the four-legged variety."

Andrea swallowed, and he saw goosebumps rise on her arms. "Thank you," she managed.

The woman nodded and sat back in her seat, turning her attention back to her husband.

Kallan scanned the occupants of the small bus more closely, trying to ignore the way his pulse hammered in his ears at the woman's odd warning.

Andrea touched his hand lightly, and he looked at her. She lifted her chin slightly in the direction of a man sitting in the back of the bus, hunched down in his seat and wearing a baseball cap that shadowed his face on the already-shadowed shuttle. Kallan opened all his senses, but he didn't get anything. He shook his head once, but Andrea frowned, still watching the man who, strangely, had no bags.

Kallan wondered if any of his cousins had the ability to cloak their presence. That would be very, very bad.

Andrea shouldered her backpack when the bus slowed down, then picked up the other pack, and Kallan grabbed the suitcase handle. He stood as the shuttle stopped, keeping an eye on the man in the back. He guided her off the bus, noticing that the man got to his feet slowly.

Their car was first in the row, thank the Goddess, he noted as he stepped onto the asphalt. "Just get in," he breathed. He hit the button on the keyring to unlock the doors.

She clambered into the backseat rather than try to get out of her pack. He tossed the suitcase in after her, then slid into the driver's seat and locked the doors before starting the car.

He could see the other man in the rearview mirror, holding his own key and paper from the rental agency and seemingly looking around for his car.

Something didn't feel right, though.

"Go, Kallan," Andrea said from behind him, and he could hear her shifting to get the pack off.

He put the car in gear and his foot on the gas. And in the

flash of headlights from someone else's rental car, the man turned just enough that he could see his cousin Theo.

"Son of a bitch." He pressed harder on the pedal and guided the car out of the parking lot, watching in the rearview mirror as Theo ran to his own car. "Put on your seatbelt, *meli*," he said. And pushed the car up to the speed limit on the ramp to the highway. Higher.

In the rearview mirror, he saw distant headlights coming up quickly, so he went faster. There was a cluster of cars ahead. If he could get to them, blend in, then get the hell off the highway and into the city for a while, he could lose his cousin.

He wove in and out of the traffic once he caught up to the other cars, but one set of headlights in his rearview mirror kept coming in a hurry. Kallan sped up, not sure if he should wish for a traffic officer to pull them over or not. The speeding car drew nearer still. He kept their rental car ahead of his cousin for several miles, weaving in and out of the light evening traffic far faster than he normally would have. Theo kept up easily, then started closing the distance. Now only four cars between them.

Kallan started watching the exit signs as they flew past, his rapid heartbeat thumping in his ears.

Now three cars between them.

He was too aware of Andrea in the backseat, trusting him to protect her. His pulse quickened still more.

Now only two.

His cousin cut into the right lane, and silhouetted in the headlights from cars behind Theo, Kallan saw the shape of a gun coming out of the driver's window. Kallan pressed harder on the accelerator, but there were more cars ahead, and he wasn't sure he could get through them without slowing down. If he slowed down, Theo was going to catch them.

Something hit the car roof, and Andrea made a startled sound in the backseat at the same time his breath snagged in his chest. "Is he shooting at us? He is. Dammit."

"Stay down, *agaph*. Please." He watched the flash of another shot brighten for a moment in his rearview mirror before something dinged the side of the car.

Apparently shooting was necessary to slow the traffic, because now the second car back slowed down, and Theo zipped into the space. Only one car between them now.

Kallan hung in the passing lane, waiting until the last possible second, then veered across the right lane—his rear bumper far too close to the front bumper of a tractor trailer— and onto the exit ramp as the truck driver blared his horn, the sound almost loud enough to drown out his thudding heart.

Too late for Theo to follow them. He breathed a little sigh of relief and randomly chose a direction at the bottom of the ramp.

"We did lose him finally, right? Who is it?" Andrea asked after they'd driven around in the city for nearly half an hour. "I was trying not to distract you in case he managed to keep up."

"Theodore. He's a west coaster. He's out of his usual territory." Kallan had to wonder why. And when had Theo developed the ability to cloak his presence? And how many other cousins could do it too?

"If he's here, then he's not alone." His Medusa was smart. Only one of the reasons he loved her.

"A fair guess." His gut told him Ari had called in some extra help. Which meant that whoever tracked them to Scotland knew when they returned. Probably Phillip. He was a serious computer hacking genius. Obviously, they knew when he left his house with the tracker in the phone and probably one in the car too, so they could find him no matter what.

And with Theo in Philadelphia instead of Reno, he would have brought his brother Sebastyen and their cousin Kosmo with him from the other end of the country to bolster the Philly crew. Which meant Stavros was still in Maine. Waiting for them.

He swallowed. His Medusa was in a lot of danger, and he hadn't done enough to keep her safe.

"I think I'm going to want to pick up a gun when we get to Maine," Andrea said from the backseat.

Kallan laughed, a tiny bit of tension escaping with the sound. "I think that might be a good idea, *agaph*. But I think we may need the big guns, and those will take a little too much time to track down."

"We're still heading to New York, right?"

He considered that. It would be a gamble now, with his cousins so close, plus all of the rest who were normally in New York. The question was would they expect him to try something else and focus their attention elsewhere now, or would they figure he'd stick to his plan?

His family knew him well enough to know he always had a plan, and most often his plans were direct, rather than roundabout.

"No, I think we're going into Harrisburg instead." They wouldn't have figured he'd detour so far off plan.

He hoped.

His Medusa's life depended on it.

CHAPTER THIRTEEN

A ndi woke with a start, then winced when the sudden movement pulled a muscle in her neck painfully. She'd clambered into the front seat while they were still in Philly last night, and Kallan refused to let her drive—his foot heavy on the accelerator when he steered the car onto the Pennsylvania Turnpike.

Now, though, he'd stopped the car, which had wakened her.

She looked around them and found not much of anything.

He smiled a little when he met her gaze. "It's time to rent another car." He pulled out his new cell phone.

She nodded and shifted in her seat. He'd driven well beyond Harrisburg. Around Harrisburg, actually, for the remainder of the night. She craned her neck to see the road sign ahead.

They weren't too far from the capital now. It just *looked* like they were in the middle of nowhere.

She sat back, twisting and stretching as much as she could in her seat. Sleeping sitting up in a moving car left a lot to be desired.

But it beat being dead.

She curled her fingers into fists. It looked as if Kallan's great-uncle had called in the troops. Just for her. How lovely. But not the sort of lovely that made one feel all tingly and happy.

Kallan must be exhausted. Dark smudges marked the skin beneath his green eyes, and she wanted to drag her fingers through his mussed hair to try to make it neater. Or just to touch him.

She gave in to part of the urge, setting one hand on his knee as he finished his phone call.

He smiled over at her, though strain bracketed his mouth. "Good morning."

"Why don't you let me drive?"

He looked as if he wanted to argue, but he shifted his gaze to the field beside the road. "After we get the new car. We should get some breakfast. Check the laptop for a tracking device too."

She shut her eyes. That hadn't occurred to her last night when they were destroying his old phone and abandoning his car.

"I should have thought of that earlier. I'd hate to have to ditch it, but if we have to, I will." He covered her hand with one of his. "I don't know why I didn't think of that before this morning. They may know exactly where we are right now. Or when we boot up the system, depending on what they're using." His other hand slid up the side of his face to his rumpled hair. "Okay, this is our current plan. Get the new car, find somewhere to eat, then head north." His bright gaze swung back to hers. "And we'll find somewhere to spend at least the next night. I'm beat."

She leaned over to kiss him lightly. "If you weren't such a guy, you would have let me take a turn driving last night."

A ghost of a smile touched his lips at her teasing, as she'd hoped. "You like that about me."

"Most of the time." She squeezed his knee. "How long are we going to drive before we stop?"

"Depends on what I find in the laptop." He pushed his door open and climbed out slowly, then stretched.

Andi watched him root through the backpack for his computer before he returned to his seat. He pulled a multi-tool gadget with a tiny screwdriver from his pocket and undid all the screws holding the laptop case together. He held out the screws, and she opened her hand for them.

Then he carefully lifted the bottom off.

She leaned closer to look. She didn't see anything that looked like the device in his cell phone. Nothing blinking that it was sending out a signal.

His mouth turned down. "So when we boot up then." He sighed, sliding one hand over his eyes.

"If it's a tracking program, we can disable it."

"If we had a computer expert. I can do what I need to, Andrea, but I'm not a computer geek."

She didn't like the defeat in his eyes. "I know one."

He lifted one eyebrow, a little of the disappointment leaving his face.

"Give me the phone." It was early, but this was life or death. She traded the screws for the cell. She punched in Thalia's number and held her breath.

Four rings. Five. Finally a click. "Hello?" It sounded as if her cousin had just rolled over in bed and snagged her phone.

Andi shut her eyes, relief welling in her middle. "It's me."

"Andi? Where are you?"

"Never mind. I have a problem you can help me with, though." She explained quickly, offering only details pertinent to the laptop issue.

Thalia was silent for a long time. "If booting up the system triggers the tracking, you won't have much time to disable the program. Unless you can scramble the signal."

"How can we do that?" Her heart pounded in her ears, much too loudly. She shot Kallan a quick smile when he set his hand on her thigh, squeezing lightly.

"Let me think for a minute. I'm still not awake." Thalia yawned, and there was rustling from her end of the line.

Andi dropped her head back against the headrest.

"We?" Thalia asked after a minute.

Andi laughed. "The laptop, T."

Her cousin hummed, clearly dissatisfied with that response. "How close to an airport are you?" she said finally.

"Not very far, actually." Andi sat straighter in her seat.

"Get there and call me back. I'll be awake, I promise."

"Okay." She clicked the off button. "We need to be at the airport."

"Lucky for us, we were heading there." He handed her the laptop and restarted the car. "We'll do this first and then get the car, I think."

She nodded, her mind racing. If Thalia could fix this, they would still be able to access things they might need, like email. She hoped Aunt Lydia had finally spoken to Celosia.

Her stomach rumbled, interrupting her pondering.

"And breakfast immediately after we get the car," Kallan said with a grin.

She didn't even protest his teasing. There was too much to worry about now.

Kallan watched with his heart in his throat when Andrea booted up the laptop while they sat in the middle of the airport, his new cell phone tucked against her ear. Her fingers skipped over the keys at her cousin's instruction, her forehead creased with worry.

He kept an eye on the surrounding crowd, but he didn't spot anyone who looked familiar, or feel any other Harvesters nearby. Not that that meant anything, since Theo could evidently cloak his presence.

Frowning, he turned his attention back to Andrea, who was looking at a screen full of gobbledegook.

"Okay, I see it," she said into the phone. "It does have… yes, it says on the tenth. What does that… Oh. Okay. I see that, too… Yes."

He watched her type in a command after a second, his gaze flitting away to keep an eye on the people around them. They needed to get out of here. His gut knotted with tension.

"Okay, it's gone." She shot him a thumbs-up and a quick smile. Then she frowned. "Wait, I see it again."

He groaned softly.

"Okay. Tell me what the other one looks like." She scrolled through the lines of code on the screen. "Got it." She waited for instructions, then typed in something that looked like a two-year-old's attempt at writing words. "It's gone. They're both gone… Okay, rebooting." She shut the system down, then waited before restarting it.

Kallan felt like he could puke, if only he'd eaten something since supper last night.

When Andrea executed the steps her cousin described, her shoulders sagged with relief. "It's gone. Thank you so much, T."

His breath rushed out, and he unclenched his fists. *Thank Goddess.*

Andrea said her goodbyes to her cousin as she packed the laptop into the backpack. When she held out the phone, she looked wiped out. Still paler than usual—she had dark smudges under her eyes from lack of sleep. He guessed he had them too. "Let's get the hell out of here, Harvester."

He nodded his agreement and steered her to the rental counter downstairs where he signed the waiting agreement and took the key from a slow-moving young man who looked as if he needed a caffeine injection.

"Can you wait until we get onto the interstate?" he asked when they climbed into the new car. "For breakfast? And to check email?"

She nodded as she settled into her seat. "Yes. I just want to get away from here before someone who was able to catch the signal before we disabled it comes looking for us. Whoever installed the tracking program activated it just before we went to Scotland."

He didn't find that shocking. Not since they'd found the device in the phone. But he didn't like it. He floored it when they hit the highway, guiding the car northeast, away from Harrisburg. No car appeared to be following them, and he forced himself to relax a little bit as he drove. "Your cousin is a genius."

Andrea's smile was tired, but still affectionate. "She is. Good thing, too. Who knew someone could create a tracking program that would replicate itself if you tried to delete it without catching the second portion?"

He didn't have to imagine who. Ari had his fingers in all the pies of the searches for the Medusa. He encouraged his nephews to use the most advanced technologies available to them, and to hone their individual skills. But Kallan had never imagined his great-uncle would use those same tools against his own family. Then again, he supposed Ari didn't trust any of them to do the job properly. Which made him wonder why.

About an hour north of the capital, he finally pulled off

the interstate and into a truck stop so they could eat. Andrea returned from the ladies' room with wet hair and pink in her cheeks, and slid into the booth across from him. "I am starving."

"Good. I ordered you a huge breakfast." He smiled at the arch of her eyebrow. "I didn't think you'd want to wait any longer than absolutely necessary."

She sighed. "You're right." Her gaze skittered around the restaurant, over the truckers and the tourists before returning to him. "Do you think we got everything now?"

"I hope so." He didn't tell her he'd searched through his backpack after she headed to the bathroom, just to make sure.

Her dark head bobbed once. "Would you reconsider waiting just a little longer?"

He laughed. "You are persistent, *agaph*."

One of her shoulders lifted. "I really think it would be the most effective way to deal with them."

He rested his forearms on the table and leaned toward her, searching her face for a few seconds. "If you'd let me, I'd take you somewhere far away right now," he said, low. "I can keep you safe." Now that no one could track them, that was.

Her expression softened, and she leaned forward so she could reach his hands, clasping them with hers. "I know. I appreciate it. But we can't run forever. And you hate running as much as I do."

He couldn't argue that. "I want you alive more than I hate running," he said finally.

The waitress rushed up to their table, nearly dropping a big plate on his head. "Oh, sorry. I've got your breakfasts. You wanted the farmer's platter." She set one of the plates in front of him when Andrea released his hands. "And the same for the lady. Can I get you anything else?"

He shook his head, and the woman hurried away.

Andrea touched the back of his hand when he reached for his fork. "I love you too."

Warmth spread up his arm from her fingers, and expanded in his chest from her words. Smiling, he lifted her hand to his mouth, briefly.

After breakfast, they drove north. He set the GPS to avoid New York, since he imagined his cousins would be waiting there—watching, expecting him to want to blend into the crowds. And he let Andrea drive, both to stop her arguments and because he truly needed a nap.

"We should find somewhere not too far off the interstate to stay," she said after they'd been on the road a while. "But not too near a big city. Unless you know you have cousins in some little town north of New York."

He shook his head, trying to relax into the seat. "Not that I'm aware of." He eased the seat back so he could stretch out his legs a bit. Much better.

"Okay. Then when I see some likely spot, we'll get off. You should try to rest in the meantime." She patted his knee, then put her hand back on the steering wheel.

"I'm sorry, Andrea."

Her bright gaze slid away from the road and onto his face. "For what?"

"For not realizing just how much danger I was putting you in."

She turned her attention back to the road, frowning. "You had no idea what you were in for when you came hunting me, Harvester." Her tone was light.

He set his hand on her thigh. "I mean I didn't know how desperate Uncle Ari is to kill you, desperate enough that he doesn't trust any of us apparently."

"He'd take the credit, too, wouldn't he? The miserable old bastard."

He inhaled slowly. "Probably. He's shepherded all of us over the years. Everyone looks to him for guidance." He shook his head. "I'm sorry."

"We all have relatives we'd rather not acknowledge." She sent another smile toward him.

Reluctantly, he smiled back.

"Now get some sleep. You look like hell," she teased.

He shut his eyes, but his mind was whirling in too many directions for him to possibly take a nap.

Andi hated to wake him when she stopped the car at the little motel off the highway—especially when it had taken over an hour for him to actually get to sleep. They'd left the interstate behind hours ago for a state highway, and this motel sat just outside a tiny town whose exit sign boasted "the best hot cakes in the state". She hesitated, then put her hand on his shoulder, lightly.

He jerked upright instantly, and guilt lanced her belly. "Are you okay?"

"Fine. But I found us a place to spend the night." She let her hand rest on his shoulder, feeling the tension in his muscles ease a little.

He sighed, rubbing his face with one hand. "All right." He pushed his door open and got out.

Andi climbed out too, glad to stretch her legs. Upstate New York was pretty in the summer, she thought, scanning the area surrounding the motel. The trees shaded the property but weren't so thick they would hide anyone. That was a plus. And one of the reasons she hadn't stopped at the motel she'd seen directly off the highway. The trees and shrubs there were too thick for her liking right now. If she were home and safe, she'd be perfectly happy on her wooded mountain.

But she wasn't safe, and it seemed best not to give her enemies any help reaching her.

They checked in as Mr. and Mrs. Reece Levine, though she doubted the man who took their money cared what names they used, as long as their money was good.

Kallan relaxed a little more once they were locked in their room at the far end of the long, low building, the car parked directly outside their door.

Andi sank onto the foot of the bed, her gaze skimming the room. It was clean, though outdated. She didn't care as long as she could sleep. She was beyond tired.

He checked all the locks, door and windows, went into the bathroom to inspect it, and then came back out to sit down beside her. "Looks good."

She leaned against him. "You need to sleep."

"So do you, *meli*." He kissed her forehead. "I want to get a couple blades out of the suitcase and into the backpack. Just in case."

She sighed as he rose and moved to where they'd dumped their belongings when they came in—on the small table next to the window. He tugged the curtains shut and unzipped the suitcase.

"I should see if Aunt Lydia has gotten back to me yet." She thought about it for a second before she pushed herself to her feet. Sitting down on the very tempting bed had made her feel even more tired. Just this one task before she let herself crash.

She sat in one of the chairs beside the table and booted up the laptop. She ran the check Thalia had told her about just to be certain the tracking program hadn't had another backup. Still clear. Thank the Gods. Then she clicked into her email.

"About time," she muttered when she saw Aunt Lydia's email. She tapped the key to open it.

Dearest Andi,

I'm sorry it took me so long to get back to you. Celosia is sometimes so useful. Then other times, she's just a cranky old woman, and this week happened to be one of those times.

Unfortunately, she isn't much help. She said she thinks she might remember a story of one of the Medusas falling in love after the curse fell on her shoulders, and the curse then moving on to someone else, but she isn't sure. She said Sophronia would remember. I think she's lost it if she can't remember Sophronia's been dead for twenty years. Good Gods.

Anyway, when she gave me that very useless answer, it reminded me of something. It's been years since I thought of it, but there's a book chronicling some of the past Medusas. Nothing recent that I'm aware of, though we really should remedy that, dear girl. But back to the book. I know who has current possession of it, though she really only borrowed it fifteen years ago from the person who should have it, and I'm making a trip to see her right now, since this could be extremely important for you from the sound of things. I'll contact you as soon as I get a look at it.

Please be careful, dear. I spoke to Thalia the other day, and she told me she's had one of her premonitions. (Though one of these days, we really have to tell her she's often late with those.)

Much love,

Lydia.

Andi sat back, chewing on her lower lip, and heard footsteps behind her.

"Well, that isn't really an answer, is it?" Kallan asked after a minute.

She shook her head. "But it's better than nothing. At least

I know she's trying and there might still be an answer." She rubbed her forehead.

"Shut that down, *meli*. We need some rest." He brushed one hand over her hair to her nape.

She closed it down, thinking about her aunt's message. There might have been a Medusa who fell in love, which sent the curse on to someone else.

She might be free of the curse.

She frowned as she kicked off her shoes. But she still had the amulet, which meant she was still the Medusa.

Kallan touched the spot between her eyebrows lightly, making her force the frown away. "You're thinking way too hard for someone so exhausted." He bent to kiss her in the same spot. "Don't worry about it now. When she gets an answer, she'll email you." He smiled gently, encouragingly.

She nodded. "I know." She let him gather her close, rubbing her cheek against his soft shirt and feeling his steady heartbeat beneath her face.

"Get in." He kissed the top of her head and released her. "I'll race you to see who gets naked first."

"Naked? I thought you were tired." A slow heat bubbled in her belly at his words.

"I am. But that doesn't mean I don't still want to hold you. Naked." He winked at her.

She smiled back in spite of the worries rushing around in her head. "You are such a man." Nevertheless, she tugged her shirt up and off, then undid her jeans.

He won. But then, he wore less clothing than she did. She was still unhooking her bra when he dropped his cargo pants to the floor. And for a man so tired, he was still beginning to be aroused.

She shook her head. "Really?"

His smile turned wicked. "Even when we're old, *agaph*."

He tugged the blankets back and climbed into the bed, yanking the covers down on the opposite side as well, so when she kicked off the rest of her clothing she could slide in too. He pulled her tightly to his side, and she relaxed fully for the first time in over twenty-four hours.

"Sleep," he whispered, kissing his way down her cheek to the corner of her mouth.

She turned her face to catch his lips, just for a second smiling against him.

Kallan smiled back and shut his eyes.

Andi shifted so she could wrap her arms around him and closed her eyes too. Maybe when they woke, they'd have not just an answer to her question but a better plan than the one they were currently working with.

Kallan woke first, inhaling deeply and rubbing one hand up the side of his face to shove his hair away from his eyes. Andrea still slept, wrapped tightly around him. The scent of her teased his nose, making his body surge to life. Slowly, he turned to look at the clock on the nightstand: nine p.m. They'd slept away the afternoon and evening. His stomach rumbled and he winced. The motel restaurant closed at six. He wondered if anything else in the little town stayed open this late.

And if anyone hunting them was nearby.

Andrea stirred, and he slid his hand down her back, keeping her close.

She hummed against his chest. "You're noisy."

He laughed. "Sorry. I have no control over that."

Her fingers wrapped around his erection. "Or that." She squeezed gently, making him groan. "I like waking with you this way."

His body pulsed in her grip, and he swallowed. "Well, it's entirely your fault."

He felt her smile on his skin. "Really?" She stroked up to the tip of him, her thumb caressing there lightly. "Well, I don't know if you can wait for supper that long."

He rolled her beneath him in a flash and wedged his knees between hers. Her laughter was surprised. "Screw supper." He slid one hand between her thighs, finding her damp already. He eased one finger inside her, felt more moisture rush to meet him, so he shifted to position his cock there instead.

Andrea sucked in a quick breath, bending her knees at his sides. "Yes."

Kallan eased into her rather than just thrusting to the hilt as his body demanded. Her sheath clenched around him, then relaxed to allow him to slide deeper.

She cupped his face, drawing him down to kiss her. "I love you," she whispered against his lips.

He settled as deeply as he could, then set his jaw to resist the need to move. Not yet.

She tightened her inner muscles , a faint smile touching her lips. "It's all right."

He kissed her again, rolling his hips in a slow circle against hers.

She moaned her approval.

He slipped one hand between them to stroke her clit, making her hips jerk up toward his. The hot wet silk of her body around him contracted harder. He groaned.

She wrapped her legs higher around him and nipped at his lower lip. "Please, Kallan."

He withdrew just a little, then pushed back into her welcoming sheath. Over and over until they were both breathless and dripping perspiration. Until they were both shaking with release and relief.

He rolled to his side, bringing her with him, kissing her cheeks, her forehead, her mouth.

He couldn't lose her. Not now.

Her warm fingers massaged the muscles at the back of his shoulder. "You're thinking too much."

He grunted into the side of her neck.

"How about neither of us does that until we get some food? Deal?"

"I think I need a shower before we can get food," he murmured, sliding his hand down her damp back.

"We can do that too." She tipped her head back to look at him. Her blue eyes didn't miss anything—even things he intended for her to not see, he was sure.

Her breasts lifted against his chest with the deep breath she took. "Promise me something."

He frowned.

"Promise me you won't step in the way if they get to me. I don't want you to die for me."

His heart constricted with pain. "I can't promise that." His words came out raspy, hoarse.

Her gaze was somber. "I don't want to see you die."

"Any more than I want to see you die."

Her mouth pursed a little at that, and she looked away.

"Andrea."

Reluctantly, she looked back up at him.

"If we leave now, we can be all the way across the country in a few hours. Or we can drive. I don't care. But we'll be away from the ambush waiting for us at your house."

She shook her head. "No. We have to go back."

He kissed her gently, and her eyes fluttered shut, but when she opened them, they were shadowed, troubled. "We'll deal with them." He didn't know how, but they had to. He wasn't going to lose her.

Andi felt both better and worse in the morning when they got underway, Kallan behind the wheel of the rental car. She was rested now. Not only had they slept away the afternoon and evening, but after they'd found a pizza shop open in town and picked up a loaded pizza to take back to the motel with them, they'd slept again until nine a.m.

But she'd hoped to make him see it wouldn't do her any good to have him die in front of her. That he refused to consider her request made her heart ache. And annoyance bubble in her middle.

He was such a man.

Sure, the protectiveness was nice. But she could do some of the fighting too, dammit.

She propped her chin on her fist and stared out the window at the passing blur of homes and trees.

His old cell phone vibrated on the console between them.

She shot him a questioning glance when he picked it up to look at the screen. It was a wonder the thing still worked with half its case missing.

He shook his head. "In case there's some way they can track while I'm on the line."

Which there probably was.

Andi frowned out the side window. By now, his cousins would have figured out their tracking program in the laptop was gone. They would also know the device they'd planted in his phone was lying along the interstate outside of Baltimore, and his car sat at the airport in Philadelphia.

These guys were persistent, even when one of their own was the quarry.

That didn't bode well for her.

She booted up the laptop after they'd been on the road for a while, checking again for the tracking program and coming up clean. *Good.*

No email from Aunt Lydia. *Not so good.*

"*Agaph.*" He touched her balled-up fist on her thigh.

She shot him a glare.

He smiled anyway. "Give her some time."

"We don't have time." In a few hours, they'd reach Boston. Then they'd be back in Maine a little while later.

And she needed to know what the changes to her tattoo meant.

She'd looked at it again that morning in the mirror, surreptitiously. It was still there, outlined, but flesh-toned. Something was keeping it with her, and she didn't know what. The curse? Maybe.

She did know, though, that she loved Kallan. It wasn't that.

So maybe really she *was* stuck with it.

He touched her fist, insinuating his fingers into hers and lacing them on her leg. "I think we should wait till tomorrow to go to your place."

She met his gaze, her brain shifting gears. It would be smarter to go in during the day, when they could see just what they were up against. If they went in later today, or tonight, there would be plenty of places for Stavros and his crew to hide.

That made her blood bubble in her veins. *On her mountain.*

She wanted them off.

She glared at the dashboard. Bastards.

A tiny ding appeared in the plastic.

She blinked, startled.

It was too soon for *that* again.

Kallan glanced over at her, and she forced a smile for him, giving his fingers a little squeeze.

When he turned his attention back to the highway ahead, she shot a surreptitious glance at the dashboard. Yep. Right there. She inhaled unsteadily. The stress. Usually, she was pretty regular. Most of the time, she amended silently—once she'd adjusted to her life After the Curse. For almost the first year of being the reigning Medusa, it had been a very irregular thing. But not in a long time.

She did a quick mental count in her head. *Way* too early. But it might be a good thing for when they got onto the mountain tomorrow.

In spite of herself, she felt the smile curving her lips. "Okay, tomorrow it is."

Then she could take care of Stavros and whoever else he'd brought in to kill her.

CHAPTER FOURTEEN

Kallan frowned as he maneuvered the car off the highway. Andrea was very quiet, though not seething as she had been that morning. The smile on her lips earlier had made the hair on the back of his neck stand up. When he caught her hand in his, she'd jumped a little, a guilty look flashing over her face before her smile shifted to something gentler.

But she'd been plotting. He'd bet on it.

His jaw tightened. She was not going to get herself killed if he could prevent it. He wouldn't allow it.

Then again, he didn't see how he could prevent his cousins from killing both of them.

That wasn't any comfort.

He eased the car into the parking lot of a diner. She sat up a little straighter, her eyes focusing as if she'd been daydreaming. "Supper," he said.

She nodded.

He met her at the front of the car and caught her hand in his. They were just north of Portland—blending in, he hoped, with all the summer tourists. "Some supper, and then a little more driving before we find someplace to spend the night." He held her gaze until she nodded, her blue expression quizzical. "And I want to know what you were thinking about earlier."

A smile tugged at one corner of her mouth. "I was thinking about what I'm going to do to you later." She winked up at him.

While her statement heated his blood, he knew it wasn't the truth. At least, not the whole truth. "And the other thing."

Her smile faded. "We'll see."

That wasn't good enough. "Do I need to handcuff you to the hotel bed?"

Blue sparks flashed in her eyes. "You wouldn't dare."

He lifted one eyebrow. "We'll see," he parroted. He led her inside before she could answer and found them an empty booth at the back corner. It looked as if the dinner rush was mostly over, but there were still tourists in several other booths and locals at the counter.

Andrea folded her arms on her chest when she sat opposite him, her eyes averted.

When the waitress came, they glanced over the menus and listened to the specials before ordering. Then, after the waitress bustled away, he leaned on the table, arms folded on the cool surface. "I would dare, Andrea," he said, low. "Because I want you safe."

She didn't look up, but her mouth tightened.

"I've been racking my brain all day long trying to think of a way for us to go up there and not get killed, and I can't do it." He stretched over the table to touch her clenched hands. "I'll kill my cousin myself before I let him kill you, and if I have to lock you up to do it, I will."

She glared harder at the table to her left.

And he saw the ding appear.

"Andrea." His voice trembled, much to his shock.

She shut her eyes, her expression softening.

"It's too soon, isn't it?" He kept her hands covered with his, feeling a shudder ripple through her.

"It should be, but the first year—when I was super-stressed—it wasn't a regular thing." She met his gaze. "If this isn't stress, I don't know what is."

Kallan considered that. In less than twenty-four hours, she'd be curled into a fetal position wherever they were, unable to run. But still fully able to defend herself without lifting a hand. He took a slow breath. "We need a new plan," he said after a moment.

A hint of a sad smile touched her lips. "I think that *is* our new plan, Kallan." She freed one of her hands to cover his. "We don't have a choice now."

"Of course we do." He bit off his next words when the waitress sailed toward their table with steaming plates. He waited while the young woman served them and topped off their water glasses. After she'd finally hurried off to another table, he studied his plate for a moment, his appetite gone. "We'll have to think about this. We can figure it out once we stop for the night," he said at last.

Andrea nodded once, but he didn't think he'd have an easy time convincing her to wait. Or to let him face his cousins alone.

Picking up his fork with his free hand, he began to eat, but he didn't taste a bite.

By the time he finished, his meal sat like lead in his gut, and Andrea had done no more than pick at her own, her face wan and lined with strain. "You should eat more, *meli*." He nudged her foot under their table.

"I'm not hungry." She dropped her fork onto her plate and sat back.

He didn't argue, nor did he argue when they got back in the car and back onto the highway. That would wait.

By the time he'd found them a vacancy in a touristy motor lodge near Bath, the tension in his gut had tightened like a vise. He parked the car in front of their room after checking them in, then shot a quick glance at her. She sat with her eyes closed, worry lining her forehead. "Come, *agaph*. Let's go in."

She opened her eyes slowly and pushed her door open.

This wasn't like his Medusa.

He gathered the suitcase and the backpack she hadn't yet grabbed and met her at the door to their room. He stuffed the key into the lock and pushed the door wide. Then froze. "Get in the car," he breathed. Another member of the Tassos family was in the vicinity. Very, very close by.

Standing on alert? Or on their way to join Stavros?

Her eyes went wide at his command, and she backed up a step, then another, until she came up against the hood of the car. He jerked his head. She rushed back to her side, fumbling for the door handle for a second, then slid in, her backpack slowing her down.

Kallan dropped onto his seat and started the car at the same time. Andrea wrestled his bags into the backseat while he reversed the car out of the parking lot.

He drove quickly up the coast road, keeping his senses open. He'd been sloppy, he realized, his heart still beating into his throat fifteen minutes later. No one followed them. At least, no one he could feel.

He shot a glance over at Andrea. In the light from the dashboard, she was pale, but her jaw was set.

He might have no choice but to let her fight with him, in her own way.

The notion sent ripples of fear down his spine.

His old phone rang, making her jump in her seat. He touched her knee before he picked it up to see the screen. Stavros again.

Bastard. There was no way in Hades his cousin was getting his murderous hands on Andrea. *No way.*

Aristotle reached automatically for his phone while looking over the papers in front of him. "Yes?"

"We have reason to believe they're heading north."

"Stavros." He set his pen down and focused his attention on his nephew. He hoped Stavros had sobered up since their last conversation. "How do you know?"

"Theo lost them in Philadelphia."

"Lost them?"

Stavros cleared his throat. "Yes, sir."

Aristotle inhaled slowly. "I see." Somehow, he didn't believe he was hearing all the details. "Why would they be returning?"

"Kallan never can leave well enough alone. Who knows why she'd come back. The monster probably thinks she can kill us."

Aristotle shut his eyes. Stavros was far too arrogant. Too reckless. He was also the most ruthless of all of the nephews, and right now that ruthlessness was their best opportunity to finally kill the Medusa and get the protective goblet away from her family. "Keep me apprised, Stavros. And be careful. If Kallan would abandon his family for this monster, there is no telling what else he would do."

His nephew laughed. "We outnumber them greatly. We cannot fail."

The older man winced. "A little humility would serve you

well, Stavros," he said firmly. "The Goddess does not like so much arrogance."

Stavros sighed. "Yes, Uncle Ari," he said after a moment, his tone sullen.

Aristotle hung up and closed his eyes for a moment. "Forgive him, my Lady," he murmured. "I have made mistakes with that one, I think."

He opened his eyes. He could not fix his previous mistakes with Stavros, but he would make certain he did not repeat them with any of the younger nephews.

Andi persuaded Kallan to let her drive after they stopped for gas in Rockland. "You've driven most of the day again. I'm tired of sitting here doing nothing."

He gave her a measuring look before he nodded. "All right. Let's head into Belfast and try to find another motel."

She swallowed and nodded. "Okay." Maybe by the time they arrived, her brain would be tired enough to let her sleep. As it was, she'd spent far too much time thinking in circles all day long, about two things: the tattoo color and his cousins waiting to kill her.

Aunt Lydia needed to get back to her on the amulet.

As for his cousins, she kept coming back to the curse rearing its ugly head. It was the only way.

Getting Kallan to agree would be the challenge.

She tried to marshal some convincing arguments while she drove. And was pretty sure she'd failed. By the time she found a small motel along the road, she'd started tapping her fingers nervously on the steering wheel.

Of course he noticed. He slanted her a knowing smile when she parked. She tried to smile back but didn't quite manage that either.

This time when they got to the room assigned to them, Kallan nodded that the area was clear, and she went inside on shaky legs.

The room looked a lot like the one where they'd spent last night. The only thing really different was the scent of the sea air, which was still strong even with the windows closed.

She busied herself taking toiletries out of the suitcase, then brushed her teeth and combed her hair. She froze with the comb in mid-air over her head, her fingers trembling as the realization emerged. She lowered her arm and walked out of the bathroom to where Kallan stood in the center of the room, looking deep in thought. He glanced up when she stepped out, then frowned when he saw her face.

"What's wrong?"

"I need a pair of scissors."

His eyes lit with understanding, but his mouth turned down. "I don't have any." His tone was apologetic.

Her eyes stung a little, but she blinked hard, determined not to cry. Not right now, no matter what her hormones thought. If she had to cut her hair off with her dagger, she'd do it.

He snapped his fingers. "Wait a second." He rummaged in his pockets and came up with the multi-tool gadget, then rifled through the tools before he came up with an even smaller pair of scissors than he'd found for her the last time.

She took the tool and curled her shaky fingers around it. "Thank you."

He caught her wrist before she could retreat to the bathroom. "Come here, *meli*." He pulled her closer so he could wrap his other arm around her.

She heard his steady heartbeat under her ear, and she took a deep breath, willing some of the rush of nerves to settle down inside her.

laptop, though she felt his gaze following her movements. When she couldn't stand it any longer, she looked up and he smiled at her, just a little.

She smiled as she turned her attention back to the computer screen, bringing up her email program.

Nothing from Aunt Lydia.

She sank back in her seat, smile fading. She'd so been hoping…

"I'm sorry, *agaph*," he said.

She *needed* that information, even if it didn't help them tomorrow. Her eyes burned. She needed to know if she was stuck with this forever, even though she had Kallan now.

It wouldn't be fair to ask him to stay with a monster forever.

"It doesn't matter."

She blinked, then turned her blurred gaze in his direction.

"I don't care about the curse, Andrea. We'll deal with it."

She dropped her chin, feeling her lower lip wobble. The first hot tear splashed onto her cheek, then down onto her shirt. Damned hormones.

Kallan's hand appeared in front of her, holding out a tissue. While she swiped it across her cheek, he shut down the laptop, then tugged her out of the chair.

She let him steer her toward the bed, swallowing to try to make the lump in her throat go away. It refused.

He gave her a gentle nudge onto the edge of the bed, then knelt in front of her to untie her sneakers, before pulling them and her socks off. He eased her to her feet, then stripped her bare and yanked the blankets back on the bed. "Climb in, *agaph*."

While she did, he tossed his own clothing aside, then slid in beside her. He settled her on his shoulder, allowing her to hide her face there against his warm skin. She inhaled unsteadily. Spice and musk. She'd know his scent anywhere.

"I don't care if you have a thousand snakes on your head every day of the year," he said at last, one big hand sliding down her back. "I don't care if our families stay enemies for another three thousand years. As long as you love me, we can do anything together."

A sob rushed up her throat, tried to get past her lips. She pressed them tightly together to keep it contained.

"I would fight anyone to be with you, Andrea. I love you."

The sob won, bursting free, and she squeezed her eyes shut tighter.

His hold around her firmed, and his lips grazed her temple.

Andi fought to keep another sob in, but it brought friends, dammit.

"It's all right, *agaph*," he whispered. "I'll hold you as long as you need me to."

She gave up, letting the tears and the sobs have free rein. And all the while, she knew Kallan was there, surrounding her, soothing, protecting.

When the tears finally stopped, her throat was raw from crying and her eyes ached. And he continued to hold her tight.

An idea occurred to her then.

The curse remained with her because she still doubted.

Her eyes popped open, and she stared at the hollow of his throat, her pulse pounding crazily.

She loved him, yes. That still surprised her. And she knew he loved her. But some small part of her didn't trust that he'd be there no matter what. No matter how many times he told her he would.

She closed her eyes, feeling a fresh wash of tears. She didn't need Aunt Lydia to tell her that. She didn't need Aunt Celosia to remember, or any book of family lore that somebody had borrowed from someone else. She just needed to believe in him.

Under her cheek, his chest was slick with her tears.

Andi felt horrible. She needed to find a way to let that last piece of mistrust go.

Kallan kissed the top of her head. "It's all right, *meli*. Whatever it is, we'll deal with it."

Tears pooled under her cheek, burning her skin. "Thank you," she choked out.

For a long time, they stayed there, her breathing gradually evening out, the tears eventually running dry, the yellow light from the lamp illuminating the side of the bed where they lay and casting shadows around the rest of the room.

"We can do this any way you want," she said at last, her voice raspy. She sniffled.

His hand on her back went still. "Do what?"

"Tomorrow. I'll do whatever you want me to do." She held her breath.

For a long time, he was silent. He went back to stroking her spine slowly, as if he were pondering. Planning. "I think we have to go up there," he said finally. His fingers caressed her skin, occasionally lingering over one spot before moving on to another. "And I'm not sure we can really plan. We might have to wing it."

She lifted her head in shock, forgetting how messy she must be. "What?"

He gave her a crooked smile.

"Who are you, and what have you done with Kallan?" She swiped one hand over her wet cheek, then over his chest.

"There is no way to predict what we're going to run into

up there," he admitted. "If I tried to strategize for a month, I still couldn't come up with every possibility, and inevitably we'd run into one of the scenarios I'd failed to imagine." He touched the corner of her swollen lip. "We'll have to improvise."

Andi stared up at him, aware her mouth was hanging open. "You must be more exhausted than I realized."

He chuckled and drew her on top of him. "Then you should help tire me out so I can stop thinking and get some sleep. I have a feeling we're going to need all the rest we can get tonight. Besides, I'm sure your hormones are starting to fire up now too. We can kill two birds with one stone."

"How romantic of you," she murmured dryly, letting him settle her over his chest, her legs opening to fall on either side of his hips. Between them, his erection thickened with his desire. "And whose hormones are getting happy?"

He laughed and caught her nape, jerking her against his mouth.

She let him, opening for him when his tongue slid along her lower lip. Heat burst in her middle, sliding down her spine. She glided her hands up from his shoulders, into his hair, stroking his scalp and neck until he purred into the kiss.

Kallan took charge of the next kiss, and the next and the next, devouring her—claiming her—as he pressed his fingers into her tight sheath. She wedged one hand between their bodies to curl her fingers around his shaft, stealing his breath for a moment. His hips rocked into her touch, and while he thrust his fingers inside her, he pressed his thumb over her hard little clit, making her moan.

He rolled her over and caught one of her legs, then hitched it up and out over his arm, higher until it rested on his shoulder.

She opened her dark eyes slowly, the desire and emotion mingling there for him to see. To feel.

He forced her to unwrap her fingers from his erection, and guided the head along her outer lips several times, until her hips rocked up toward him.

"I love you, Andrea Rosakis," he whispered, his mouth an inch over hers.

Her smile was breathtaking, making his already-racing heart stop its crazy pounding for a second before tripling in pace. "I love you too, Kallan Tassos." She used the hand still tangled in his hair to draw him down, brushing her lips along his. "Come inside me now, please."

He didn't make her wait. He let his heavy length slide deep, until he could go no further. Her inner muscles fluttered around him, making his pulse skip and quicken even more.

They rocked together slowly, smiling into each other's eyes for what seemed like hours. Or maybe only a few minutes. When her first release rushed through her, he gritted his teeth against the need to let go and watched pleasure wash over her face. Her next orgasm triggered his own, so he could do nothing but feel for a very long time.

He realized much later that he'd collapsed on top of her, and he tried to shift away, but she held on. "Don't move yet," she whispered.

He stopped trying to roll onto his side, though he did ease her leg off his elbow.

For a long time, he listened to her breathing as it evened out, feeling little aftershocks clench her body around his, gently. Eventually, he lifted his head far enough to look into her still-flushed face. Her eyelids fluttered up, and she smiled up at him.

"Hi." He kissed the tip of her nose.

"Hi." She slid one hand up from his arm to his nape. "Are you tired yet?"

He huffed out a laugh. He'd forgotten his challenge to her. "Not tired enough to sleep," he admitted.

"Then we have to try harder." A sly smile curved her lips this time, and her foot slid up the back of his thigh.

Heat burst at her caress, rushing up to his groin. "You don't need to—"

She touched her lips to his. "I want to." She rolled toward him, and he let her tumble him to his back.

This amazing woman was his. And he'd do whatever he had to do to keep her.

But right now, he simply let her do whatever she wanted to do *to* him.

Andi stretched in the shower in the morning, feeling some achy muscles complain about overuse. She smiled as she put her face under the spray. Kallan's arm brushed her back. But when the faint twinge in her belly echoed the complaint, her smile disappeared.

They didn't have long.

"We need to get moving," she said, turning blindly toward him.

He caught her and pressed a kiss onto her lips. "Okay." He shut the water off and grabbed two towels.

Andi dried quickly, dragging the towel over her head. She tugged on clean clothes and went to check her email one more time before they got on the road.

She sighed. Still nothing from Aunt Lydia.

"Do you have a plan in that gorgeous head of yours?"

She hesitated. "I know we can't just go on up the driveway."

He shook his head. "They'll be waiting."

"Exactly. Which means we need to hike in." She chewed on one corner of her lower lip. "I kind of wish we'd brought one or two of your guns."

He smiled a little. "It's too late to pick one up now. Besides, once we fire, everyone else will know we're there."

She knew that. "The blades are silent," she agreed reluctantly. "But we do have to get in close." And she wasn't sure she could do much damage yet with her curse. Just thinking about it, she felt her gut tighten reflexively. "If I can't go in on my own, leave me behind. Or if I have to stop, don't wait."

His smile vanished in a flash. "Won't happen."

"Kallan." She turned fully toward him. "They're going to be after you as much as they're after me now." She lifted her hands to cup his face. "I'll get there eventually." She winced involuntarily when her belly cramped. "We need to make a stop at the drug store."

Some of the annoyance in his face faded, and he set his hands gently at her waist. "All right. Let's get out of here."

They got everything into the car in one trip.

Andi stewed as he drove, watching out the window. It was still early, so the tourists weren't up and out yet, and only a few locals were on the sidewalks. She rubbed her belly, determined to resist the urge to curl into a ball in her seat. Not yet.

After they made a couple stops for supplies—for her and for their trek into the woods—she guided him along back roads to her mountain. The familiar area made her tension ease just a little, though knowing someone was waiting at her home to kill her wouldn't let her fully relax.

Kallan's fingers tapped on the steering wheel as he drove, almost nervously.

She smiled to herself. Even the big bad Harvester was worried.

He set one hand over hers on her thigh, giving her fingers a gentle squeeze. "This time tomorrow, we can be on our way anywhere you like."

She shut her eyes. It was a nice dream.

Kallan didn't like the pallor of Andrea's face. Or the way she was rubbing her abdomen. He frowned as he maneuvered the car along the twisting back road. Well, it was almost a road—oiled-down dirt and gravel nearly wide enough for two cars to pass one another.

He grimaced as the car hit a pothole and bounced. Andrea's knuckles whitened for a second on the door handle before she resumed massaging her belly.

He steered the car around the next dip, then back onto the right side. "Are you sure you're up to this?"

She nodded. She had her eyes shut tight, and he realized they hadn't brought her sleep mask. Neither of them had thought about it when packing for their first flight. He wondered if he had anything they could use. It would be bad if he got in the way.

At last, he reached the turn-off she'd told him was coming, and he pulled in to park the car. He considered the woods surrounding them.

"How long do you think it'll take us to hike in?" he said at last.

She inhaled slowly, as if she were concentrating on the pain gathering in her belly. "An hour or so. Maybe longer, depending."

Depending on how she held up. He stifled a sigh. She was right. He wasn't a runner. But for her, he'd run far and fast. She had made it clear that wasn't an option, however, so they had to do this.

He took the keys from the ignition and stuffed them into one of his pockets.

"You'll have to let me lead," she said.

He studied her pale face, the sweat beading on her brow. And swallowed back the words that wanted to come out again. She'd never agree to leave now. "Okay." He pushed his door open and climbed out, stretching, trying to twist away the anxiety knotting his muscles.

She did the same on the other side of the car, though her stretching was less vigorous than his.

He pulled the backpacks from the backseat, double checked the things they'd picked up in Bath, and locked the car. Andrea stood with her face toward the forested slope ahead of them, and he helped her into her backpack.

"I love you." He kissed her temple.

A small smile curved her lips then. "I love you, too, Harvester."

"Let's do this." He shouldered his own pack and followed her into the woods.

They walked in silence, avoiding fallen twigs and dry leaves. He listened, his senses open. His cousins weren't very close yet. But they were there, waiting.

When she stopped walking and bent over, one arm across her middle, Kallan slid his hand to her waist. "Let's sit for a minute. Get you a drink of water." His heart ached.

She shook her head, eyes shut tight. "There's a spot a little way ahead we can sit."

"How far?"

"Not too much." Still, it was a moment before she straightened.

He waited, feeling helpless. He'd felt it when she went

through this last time, and he hadn't liked it then. He hated it now. He wanted to make her pain stop. *Now.*

Taking a deep breath, she patted his hand at her side before moving away. Slowly. Carefully.

He stayed close, wishing he could see her eyes.

"You know what?" Strain was obvious in her voice, despite her effort to keep her tone light.

"What?"

"We could go in there with me blindfolded and hand-cuffed. Make them think you've captured me. Lull them into a false sense of security for a few minutes, then take them out."

He watched her feet as she stepped over a fallen tree, considering her idea. "They might believe that, but if you're handcuffed, how do you think you're going to get rid of the blindfold?"

"Mm. Yeah. I guess the handcuffs would have to be behind me, wouldn't they—for them to really believe." She sighed audibly.

Kallan thought hard. "What about rope?"

She paused before stepping over another limb on the ground. "Rope. If you have a long enough piece, you could tie my hands in front and keep hold of the other end. Then they wouldn't think anything of it."

He didn't want to do it. It would involve her getting far too close to Stavros.

She stopped walking and doubled over again, almost stifling a moan of pain.

He bent closer to support her while she breathed through the cramping.

After a few long minutes, she eased upright once more.

"*Agaph.*"

She smiled faintly when she turned her pale face toward

him, eyes shut. "I know." She let him gather her close for a moment. "It'll be all right."

He wanted to believe her. But he couldn't see how this would ever turn out all right.

When she took a deep breath and pushed away, he let her, though it was a challenge not to hold on.

He kept his eyes peeled for movement as they made their way up the side of her mountain. "Stop," he breathed.

She froze, one foot in mid-air.

His cousins were closer now. Much closer. He could feel them. "Four."

She set her foot down carefully. "All together, or can't you tell?"

"Three are together." The other was some distance from the others, but closer to where he stood with Andrea. Probably keeping a lookout. "We'll have to deal with the one alone first."

"I can do it."

He exhaled slowly and moved to stand at her side. "They'll be armed."

"So am I." Though her eyes were closed, he knew the stubborn look he'd find in them. "We just have to get close enough to him before he alerts the others."

Kallan dropped his head back far enough to look up into the green canopy overhead. Birds flitted there, from tree to tree, singing and scolding. He knew what they had to do, but a voice in his head pointed out this was his family—it sounded very like Great-Uncle Ari again. He reminded himself that they'd tracked him as if he was their enemy. Clearly, he was, which meant he owed them no allegiance any longer.

His blood family was trying to kill Andrea, and he couldn't allow them to succeed. She was his real family now.

"All right."

"You'll have to let me know when we're close enough to have to sneak around him."

He grunted his assent as she started walking again, more carefully this time. His gut was tight with the mounting tension, making him glad breakfast had been just an energy bar several hours ago.

It took them fifteen more minutes before Kallan decided it was too dangerous to continue directly. Instead he guided her off to their right. He couldn't tell which of his cousins it was —not yet. Finally, after another ten minutes of almost crawling around the other man, they came to a spot where he was visible from behind some scrubby mountain laurel and fallen trees.

Piers.

His cousin stood against a tall pine, arms folded over his chest, looking bored. He wore no weapon except a blade at his waist. He wasn't even carrying a radio.

That was good for them, bad for him.

Kallan swiped his sweaty palms down his thighs. "You're going to have to be careful to get him before he gets his dagger unsheathed," he breathed in her ear.

She nodded, opening her eyes just a little to see her target's location. "You should stay put while I deal with him."

His jaw tightened. "Why don't you let me get to his other side and we can both be ready, just in case?"

"What if he ducks?"

Well, that would suck. He exhaled softly. He didn't want to let her step out there. Not without him.

But she didn't wait for his permission, getting to her feet and moving around him before he could think of another argument, her steps sure and quiet on the forest floor.

He held his breath as she crept behind his cousin, Kallan's

heart drumming so hard in his chest he thought it might have broken a rib or two.

Finally, she stood only a few yards away from Piers. She shot a thumbs-up toward Kallan, who shook his head even though she couldn't see it, and then she cleared her throat.

Piers whipped around, and then fell as solid stone against the tree he'd been leaning on before tumbling onto the ground. Even as rock, his expression was shocked.

Kallan saw the shudder ripple over Andrea. Guilt and horror were in her expression, even in profile, even with her eyes squeezed shut.

He left the hiding place behind the bushes and went directly to her, avoiding his cousin to wrap her in his arms. "It's all right, *agaph*," he whispered into her short hair.

She shivered and slid her hands to his waist. "Well, that sucked." Her voice was choked.

He closed his eyes and stroked her back. "I know." He kissed her head and leaned away to look into her face. Still far too pale, and now tension bracketed her mouth and the corners of her shuttered eyes. "We can still leave."

She shook her head before he finished speaking. "No."

He'd known that. "Okay, then we have to keep going." He let out a short breath. "I think it's best if we don't try to take them all on at once."

Her mouth twisted to one side as she considered that. "It would be faster."

"And more dangerous." He did a quick check. All three were still together. Probably at the house.

"They'll be more dangerous one-on-one," she argued. "I'd bet at least one of them has a gun."

"You may not be able to take out three at one time."

She closed her mouth on her next argument, gave it some

thought, then sighed. "Okay. You may be right." She bit her lower lip. "Then how are we going to do this?"

He lifted one eyebrow. She was actually going to let him make the decision? He smiled. Then frowned. How *were* they going to do this? "Dammit, this is why I always make a plan," he muttered.

Andrea laughed softly, then sucked in a quick breath, her smile disappearing as she bent forward again.

He rubbed the tight muscles at the small of her back, trying to keep half his attention on their surroundings while comforting her. He knew just walking into the house would be bad for them. They'd be outnumbered and with no place to hide if they needed to duck gunfire.

But how to draw his cousins out?

He kept massaging her back while he dug into one of his pockets for the old cell phone. Stavros.

Andrea eased to an almost-upright position, her breathing ragged.

"Are you going to be able to go the rest of the way, *agaph*?"

She nodded. "If I have to crawl."

Of course she would. While he wanted nothing more than to protect her, to whisk her back down the mountain and away, he knew he couldn't. She had to stay with him—to finish this—one way or another. "All right." He thumbed the phone on, then realized he hadn't charged it in days. He hoped there was enough battery power left for this call. He shifted position, hoping for a tiny overhead clearing to get his satellite signal, then pushed the button to dial his cousin.

"Kallan?" His cousin sounded surprised.

"Yes. Just wanted to give you a heads up, I'm on my way up the mountain with her." He continued to rub her back, feeling the muscles under his fingers tightening.

There was a moment of silence. "Well, good job." That sounded completely insincere. "Dead or alive?"

"Alive, but just." He wrapped his arm around her when she stepped closer, her damp face burrowing into his shirt.

Again, Stavros was silent, either in distrust or elation. "I'll meet you. Tell me which direction," he said finally.

"There's a path behind the house that heads into the woods. I'm heading up from there." *Not.* Instead, he'd make sure they circled around from the other side and came at him from the back. And hope all three cousins were together.

Andrea's breath caught against him, and her fingers dug into his back as her body tried to curl in on itself.

This was *not* good.

Kallan shut his phone, not waiting to see if his cousin had anything else to add, and turned it off before he stuffed it back into one of his pockets. "*Meli.*" He scooped her up in his arms, and a soft moan escaped her. He pressed a kiss onto her forehead, tasting the salt of her sweat. "We need to be on the opposite side of the house from where Stavros is heading. Can you get us there?"

She inhaled shakily, then nodded. "We're nearly there now," she whispered.

He concentrated on his cousins. All three were still together, for the moment, and they hadn't left the house, apparently, as they were exactly where they'd been last time he checked. Probably trying to come up with their own plan.

He just hoped his was better.

CHAPTER FIFTEEN

Andi concentrated on breathing evenly as she instructed Kallan which direction to go with her eyes barely open. She needed to be able to stand up for what was coming.

Her stomach rebelled at just the thought. When she'd taken out his cousin, she'd been very, very happy she'd only had half a granola bar for breakfast. It had been bad when she'd accidentally killed the rabbit. Deliberately killing a human being was a thousand times worse, even if he had been plotting to kill her.

When she directed Kallan to stop, she pushed away, and he let her ease to her feet. Her knees wobbled, and she locked them to stay upright. Her belly cramped harder, making her clench her jaw against the pain.

"Do you think you can get to the house, *agaph*?" he breathed near her ear.

"Why?"

"For cover," he said after a second, and she knew it was a lie.

"I'm not going to hide in the house while you deal with them," she whispered.

He huffed out a short breath. "Can you trust me on this?"

She started to say "of course" but she stopped, remembering the revelation she'd had about the curse. "I do trust you, Kallan," she said on a breath, "but I feel like this is my fight too."

"And you've contributed to the fight very nicely." His breath warmed her ear. "But I can deal with the three of them myself. Quickly."

She heard the front door of her house open, then close, and she turned her head to look. She couldn't see the men, though heavy footsteps sounded.

"That's only two," he breathed. "The other one is heading to the far right corner of the house. Of course they won't believe me." A humorless laugh escaped him.

Andi turned back to him, eyes shut, and slid one hand up his chest to his neck, the side of his face. "Let me deal with the one."

Kallan was silent for a long moment, and she knew he wanted to say no.

"I trust you to deal with them, but I need to help. This is my life, after all."

"You don't play fairly," he complained, but brushed a kiss on her lips. "Fine. I'll deal with the other two. I just wish I knew which ones were where."

"It won't matter. I'll wait till you go, then I'll move around the house." She stretched up to kiss him back. "I love you." She released him.

His hand lingered on her spine for several heartbeats, warming her, then he stepped away. "When you're done, stay put, and I'll meet you there." Then he was gone.

She only heard a few of his footfalls before he disappeared into the trees. He was silent in the woods. That was good. She needed to be just as quiet. She opened her eyes slowly, listening. The other man was still on the opposite side of the house, as she couldn't hear him either. So she made her way around, deeper into the forest so she could blend into the trees and shadows but still see the edge of the trees and her house.

When she finally made her way to the other side of the house, her heart was pounding harder, almost in time with the cramping low in her belly.

There.

A big, dark man stood with his back to her, watching the woods at the other end of the house where the pathway disappeared into the trees. At his waist, he had both a gun holster and a knife sheath. Not taking any chances.

She sucked in a quick breath and froze, feeling sweat roll down her chest with the fresh onslaught of cramps. *Bitch.*

She waited until they eased off, though the easing off wasn't very noticeable. Then she took a few more paces toward him, careful where she stepped. She imagined Kallan stalking his own prey. Just thinking about what she was going to do made her stomach flip over, but the queasiness only distracted her from the cramps momentarily.

She paused when her belly tried to curl her in on herself from the giant fist squeezing her guts. The pain was excruciating, making her lungs freeze, her heart thud harder, and sweat break out on her face. She felt it running down her scalp to her nape, dampening her T-shirt beneath the backpack, and wished she'd thought to set the pack aside before she came after this one.

Andi forced herself to breathe quietly, evenly, through the cramping. And swore she'd never have children even if the Medusa were able to have them. If her period was this bad, labor would be a million times worse, and there was absolutely no way she was going through that.

It seemed like hours, but she knew it had to be just a few minutes before the fist eased its grip on her insides just a little, and she moved forward again, her gaze shifting between her prey and the forest floor ahead. The last thing she needed to do was alert him to her presence by stepping on a twig or dry leaf.

Somehow, between bouts of gut-wrenching cramps, she made it to a spot a few yards behind the hulk. He still stood there, arms crossed on his chest, white cotton shirt stretched over his wide back. He stared across the small backyard to where he had a clear view of the trail leading into the woods. She took a shallow breath, then another, bracing herself with one hand against the nearest tree when her body rebelled again. *Bitch,* she thought. *Athena, You are the biggest bitch ever.*

This round of cramps was far worse than its predecessors, and it was all she could do to stay semi-upright against the tree. She really, really wanted to get inside her house and curl up in her bed after a nice hot shower.

But she had a job to do first.

"Hey, jackass," she said hoarsely.

He whirled around, hands going to his waist, but too late. He'd already looked at her, and toppled to the ground, solid stone that cracked into three big pieces and several smaller ones when it hit.

Andi slid down the tree and curled into a ball, panting for a moment. She wondered if Harvester training covered *not* looking when someone called you names in the woods. If so, he had clearly failed that test. Then she crawled to where the gun holster had landed when the stone man had broken. *Good thing only the body turned to stone.* She took the gun out with shaking hands. Then, for good measure, took his knife too. Just in case. She had to believe Kallan was successful on his side of the forest.

Kallan crouched behind a small stand of young trees, watching his cousins. Stavros wasn't here—just two of Stavros's favorite cousins, Theo and Kosmo. Which meant Stavros was the one waiting on the other side of the house. For Andrea.

His heart pounded faster, echoing in his ears. He hoped they couldn't hear it.

She'd deal with his cousin. She'd be fine. He'd like to convince himself, but he realized if he kept thinking about it, he'd never do what *he* had to do.

He took in a slow breath, then glanced around. He found a small rock nearby and picked it up. He hefted it for a second, then lobbed it to the other side of his cousins, satisfied when it hit a fallen tree and made a dull thud even he could hear.

Theo gestured for Kosmo to check it out while he glanced around them. Scowling, Theo continued to pick his way along the trail, looking for signs of their quarry.

Kallan made his way along the slope until he was about five yards away, then took one of the daggers he'd stuck in his belt that morning and hurled it into the left side of Theo's back. Heart shot.

His cousin went down with a soft thump.

Then there was one.

He made his way back up the hill, watching for Kosmo, who was still investigating the area of the sound. Kosmo wasn't the smartest of the cousins, he mused, moving into a position just below the other man, behind a small mound of young trees that had fallen during some rainstorm, their roots not deep enough to hold them in place.

Kosmo muttered under his breath, his gaze skittering around the area and his brow damp with sweat. Nervous.

Kallan smiled to himself as he felt around for another small rock.

Kosmo was a city boy—not a country boy—and he jumped, whirling in a circle when the stone cracked hard into a tree trunk several feet away from him. He drew his own blade and scanned the surrounding area. A squirrel overhead chattered at him, startling him again.

Kallan took the opportunity to hurl his next dagger into the front of his cousin's white T-shirt. A red stain spread rapidly over the cotton from the blood pumping out of his heart. Kosmo dropped to his knees, looking shocked, then onto his face in the soft blanket of decomposing leaves on the forest floor.

Two down.

He retrieved his daggers, cleaning them on his cousins' shirts before replacing the blades in their sheaths. Feeling only slightly better, he made his way back up the slope toward the house.

Andi heard the footsteps coming through the trees and her head shot up before she realized it was probably Kallan.

"Andrea?"

She shut her eyes, relief rushing along her veins and easing her cramps just a tiny bit. "Here."

The footfalls grew nearer, and then he was there, kneeling in the dirt beside her. "Did you—"

She nodded. "I need a shower and my bed."

He brushed one hand over the top of her head. "I'll see what we can do about that, *agaph*."

"Kallan!"

She jerked under his touch, hearing the other man's deeply accented voice nearby, and her pulse doubled its pace.

"I thought you dealt with Stavros." His whisper was harsh.

"I got somebody," she breathed. "Back at the edge of the tree line."

He shifted beside her, then blew out a hard breath. "Not Stavros. Sebastyen. That means Stavros can cloak his presence too." Now that his cousin knew Kallan was his enemy, he was clearly taking no chances.

"I know you're there, Kallan."

"We need to move," he breathed against her ear, easing one hand under her elbow to help her up.

"Did you kill your own family? For a monster?"

She could hear Kallan grinding his teeth, and touched his forearm blindly. "Where?"

"I can't see him from here."

She swallowed. "Let me go."

"No."

"I can deal with him."

"He'll be armed." He grasped her hand, tight. "We need better cover."

Andi balked. "I'm armed, too. I took a gun and another knife from the big guy. I'm done running."

"Then *I'm* going to deal with him." He kissed her forehead, cupping the side of her face. "Don't move."

"Uncle Ari will be very disappointed in you, Kallan." His cousin was nearer now, not bothering to be quiet as he moved among the trees.

She tensed, ready to turn to face the cousin, but Kallan's breath brushed her ear. "Trust me, *meli*. Promise."

She let out a slow breath. It was now or never. She nodded. "I do."

A small smile curved his lips along her skin. "I'll be right back."

She leaned back against the tree as much as her backpack would allow, feeling the rough bark under her fingertips. *Please Gods, keep him safe.*

He was silent as he moved away from her, and her heart raced with fear for him.

"Just give her to me, Kallan." Stavros was farther away now—more toward the tree line, she realized. "I'm sure the family can forgive you. Somehow. Someday."

"I don't need forgiveness, Stavros." His voice rang out confidently.

Her eyes shot open, and it took tremendous effort to stay right where she was, to not rush out to his aid. Her fingers dug harder into the bark.

"Of course, you do. You lied to Uncle Ari. To me. You helped that monster escape her rightful end."

"I helped the woman I love."

"Love?" His cousin laughed, and it wasn't a pleasant sound. "You can't love her. The Tassos family has been tracking these monsters for centuries to expose them to the world. They aren't women, and they can't be loved. They're not worthy of it."

"They aren't monsters, just women dealing with something they shouldn't have to. But I don't expect you to understand them."

She shut her eyes. Judging by the sound of his voice, he was standing near his cousin—probably face-to-face. *Gods, don't let him die for me.*

Stavros sighed dramatically. "What have you done with our cousins?"

Silence.

"You *have* killed them." Surprise tinged the other man's

voice this time. "I wouldn't have believed it of you, Kallan. Never you, always the good Harvester."

"How long have you been able to cloak your presence?"

It was Stavros's turn to be silent for a moment. "So you can sense other Harvesters. I wondered. Theo seemed to think so."

"Enough talking, Stavros. No one is coming to your rescue this time."

"You might be surprised. I believe Piers…" His voice trailed off. "You realize everyone knows where she lives, don't you, cousin? I've made certain of it. If you kill me too, someone else will just come here to finish the job."

A thud reached her ears, the sound of flesh meeting flesh, and she huddled there, wanting badly to go out to him, despite the cramps that made her also want to curl into a ball where she stood. Despite her promise. But she waited. Kallan had asked her to trust him, and she had to believe he'd come back to her alive.

Still, the sounds of their fighting made her curl her fingers tighter into the tree.

"Bastard," snarled Stavros several minutes later, his accented voice muffled. She hoped Kallan had knocked his teeth out.

More thumping as fists met flesh. Soft grunts accompanied each one, and she swallowed back a cry.

"Of course you won't make this easy," Stavros growled, and she heard the sound of metal sliding out of leather.

Her knees buckled, and she slid down to the dirt, biting her lip.

Metal clashed with metal this time, and she curled forward until her forehead rested on her knees, both in relief at knowing Kallan was still fighting, and to ease the fisting in her abdomen.

Someone hissed in a breath, then there was nothing but the sound of footsteps, probably as they circled one another.

Oh dear Gods, not Kallan.

"Can't you find a suitable woman?" Stavros panted some time later. "You have to settle for a monster?"

His taunt was followed by a surprised hiss, which she hoped was from Stavros being cut.

"It's a shame you need so much help to do a job and still can't manage it." Kallan laughed a little while later, then laughed again when his cousin growled at him. Heavy footsteps thudded on the ground, and she guessed he was charging Kallan.

Andi couldn't stand it. She forced her wobbly legs to push her upright once more, using the tree for support. Her belly clenched tighter, but she ignored it.

A heavy thump met her ears, and Stavros cursed, then sucked in a harsh breath. "You would kill me, too? Your own blood?" His words were slurred, making her think he had indeed lost some teeth.

Kallan was silent for a moment. "If you had asked me that a month ago, I would never have said yes. Not even knowing everything I knew about you already. But now…" There was a brief pause. "I feel sorry for you, cousin," he finished more quietly, his breath still coming quickly.

She made her way to the next tree, catching it to remain upright, her cramps tightening like a vise. He could deal with Stavros. She just needed to get in the house and collapse somewhere clean and comfortable.

Another sharp pain, this time from her back. Her knees gave out again, and she landed on all fours in the shadows of her forest. *Oh Gods!* This was worse than even her cramps. She lowered her head to the back of her hands and panted, feeling as if a hot knife now pierced her skin. Her entire focus centered on the pain there, fiery and jagged. She thought she might have moaned, but she couldn't be sure.

It went on for an eternity, and when it finally vanished—as suddenly as it had started—she found herself sprawled flat on the ground, panting, her clothing soaked with sweat.

Footsteps pounded toward her, and she shut her eyes automatically.

"Andrea." Kallan's hands eased her backpack from her shoulders, down her arms. "*Agaph*." He knelt at her side, one hand stroking over the back of her head and nape. "Can you get up?"

She shook her head. "Give me a minute," she whispered.

He ignored that and rolled her to her side, then her back, and then scooped her into his arms. She put her wet face against his shoulder, relaxing. If Kallan was here now, it was over. At least for now.

She realized when he started climbing that he'd carried her inside the house, and she smiled into his shirt.

When he set her on the closed toilet, she took a slow, deep breath. "Are you all right?"

"Just a scratch or two," he muttered, tugging her boots and socks off, then going to turn on the shower. "Let's get you in here."

"I feel better." She let him pull her to her feet, realizing it was true. Her cramps had stopped. She frowned. That had never happened before.

She raised her arms when he tugged her shirt up, then let him unfasten her jeans. "I'll grab something clean for you." His footsteps left the room, and she finished undressing so when he returned, he could herd her into the shower.

When he sucked in his breath, she went still. "Kallan?"

"It's gone." His fingers stroked over her back, where the sharp pain had been minutes ago.

"What is?"

"The amulet."

Her eyes popped open, and she stared at the tiled wall of her shower. "Oh my Gods," she breathed.

"Come here." He pulled her back out of the shower, and she closed her eyes automatically. "I think you can open them, *agaph*."

She opened her eyes cautiously, looking over her shoulder at her reflection. Her mouth went dry.

The tattoo was changed. No more snake wound around the stem of the goblet. No goblet. Just the flowers blooming in bright pinks and reds on her lower back, fuller now that the cup was gone from the middle.

She met his gaze in the mirror, and found him smiling. "My cramps are gone, too," she said unsteadily.

His smile widened further. "Really?" One of his hands settled low on her belly, over the spot that had been so painful just ten minutes ago.

She nodded, turning her head around to look up at him. Nothing happened to him. Her legs started shaking, and he eased her backward to lean against the counter, then moved in front of her to wrap his arms around her. Her fingers trembled when she lifted them to grip his shoulders.

"I think the curse has moved on, *agaph*," he whispered on the top of her head.

She closed her eyes and felt them stinging. Her whole body was quaking.

She was no longer the Medusa.

Kallan held onto her until the trembling eased, and when she lifted her head, she noted the wet spot on his shoulder from her tears. And the bloody spots beneath the slashes in his shirt.

"Are you all right?" She eased away, reaching for the hem.

"I'm fine. Just scratches." He let her raise the garment to inspect them.

They looked like more than scratches. One was about six inches long and still oozing blood. Another was a shorter slash, but it was apparently deeper, as the blood flow there was steadier.

"I promise, they'll be fine later." He tipped her chin up and kissed her lightly.

"You need to clean them." She lifted his shirt higher, until he had to release her to take it off.

"Fine. Get in the shower, and you can help." He winked at her.

She wasn't about to argue with him, and watched while he kicked off the rest of his clothing. "We have clean-up to do, don't we? Outside?" She hated to think of that, but knew it would have to be done before she could sell the house.

"Later." He pointed, and she stepped into the shower. He followed her, then turned on the water and adjusted it to a comfortable temperature before guiding her under the spray. He sighed, then hissed in a breath when she slid the soap over one of his wounds. "Bloodthirsty," he teased.

She shook her head, lathering up her hands to carefully wash his cuts. "You're supposed to get out of the way when someone swings a dagger at you."

He laughed, his fingers catching her wrists. "I'll keep that in mind."

She let him press her against the cool tiles, loving the feel of his body along hers. "I didn't want to lose you."

"You haven't." He kissed the tip of her nose, then met her gaze. "And now you're stuck with me."

She inhaled slowly, her heart full to bursting.

She met his kiss and the next and the next, and all the rest, until the pleasure exploded for them both, and they slid down the tile to the floor of the shower, where the water pounded on them while they caught their breath. She smiled against his mouth when one of his hands slid lazily up her side.

"Thank you."

He lifted his head just a little, his green eyes slow to focus, but intense when they did. "*Agaph*, I wasn't going to let him have you."

"I know." She stroked his wet hair away from his face. "I think that's when the amulet disappeared." She told him what had happened, and when she finished, he frowned thoughtfully. "I need to let Aunt Lydia know, because if that's not in the book of family lore when she gets her hands on it again, it needs to be."

He nodded slowly. "We can't stay here."

Her smile faded. "I know." She glanced away for a second. "How long before someone else comes looking, do you think?"

"A day maybe." His expression was somber. "Possibly less, depending on who was at the motel last night. I'm sure he's been in regular contact with Ari."

"Okay. Then we need to move." She tried to shift to her feet, but he held onto her. She lifted one eyebrow.

"We aren't going to need to run for long. They'll know someone else is the Medusa and start the hunt for her."

"How?"

He shook his head. "I'm not sure how it works. But Ari will know the amulet has moved on. I don't think he can sense the cup—or we would have found you long before now —but he knows somehow when there is a new Medusa. Perhaps the Goddess knows."

She bit her lower lip. "I wish the amulet and the curse would just go away forever."

Kallan smiled faintly. "I don't think the Goddess has forgiven the original Medusa yet."

"What about Ari? He won't be happy with you. We did kill five of your cousins." Andi could live in hiding—she'd done it for years, but she didn't think Kallan would enjoy it.

He considered that. "I imagine he will be very angry. But I don't think he's going to waste resources hunting for us when he has to start a brand new search for the Medusa. The Goddess will be angry with him. With all of my family."

"After all of this, you just really believe he's going to let you go?"

"I think he'll want to find us, but I believe Athena will make sure his focus remains on his hunt. She is determined."

Her eyes narrowed, making his smile widen.

"Don't say it." He kissed her hard, then released her, easing to his knees while she got to her feet, both wincing as their bodies parted. "Where do you want to live?"

Andi stopped moving, her hand halfway to the faucet. "Can I think about it?"

"As long as I get to go with you."

She shut off the water and straightened. "I expect you to be with me forever." She slid both hands up his wide chest to his shoulders.

"Good. Because I'm not leaving you." His green eyes swirled with emotion.

"I love you, Harvester," she whispered, going on tiptoe to kiss him.

"No, no Harvester here. Just Kallan Tassos." He held her gaze. "Part of your family."

Her eyes stung with tears. "I like the sound of that."

Athena scowled at the old man on his knees before Her. "You assured Me you would take care of the Medusa, Aristotle."

"I am sorry, My Lady. My nephew betrayed not only You, but his family. He killed his cousins to protect the monster."

She knew perfectly well what had occurred in Maine. Knowing didn't make Her happy. "Now you must begin the search anew." That made Her even unhappier.

Aristotle Tassos bowed lower, his forehead nearly touching the floor now. "I have already, My Lady. We will do better this time."

"You told Me that only weeks ago, Harvester." The Goddess tightened Her grip on the bow She held in Her left hand. "You cannot fail Me again."

He nodded once. "I vow I will not."

She knew his words were heartfelt. If he were much younger and still actually in the hunt, She'd feel better about the promise. But Aristotle hadn't been in the hunt for many years, and She had Her doubts about his current generation of hunters. "If your family fails Me, Aristotle, there will be consequences."

He shuddered a little below Her. "I understand, My Lady," he said hoarsely.

Andrea straightened from the suitcase she was unpacking, and Kallan smiled at her when she caught him watching her from the doorway. "You could help with this, you know."

He winked. "I was enjoying the view."

Color tinted her cheeks. "Such a man," she muttered, even though she was smiling as she said it.

He crossed the room to her and slid a kiss along her cheek.

"Do you think she's okay yet?" Her blue eyes were shadowed with concern.

He lifted one shoulder. "I hope so. But I can't say for sure."

"I remember it really sucked." She caught the corner of her lower lip in her teeth. "Maybe I should have gone—"

He touched one finger to her lips. "Your mother said she asked you not to. She said she'd deal with it." He knew she was worried about her cousin.

"But she's young. And Mom knows how bad it was for me. She should have told Philomena I would come. She's so young."

"So were you."

Andrea sighed and turned to wrap her arms around his waist. "I know."

"We can visit her when she'll let us. Maybe by then Lydia will have finally tracked down the book so we can share it with her." He rubbed his face against her hair, marveling at how long it was already, past her nape and nearly to her shoulders, glistening like black silk in the sunlight streaming in the window.

"I know," she said again, her fingers tightening on him for a moment.

"So, how about getting this honeymoon started?" he said, keeping his tone light.

Her smile curved against his chest, through the light shirt he wore. "What did you have in mind?"

"Well, wife, I was thinking about trying out that great big bed over there." He scooped her up, startling a laugh out of her.

"What did you think we might do in it?" Her fingers sifted through the hair at his nape, making him shiver.

He nuzzled her ear, and then whispered a suggestion.

A throaty laugh escaped her, and when her head tipped back, he took advantage, sliding his open mouth along the creamy skin of her throat so a shiver made her tremble in his arms. "Really? Well, I suppose we could. If you insist," Andi said.

"Oh, I insist," he growled, carrying her down onto the bed. "*Sas agapw*, Andrea. I love you. Forever."

The Legend

Millennia ago, a beautiful young Gorgon made a fatal mistake—one her descendants are still paying for today. She so angered Athena that the Goddess cursed Medusa, changing her lovely hair to snakes and causing her gaze to turn any living thing to stone. As if that wasn't bad enough, she then sent Perseus to kill the unfortunate Medusa.

Perseus didn't know, however, that Medusa had already found a way to protect her descendants from a part of the Goddess's curse: she created an amulet that would transfer from one future Medusa to the next, either when she fell in love or died. This cup prevents the curse from wreaking constant havoc in the women's lives, instead limiting it to once each month.

And you thought you had PMS from hell.

Along with the Goddess's curse, Perseus's descendants have also followed the Medusas through the centuries, trying to take the amulet as they hunt, or harvest the Medusas. These Harvesters have so far failed to steal the cup, and—for several recent generations—have also failed to kill the reigning Medusas.

But they are persistent and, while they have failed this

time, they are closer than in many years to killing the newest
Medusa.

Elizabeth Andrews has been a book lover since she was old enough to read. She read her copies of *Little Women* and the *Little House* series so many times, the books fell apart. As an adult, her book habit continues. She has a room overflowing with her literary collection right now, and still more spreading into other rooms. Almost as long as she's been reading great stories, she's been attempting to write her own. Thanks to a fifth grade teacher who started the class on creative writing, Elizabeth went from writing creative sentences to short stories and eventually full-length novels. Her father saved her poor, callused fingers from permanent damage when he brought home a used typewriter for her.

Elizabeth found her mother's stash of romance novels as a teenager, and—though she loves horror—romance became her very favorite genre, making writing romances a natural progression. There are more than just a few manuscripts, however, tucked away in a filing cabinet that will never see the light of day.

Along with her enormous book stash, Elizabeth lives with her husband of more than twenty-five years, with two young adult sons nearby, though no one else in the family reads nearly as much as she does. When she's not at work or buried in books or writing, there is a garden outside full of herbs, flowers and vegetables that requires occasional attention.

Website: www.elizabethandrewswrites.com